Acclaim for Radclyffe's Fiction

In *Prescription for Love* "Radclyffe populates her small town with colorful characters, among the most memorable being Flann's little sister, Margie, and Abby's 15-year-old trans son, Blake…This romantic drama has plenty of heart and soul." —*Publishers Weekly*

2013 RWA/New England Bean Pot award winner for contemporary romance *Crossroads* "will draw the reader in and make her heart ache, willing the two main characters to find love and a life together. It's a story that lingers long after coming to 'the end.'" —*Lambda Literary*

In **2012 RWA/FTHRW Lories and RWA HODRW Aspen Gold award winner** *Firestorm* "Radclyffe brings another hot lesbian romance for her readers." —*The Lesbrary*

Foreword Review Book of the Year finalist and IPPY silver medalist *Trauma Alert* "is hard to put down and it will sizzle in the reader's hands. The characters are hot, the sex scenes explicit and explosive, and the book is moved along by an interesting plot with well drawn secondary characters. The real star of this show is the attraction between the two characters, both of whom resist and then fall head over heels." —*Lambda Literary Reviews*

Lambda Literary Award Finalist *Best Lesbian Romance 2010* features "stories [that] ⟨…⟩ in tone, style, and subject, making for more ⟨…⟩ ar anthologies…well written, ⟨…⟩ g, surprising twist. Best Lesbian ⟨…⟩ ffe has assembled a respectable ⟨…⟩ r's offering." —*Curve Magazine*

2010 Prism award winner and ForeWord Review Book of the Year Award finalist *Secrets in the Stone* is "so powerfully [written] that the worlds of these three women shimmer between reality and dreams…A strong, must read novel that will linger in the minds of readers long after the last page is turned."—*Just About Write*

In **Benjamin Franklin Award finalist *Desire by Starlight*** "Radclyffe writes romance with such heart and her down-to-earth characters not only come to life but leap off the page until you feel like you know them. What Jenna and Gard feel for each other is not only a spark but an inferno and, as a reader, you will be washed away in this tumultuous romance until you can do nothing but succumb to it."—*Queer Magazine Online*

Lambda Literary Award winner *Stolen Moments* "is a collection of steamy stories about women who just couldn't wait. It's sex when desire overrides reason, and it's incredibly hot!"—*On Our Backs*

Lambda Literary Award winner *Distant Shores, Silent Thunder* "weaves an intricate tapestry about passion and commitment between lovers. The story explores the fragile nature of trust and the sanctuary provided by loving relationships."—*Sapphic Reader*

Lambda Literary Award Finalist *Justice Served* delivers a "crisply written, fast-paced story with twists and turns and keeps us guessing until the final explosive ending." —*Independent Gay Writer*

Lambda Literary Award finalist *Turn Back Time* "is filled with wonderful love scenes, which are both tender and hot." —*MegaScene*

Applause for L.L. Raand's Midnight Hunters Series

The Midnight Hunt
RWA 2012 VCRW Laurel Wreath winner *Blood Hunt*
Night Hunt
The Lone Hunt

"Raand has built a complex world inhabited by werewolves, vampires, and other paranormal beings…Raand has given her readers a complex plot filled with wonderful characters as well as insight into the hierarchy of Sylvan's pack and vampire clans. There are many plot twists and turns, as well as erotic sex scenes in this riveting novel that keep the pages flying until its satisfying conclusion."—*Just About Write*

"Once again, I am amazed at the storytelling ability of L.L. Raand aka Radclyffe. In *Blood Hunt*, she mixes high levels of sheer eroticism that will leave you squirming in your seat with an impeccable multi-character storyline all streaming together to form one great read." —*Queer Magazine Online*

"*The Midnight Hunt* has a gripping story to tell, and while there are also some truly erotic sex scenes, the story always takes precedence. This is a great read which is not easily put down nor easily forgotten."—*Just About Write*

"Are you sick of the same old hetero vampire / werewolf story plastered in every bookstore and at every movie theater? Well, I've got the cure to your werewolf fever. *The Midnight Hunt* is first in, what I hope is, a long-running series of fantasy erotica for L.L. Raand (aka Radclyffe)."—*Queer Magazine Online*

"Any reader familiar with Radclyffe's writing will recognize the author's style within *The Midnight Hunt*, yet at the same time it is most definitely a new direction. The author delivers an excellent story here, one that is engrossing from the very beginning. Raand has pieced together an intricate world, and provided just enough details for the reader to become enmeshed in the new world. The action moves quickly throughout the book and it's hard to put down."—*Three Dollar Bill Reviews*

By Radclyffe

Romances

Innocent Hearts

Promising Hearts

Love's Melody Lost

Love's Tender Warriors

Tomorrow's Promise

Love's Masquerade

shadowland

Passion's Bright Fury

Fated Love

Turn Back Time

When Dreams Tremble

The Lonely Hearts Club

Night Call

Secrets in the Stone

Desire by Starlight

Crossroads

Homestead

Against Doctor's Orders

Prescription for Love

The Color of Love

Love on Call

Secret Hearts

Honor Series

Above All, Honor

Honor Bound

Love & Honor

Honor Guards

Honor Reclaimed

Honor Under Siege

Word of Honor

Code of Honor

Price of Honor

Justice Series

A Matter of Trust (prequel)

Shield of Justice

In Pursuit of Justice

Justice in the Shadows

Justice Served

Justice for All

The Provincetown Tales

Safe Harbor

Beyond the Breakwater

Distant Shores, Silent Thunder

Storms of Change

Winds of Fortune

Returning Tides

Sheltering Dunes

Visit us at www.boldstrokesbooks.com

SECRET HEARTS

by

RADCLYffE

2017

Credits
Editors: Ruth Sternglantz and Stacia Seaman
Production Design: Stacia Seaman
Cover Design by Melody Pond

Acknowledgments

I had a request for a "city" setting at the same time as I planned to write a non-series romance, but as I discovered after many years of living in a large East Coast city before returning to upstate New York, you can never really shed "all" the country. While I lived in Philadelphia, my idea of a vacation was tenting in the Poconos or running in the sand dunes on Cape Cod or roughing it in a cabin in the Adirondacks with no heat, electricity, or running water—anywhere with clear skies, moonlit nights, and frogs (turtles are a bonus). As a result, this romance, set in the heart of Manhattan, blends my desire to escape the city while capturing the unique energy and vibrancy of one of the largest metropolises in the world (a place I love to visit but wouldn't want to live).

Many thanks go to: senior editor Sandy Lowe for the astounding progress she has made in streamlining all things BSB and providing me with expert advice as a publisher and author, editor Ruth Sternglantz for never letting any loose ends slip by, editor Stacia Seaman for her careful review of the late stages, and my first readers Paula and Eva for taking time out of their busy lives to send invaluable feedback.

And as always, thanks to Lee for always looking to the next adventure. *Amo te.*

Radclyffe, 2017

To Lee, for saying "why not"

CHAPTER ONE

I've got red wine—will that do for starters?" Kip called to Julie from the kitchen, scanning the bottles in the small wine rack she'd built in to the cupboards just above the refrigerator. She took down a Merlot, figuring that was always a good bet for any casual wine drinker. One glass, a few minutes of conversation, and she could send for a car to take Julie home. Julie, yet another of Savannah's semi-blind dates foisted on her because her loving, meddling cousin thought she ought to be settled down by now. If Savannah wasn't her best friend and hugely pregnant and always there for her, she'd probably try harder to get out of these empty evenings. Rather than listen to Savannah nagging her every other day, she just surrendered.

All the same, she tried to show her dates a good time. After all, it wasn't their fault she'd rather work late than spend an evening with a stranger hoping for a connection she didn't want. This time she'd procured tickets for the final performance of the latest Broadway hit. The show had lived up to its billing, but the rest of the night had held the same sense of déjà vu most of her social life had taken on over the last few years—a *been there, done that, and don't want to do it again* quality that left her feeling oddly disconnected and adrift. "Julie? Red okay with—"

She turned at the soft laugh coming from the hall behind her and stopped in her tracks. A very beautiful and unexpectedly naked woman lounged in the doorway. Julie had looked spectacular in a figure-hugging black outfit that displayed her full-bodied assets to perfection and appeared, if possible, even more stunning without the dress.

Julie gave her a confident, knowing look. "I was rather hoping we could save the wine until later."

Keeping her eyes very deliberately above Julie's collarbone level, two very nice collarbones indeed, Kip carefully set the wine bottle on the counter. "I think we're—"

Before she could finish a diplomatic decline of Julie's generous offer, Julie took two steps into the tiny pocket kitchen and pressed against her, both arms wrapping around her neck.

"I hope you're thinking what I'm thinking," she breathed, her lips grazing Kip's ear.

Kip backed up until her ass bumped into the refrigerator, which wasn't far considering the size of the galley kitchen. Julie followed as if they were superglued together, her breasts—which deserved star billing, as Kip's brief and inadvertent glance had assured her—pressed against her chest, and a shapely thigh insinuated itself between her legs. Kip's pulse shot up higher than her temperature, which was approaching boiling.

"Maybe we should take this—"

Julie's mouth covered hers, her tongue sweeping across Kip's lower lip, her teeth tugging just a little too hard before she pulled away. "Mmm, yes. The bedroom."

A little slower? Like, some other night? Maybe with someone else?

"I think the bedroom would be the perfect place to start," Julie said, her thigh pressing harder between Kip's legs.

"Julie," Kip murmured, her nipples tightening despite her reluctance. She wasn't immune to the allure of a beautiful woman, and Julie was that and disarmingly seductive as well. Plus, the last time she'd had sex wasn't quite a distant memory, but it *was* disappearing in the rearview mirror. All the same, their signals were definitely crossed. If they fell into bed, then what? Good-bye before dawn, which would be Kip's preference? And if that wasn't Julie's picture, where did that leave them? What the hell did a fast hookup mean to Julie—because it meant nothing at all to her, as the last few times without even a hint of an orgasm or any desire to repeat the event had made pretty clear.

Julie's hand slid down between their bodies and tugged at the zipper on her trousers. "I've been thinking about this since I opened the door of my apartment. Savannah was right, you're hot."

"Thanks," Kip said dryly, doing her best not to grab Julie's wrist and forcibly move her questing hand from between her thighs, while imagining herself throttling her cousin.

"Savannah forgot to mention you're exactly my type—black hair, blue eyes, lean and sexy."

"Uh-huh," Kip murmured, finally slipping sideways and backing toward the hallway. Her third-floor apartment in the East Village was big by Village standards, but not that big. She had nowhere to run. She didn't always have to be in control in the bedroom, but she didn't give it up when she barely knew more about a woman than her name either. Usually she didn't have to worry about that—the women she slept with were generally casual acquaintances, friends who were happy to keep things light. "Let's slow this down a little bit."

Following her into the small living room, Julie laughed and gave her an incredulous look. "You can't be serious." She ran her hands over her breasts and cupped them both for an instant. "Tell me you're not interested."

"I'm breathing," Kip said honestly. Watching Julie stroke herself made her clit jump. Sweat misted the back of her neck. For a second her libido threatened to win out over her better judgment and she imagined skimming her tongue over the nipple Julie had just teased into hardness, slipping her fingers between her smooth thighs, knowing just how Julie would sound when she made her come. And then, just like so many other times—when the moment's satisfaction left her empty and confused—the feeling of déjà vu washed over her again in an icy deluge. Reason surfaced. "But I was kind of hoping we could get to know each other tonight. Relax, talk, enjoy some wine."

"I know everything I need to know." Julie resumed stalking, making Kip feel like the weakest, slowest antelope in the herd being tracked by a lioness, with nowhere to hide.

"I guess I'm not being clear." Kip smiled, hoping she could get out of this without causing a major incident with one of Savannah's friends. "I'm not—"

Kip's cell simultaneously chimed and vibrated on the coffee table. She almost cried hallelujah. "Sorry, I better get that."

With a barely muffled snarl, Julie snatched her shirt off a chair and pulled it on, leaving it unbuttoned as she lounged on the sofa, her hungry gaze fixed on Kip.

"Yeah?" Kip sent Julie an apologetic grimace.

"Hey, Kip, it's Phil."

"Hi, Phil." Kip frowned. Why was her cousin, one of the company's managers, calling her at close to midnight on a weeknight? She was labor, not management, and way down the list of family chain of command. "What can I do for you?"

"I might be out of line, but I thought you ought to know Randy is here at the Oasis with a girl. Girlfriend, I guess. It, uh, looks like he's had a fair amount to drink. Her too."

Kip's jaw clenched. "I'll be there in ten minutes. And, Phil, thanks."

"Don't mention it. I don't think he knows I'm here, but if they look like they're leaving, I'll see if I can talk them up and keep them around long enough for you to collect them. From what I can make out, neither one of them should be driving."

"I owe you one." Kip ended the call and shoved the phone into her pocket. Pushing her shirttail back into her trousers with one hand, she scooped her keys off the table with the other. "I'm really sorry, but I need to go. An emergency. You can let yourself out."

"Why don't I just curl up in bed and wait for you." Julie traced one lacquered fingertip along the inside of her thigh and tapped delicately in the area of her clit. "I can finish taking care of this for the moment, and I'll be ready again by the time you get back."

Kip paused at the door. "I don't think that's a good idea. I'm not sure I'll be back tonight. The door will lock after you when you leave. I'm sorry."

Julie shot to her feet, fire in her eyes. "Sorry? You should be sorry. You have no idea what you're missing." She shook her head and muttered under her breath, "Really, no wonder you need your cousin to set you up on a date. Asshole."

"Right," Kip muttered and let herself out. Idiot for trying to keep the family peace when she knew a blind date wasn't headed anywhere but trouble. Ruthlessly putting Julie's furious face and undeniably sexy everything else out of mind, she tapped the Uber app on her phone as she took the stairs down two at a time, and luckily, a driver was nearby. She was in the vehicle and on her way to the club in under a minute.

For the millionth time she wondered what Randy was trying to accomplish by breaking every rule and daring anyone to stop him. If he got picked up again, drinking and drugging with his seriously underage girlfriend in a club, he could be looking at real jail time, no matter what strings her father could pull. She checked her watch as the driver cut to the curb in front of the glittering sign for the trendy club on Lexington. Nine minutes. She tipped him a twenty and jumped out. "Thanks."

The club was in full swing with wall-to-wall hipsters drinking, dancing, jostling, and flying high. She picked Phil out of the crowd at the end of the bar almost at once. Tall and lanky in an open-collared shirt and slim dark pants, with blond hair just brushing his collar and high cheekbones in a narrow face, he was runway handsome and hard to miss. She arrowed through the crowd to his side. "Phil. Thanks for the call. Are they still here?"

"I lost sight of Randy a minute or two ago, but the girl he's with is still over there."

Kip followed the direction of his head tilt and sighed. Lindsay Montgomery, another spoiled rich girl looking for trouble out of boredom or rebellion, she wasn't sure which. Lindsay probably didn't know either. She and Randy were an on-again off-again couple, mostly off again, but apparently tonight was an exception. "Okay, I'll take it from here."

"You want some help?"

"No, Randy will probably be easier to handle if there's just me." She didn't bother to add he'd resent her trying to interfere with his good time, and witnesses to his perceived victimhood would only make him more resistant. She remembered when he'd been small and she'd been his hero. That seemed like another lifetime now.

Lindsay was willowy and blond, her lacy see-through top so low the pale shadows of her nipples were clearly on display. The bottom of her flimsy top rode half an inch or so above the waistband of her skinny jeans. Her heavy dark eye makeup was smeared, her mouth a crimson slash. Bangles, dozens of them, adorned both arms. She looked more like a hooker than an heiress, which Kip figured was exactly her intention. When Lindsay saw her, she cocked a hip and raised an eyebrow.

"My night just got better," Lindsay said.

"Hey, Lindsay, is Randy here somewhere?"

"Is that any kind of hello?" Lindsay feigned a pout and tapped Kip's chest, letting her fingers drop along the curve of her breast.

Kip pulled back and reined in her temper. She was a little tired of being played with. "Randy?"

"He went to the little boys' room. I don't know what he's doing in there unless it's another one of the little boys."

Kip sighed. Randy was as popular with men as women and didn't appear to have any preference for either. If it was fun, especially if it was dangerous, he was there. "Stay here, all right? I'll go get him."

Lindsay hooked a finger over the top of Kip's waistband and tugged, trying to pull her closer. "He'll be back. Why don't you keep me company. I could use a date who knows what to do with a woman."

Kip held back from mentioning at barely eighteen, Lindsay hardly qualified as *woman*. She'd likely get slugged, start a scene, and never get either of them out of the place. She had nothing against Lindsay, but she wasn't her responsibility. Randy was.

"Just do me a favor and stay right here, okay?"

"Hey, *sis*, making time with my girl now?" Randy appeared out of the crowd beside them, his dark hair disheveled, his blue eyes hazy and bloodshot even in the yellowish light of the bar. "Can't get your own pussy?"

"Come on, Randy," Kip said. "Have a little respect for your girlfriend."

He snorted and gave a pointed look to Lindsay's hand, which still rested on Kip's hip. "Yeah, like you?"

"Come on, I'll get you guys a ride home." Randy's pinpoint pupils signaled he'd been using, and Kip hoped it wasn't anything more than a line or two of coke. His grungy T-shirt and threadbare jeans looked like he'd been living in them for a week. He'd managed to talk his way out of rehab after his last arrest by swearing he'd stop using, and she'd thought he was cleaning up his game. She'd been another kind of idiot for believing him.

"We got our own ride." Randy looked at Lindsay. "So what's it gonna be? Cock or cunt for you tonight?"

Heat surging up her spine, Kip grabbed his arm. "Listen to me, you little moron. You took her out, and you're responsible for her. You don't talk to her like that."

He laughed, a dismissive, scornful sound. "Yeah, like you know so much about women. I don't see you doing so well."

"Let's go." She couldn't help trying to reason with him, but any attempt to appeal to the heart she had to believe was hidden beneath anger and contempt was wasted tonight. "We're leaving."

Randy yanked his arm away and pulled a set of keys out of his pocket, dangling them in the air. "I told you, we got a ride."

Kip snatched them from his grasp. "And now so do I. You're not driving anywhere." She glanced at the keys to a Hummer. Must be Lindsay's vehicle. "Where's it parked?"

"A couple blocks away."

"Good, maybe the walk will sober you up."

"We're not going anywhere."

"Yeah, we are." Kip pocketed the keys, grabbed Lindsay's hand, and gripped the back of Randy's shirt. "You either come with me, or I call David."

She had no intention of calling her father's security chief, but the threat was enough to get Randy moving. He cursed and muttered under his breath the entire way, but five minutes later she poured them both into a black Hummer they'd left parked on the street in a not-very-good neighborhood. "You're lucky this thing hasn't been stripped."

"Yeah," Randy said expansively, sprawling in the front seat with Lindsay on his lap. "That's me, lucky." He slid his hand under the lower edge of Lindsay's skimpy top and cupped her breast. She wiggled her ass in his crotch and kissed him.

Gritting her teeth, Kip started the engine, pulled out, and headed north toward the Upper East Side, where Lindsay lived with her parents. Or where she would have if they were home, which was rare. As near as Kip could tell, Lindsay's mother's personal assistant did most of the parenting. They were three blocks away when a patrol car pulled up behind them and lit them up with the light bar. Kip glanced down at the speedometer. Thirty-five miles an hour in a twenty-five mile an hour zone. "Fuck. Really?"

She pulled over and rolled down the window. Before she could even reach for her wallet, a voice came through the loudspeaker of the cruiser behind them. "Exit the vehicle with your hands in the air."

"What?" Kip muttered. She glanced into the side mirror and could make out two officers, one on each side of the car, approaching slowly, weapons drawn. "Cripes. Randy, Lindsay, get out of the car, nice and slow."

"Offer them a hundred bucks," Randy muttered, his hand still under Lindsay's shirt. "You weren't going that fast."

"Exit the vehicle," a voice shouted. Two more patrol cars screeched to a halt, fencing in the Hummer, and officers jumped out, weapons trained on them.

"Randy," Kip said urgently. "This is serious. Get out, both of you, and do exactly as you're told."

Something in her voice must have gotten through to him, because Randy shifted Lindsay off his lap and took a look around.

"Guess a hundred bucks won't be enough."

"Just do what they say." Kip opened the door, extended both arms into the air with her hands visible, and stepped down. A female officer a few inches taller than her, making her just shy of six feet but seeming a whole lot bigger at the moment, pushed her against the vehicle with one hand in the center of her back, grabbed her hands roughly, and cuffed them behind her back.

"What is this—?" A hand pushed Kip's head against the side of the Hummer, hard.

"You're under arrest for possession of a stolen vehicle. You have the right to remain silent. Anything you say can and will…"

"Wait a minute, wait a minute," Kip exclaimed, "there's been a—"

"You have the right to an attorney, if…"

The rest of the Miranda warning went by in a haze. She was pushed into the back of the nearest cruiser, Randy and Lindsay into one of the others. She tried to crane her neck around to check on Randy, but she couldn't turn enough to see. Two officers piled into the front, slammed the doors, and pulled away, leaving the Hummer at the curb. Kip leaned her head back and closed her eyes.

Stolen. Of course. Another perfect ending to a perfect night.

CHAPTER TWO

K ip tried watching street signs as the cruiser sped north past Central Park, but she had trouble seeing much from her cramped position in the back of the patrol car. After a short ride, the officers pulled in behind a squat brick building and the female officer who'd cuffed her initially opened her door, freed the cuffs from the restraining ring, reached in, and grasped her arm.

"Slide on out," the officer said.

Kip complied. "Where are we?"

"Twenty-fifth Precinct—8th and 119th."

Kip didn't see the other cruiser with Randy and Lindsay. That might be a good thing. Or not. She couldn't be sure of anything right then, other than she didn't want to ask too many questions—or answer any. Inside, the halls were brightly lit but relatively empty. They delivered her into a large room with a high counter partitioned into several windows like at a bank or the racetrack. Only one space was occupied.

"Name," the thin, bored-looking officer with a pencil mustache and pronounced widow's peak asked.

"Catherine Wells Kensington," Kip said.

He paused and looked up from his keyboard. "Like the apartments or the appliances?"

Both, somewhere in the family. Kip shook her head. "Rotary engines."

"Huh?"

"I'm a mechanic."

He grinned. "You like cars, I guess."

Kip unclenched her jaw and waited.

"Date of birth?"

She answered his questions, handed over her wallet and ID, the gold ring her grandmother had given her when she'd graduated from high school, and her watch. He tossed everything into a manila envelope with a printed label bearing her name and gave her a voucher.

"Sign here."

Her next stop was another beige room with a few desks, another officer at a computer, and a camera on a tripod. A few minutes later, the female officer—Winobe, according to the black plastic name tag under her badge—escorted her to a cell in a row of them. Only the front wall was barred, the other walls solid, and she couldn't see who else occupied the neighboring cells. She did catch bits of muffled conversation and the sound of someone vomiting. No one sounded like Randy or Lindsay. Before Winobe locked the cell, she removed her handcuffs.

"I'd like to make a phone call," Kip said, rubbing her wrists.

"As soon as the paperwork gets into the system, you'll be able to do that."

"How long will that take?"

The officer shrugged. "Hard to say—could be a few hours."

She disappeared and the hall fell silent.

Kip slumped onto the narrow bunk and checked her watch. The watch that wasn't there. She'd never been arrested before, but she'd thought she knew what to expect. She'd been wrong. She hadn't figured on the incredible depersonalization of the whole process. The feeling that her identity was being stripped away, one layer at a time. First her belongings were confiscated—not just her identification, her license and credit cards, but the personal items she counted as part of who she was. She'd been herded from one spot to another, told where to stand as cameras flashed, told to hold out her hand as strangers impassively pressed her digits to a screen and printed her, all the while never really looking at her. The common expression seemed to be bored, as if she were already just a number like the one on the card they handed her to put in front of her chest for the photographs.

By the time the process was over, she was numb, struggling to hold on to reality in an unreal situation, fighting to remember who she was outside these walls. If this was how she felt after a few hours, what must it be like to be cast into the system for weeks, months, years? What became of a person who was no longer a person, but simply a number, a body in a long line of bodies moving along on the tide of someone else's will? She shivered although the building wasn't really cold.

The cell held a stainless steel toilet, a narrow bunk with a gray sheet that had once been white, a thin wool blanket, and a miniscule sink bolted to the concrete floor in the corner. The wall across from the barred opening was beige and blank. Kip had to struggle to keep from feeling claustrophobic, despite the openings between the bars. She was locked in and no one knew where she was—her life outside this cell had stopped like the hands on a broken watch. Needing to move, to feel her body obey her will just to know there was one last thing she could still control, she splashed cold water on her face at the tiny sink in the corner, pulled the blanket off the bed, and wrapped it around her shoulders. Leaning back against the wall, she stared at the bars and reminded herself she was in New York City and she had rights. She would not just disappear. Her racing heart hadn't yet gotten the message.

She might've drifted, but it didn't feel like very long when approaching footsteps brought her out of her unexpected half sleep. It had to be close to four in the morning and her body had decided she wasn't in charge after all. The numbness had reached her brain, apparently. She threw off the blanket and stood, shaking her hands to get some feeling back in her tingling fingertips.

A different officer, this one young, husky, and sporting a friendly smile, unlocked the door again. "You can make three free calls. Come with me."

He led her back down the hall in the opposite direction from where she'd been before. Kip hurried along beside him, seeing figures in the semidark cells, some sitting as she had been, most curled on the bunks with their faces to the walls. He directed her into a long, narrow room with a row of booths holding landlines perched on narrow oak shelves. He closed the door and stood with his back to it.

"Thanks," Kip said. He said nothing, so she straddled the backless stool in the farthest cubicle and looked over her shoulder, judging how much of her conversation he could hear. She guessed probably all of it. She picked up the phone and carefully entered her father's private number.

He answered immediately, sounding surprisingly alert, although he ought to still have been sleeping. She resisted clearing her throat, needing to sound steady and sure, more for herself than for him. "I'm sorry to wake you, Dad. I'm at the police station, and I need an attorney."

"I've been expecting your call. Where are you?"

"The Twenty-fifth Precinct—how did…" She halted when her brain finally started working. Right. "You've heard from Randy?"

"Yes. Several hours ago."

"He's…doing all right?"

"Your brother," her father's cool voice intoned, "is currently packing his bags and will be checking in to a private facility in the morning for some long-overdue medical attention."

"Good. That sounds…best." Randy was finally going to get the help he resisted but so desperately needed, as long as she didn't mention he and his girlfriend had actually stolen the Hummer.

"I assumed you would agree. Have they charged you?"

"Yes."

"I don't have to tell you not to give any kind of statement. Jeremy Carver will be along to take care of things."

"Thanks," Kip said softly as her father said good-bye and rang off. She settled the phone back in the cradle and stared at the dull wall a foot away. He hadn't asked her if she was hurt or told her he knew she was innocent. He must know that, but then, Randy was the one who needed protecting. Not her.

She rose, turned, and nodded curtly to the guard. "I'm done."

He lifted a shoulder. "You got two more coming."

She had no one else to call. "No, thanks."

"Your decision." He pushed away, rapped on the door, and someone opened it.

Back in the cell a few minutes later, she stretched out and closed her eyes, hoping to sleep a little like most of her neighbors. She dozed for an hour, maybe a little more, she couldn't be sure, when the clang of the bars woke her. She was usually good with time, often didn't need her watch to know the precise time within a minute, but time had twisted since they'd put her in the back of the patrol car, slowed somehow. Everything was just a little skewed, as if the entire world had tilted beneath her and she couldn't quite get her balance.

They took her to a cubicle not much more than six by six—practically a booth—with a narrow table and a chair on each side. No windows, no TV, no posters on the wall. Blank, like her mind tried to be. Jeremy Carver came in a few minutes later dressed in a navy suit and tie with thin gray pinstripes. His light brown hair was trimmed close on the sides and longer on the top so it slanted just enough across his forehead to look windblown but not messy. His dark brown eyes were bright and intelligent, his face clean-shaven, lightly tanned even though spring had barely arrived, and his expression concerned and businesslike. He held a cardboard cup of coffee in his hand.

"Catherine," Jeremy said, sliding the coffee across the table to her and propping his briefcase open onto the table. He sat across from her. "Do you have any injuries—anything untoward happen during the detention process? Do you require medical attention?"

"No. Thanks for the coffee." Kip grasped the cup and sipped despite the steaming temperature. A little life returned with the first scalding swallow. Her brain started to move again like a sluggish river breaking free of an ice floe in the last days of winter. She didn't know Jeremy well, but his presence felt like a lifeline. "And thanks for coming."

Jeremy nodded. "Of course. We only have a few minutes before you're moved to central booking and arraignment is set. I'm going to push for a DAT but—"

"Wait, slow down—translate that."

"Depending on the arresting officer's report and the judge's assessment of the charges, we may be able to get you released tonight, prior to arraignment."

"I wouldn't have to spend another night here." Hope flickered, a flame banishing the cold gripping her insides.

His expression flattened. "I'm afraid it could be a bit longer than that if we can't get you released."

"Right. Okay. We'll hope for option one, then." Kip took a breath. "Then what?"

"Then we go before the judge and enter our plea." He smiled thinly. "Want to tell me what happened?"

"My brother wasn't charged?"

He regarded her steadily. "Not as far as I know. How did you come to be driving a stolen Hummer?"

Kip hesitated. Randy'd had the keys to the Hummer. She'd assumed the vehicle was Lindsay's. Wrong assumption. "I'd rather not say."

"You'd rather not say." He blew out a breath. "The Hummer belongs to Robert Ingram, who happens to live in Lindsay Montgomery's building. You know him?"

"No."

"You've been to the building?"

"Yes, for a party now and then."

"And she's your brother Randy's girlfriend."

"I guess you'd have to ask him that."

"Were you driving it?"

"Yes."

"Did you know it was stolen?"

"No, I didn't."

"Where were you going?"

Kip didn't see any reason not to answer as much as she could, short of dragging Randy back into the middle. He was on his way to rehab, which was what he needed—not a year or more in jail. "I was taking Lindsay home."

"And the vehicle?"

"I was planning to leave it there."

"You had no intention of disposing of stolen property?"

"None."

As she talked, he tapped into his tablet.

"What were you doing tonight, before they stopped you?"

"I had a date. I was out most of the evening."

"Your date's name?"

"Why is that important?"

"We need to establish whether you had access to the vehicle earlier in the evening."

Kip sighed. "Julie Rothstein."

"Number?" he asked without looking up.

She told him, wondering how pissed Julie really was over the way the evening ended. Hopefully not enough to forget the details of when and where they spent the night.

"Okay, what time did the two of you part?"

"A little while after midnight."

"And then where did you go?"

"The Oasis."

"What time?"

"Right about one."

"Why did you decide to leave your date and go to a club?"

"I got a call that Randy was there, and I went to get him."

"How did you get there?"

"Uber."

"How did you get the Hummer?"

"I'd rather not say."

"Look, Kip, I know you didn't steal it, and we can argue you had every intention of returning it. But you can do jail time if we let things stand."

Cold slithered down her spine. "How much?"

"Given the nonviolent nature of the crime and the fact that you're a first offender, probably the minimum, which still might be a year."

She swallowed against a surge of bile. With Randy's record, he wouldn't get such an easy sentence. "I was driving. I can't change that."

He set his tablet down and leaned back in the chair. "If you plead guilty, I can probably get the charges reduced and some kind of probation. We'll avoid a trial and any further investigation of the actual theft."

Translated as, Randy's part in all of it would not come to light.

"I'll plead guilty."

"You do understand there's no guarantee. Are you really willing to risk going to jail for your brother?"

Kip pushed the cardboard cup across the table toward him. "You think I could get another cup of coffee?"

CHAPTER THREE

Jordan heard the rooster crowing as soon as she got out of her truck. She hurried to the back gate, unlocked the padlock, and pushed through the wooden door, the newly oiled hinges soundless as it swung closed behind her. She noted the broccoli needed cutting as she angled through the narrow dirt aisles to the plywood and chain-link enclosure tucked under the eve of the big metal garden shed in the right rear corner of the reclaimed lot.

"Hush," she said as she got closer. "I know I'm a few minutes late, but the damn truck wouldn't start again. And you're supposed to be quiet."

The rooster, a brilliantly plumed dandy with green and purple highlights adorning his wings and tail, paced arrogantly around the six- by six-foot enclosure, his more conservatively hued brown and tan hens milling about in a patch of early morning sunlight, waiting to start their assault on the various and abundant insects populating the nascent garden.

"Just because we don't have any neighbors close enough to hear you doesn't mean you can make a ruckus." Jordan unlatched the door and the flock scampered out single file, the rooster, of course, in the lead. She paused a moment, smiling as always at their comical gaits and energetic busyness. The rooster ignored her, as usual, but at least he stopped crowing.

"It's not my fault the city has an ordinance against roosters. If you guys weren't so noisy and didn't have to announce just exactly how important you were every morning before dawn, we probably wouldn't have to worry about you getting evicted." She restocked their pellets, replaced their water with fresh, and checked the half dozen nesting boxes for eggs. Happily, the hens recognized spring had arrived and were starting to lay. Using the tail of her checked cotton button-down as a makeshift apron, she collected the eggs in the fold of fabric and carefully picked her way between wheelbarrows, tools, bags of topsoil, and loops of hose to the refurbished seventeen-foot egg-shaped canary-yellow RV she used as an office. She got them safely into the minifridge tucked under the door balanced on two stacks of crates she used as a desk without losing any along the way. They'd be able to start selling them in quantity soon, and every penny would be welcome. Although just who they'd get to deliver them was a question she didn't want to ponder so early in the day.

Chickens and eggs secured, she checked the day's agenda. She needed to make a trip to the nursery for fertilizer, peat moss, and the tomato seedlings but the truck needed gas, probably oil, and possibly divine intervention. Tomorrow would be soon enough for that trip. The nights were still cool enough they had a little window of time to get the ground ready for the tomatoes. She had an eleven o'clock phone appointment with a new restaurant in Soho that was looking for locally sourced vegetables, and another with a caterer on the East Side in the early afternoon. Their list of customers for locally sourced eggs and produce was growing, but it needed to get a lot longer if they were going to be self-sufficient by the end of the summer. Her grant money from the New York Community Reclamation Project was going to run out well before that, and she needed to demonstrate this location could generate income before the funding would be renewed for the next year. She leaned back and rubbed her eyes, columns of numbers sliding across the surface of her closed lids. No matter how she added them up, the bottom line still looked red.

"Morning," a lilting Jamaican-accented voice called from the open trailer door.

"Tya, hi!" Jordan swiveled in her chair, relieved to be free of her mental calculations and glad for the company. "You're early."

The petite woman in denim shorts and a sleeveless navy top nodded, her deep brown eyes shimmering with warmth and perpetual hope, or so it seemed to Jordan. She envied her that optimism, especially on days like this one. Tya passed Jordan a take-out cup of coffee. "Field trip—the kids needed to be dropped off an hour early today."

"Ah, thanks." Jordan pried off the lid and took a deep breath of dark-roasted beans and vanilla undertones. "Where are they off to?"

"The Space Museum. Henry isn't so sure how he feels about that, but Amalia is delighted."

"She's still planning to be a pilot someday?"

Tya laughed. "Absolutely. Henry changes his mind along with his T-shirts, but she never loses her focus." She shook her head, her expression a mixture of pride and wonder. "He can't wait for summer vacation, and she's already mourning losing time at school. If I didn't know they were twins, I'd wonder that they were even related."

"What are they planning for the summer?"

The gleam in Tya's eyes dimmed and she pulled her lip between her teeth. "The summer program at school doesn't really interest either of them, and I don't really blame them. They're both too advanced for the classes being offered. My mother offered to watch them for part of the day, but she's slowing down and though she says she doesn't mind, it's hardly fair. She did so much when they were babies, and she deserves a rest."

Jordan couldn't imagine raising two kids alone. Tya didn't need to say she didn't have the means for any kind of private day camp program. "Why don't you bring them here?"

"Oh." Tya's face lit up again. "You don't think they'd be in the way?"

"I'm sure we can keep them busy. That is, if you don't mind volunteering them."

"Consider them volunteered." Tya laughed. "That would be wonderful, and good for them too. Amalia spends way too much time in her room reading, and Henry spends his with video games."

"It's settled, then." Tya's twelve-year-olds would help counter their perpetual lack of help, plus they were great kids and they'd bring their boundless good spirits with them.

Tya sat down in the open trailer doorway and rested her back against the frame. "There's going to be a lot of work to do here this summer, especially if we're going to start making deliveries to the restaurants. Have you had any luck finding a driver yet?"

Jordan shook her head. "Unfortunately, what we can afford to pay is not very enticing for most people, especially with the kinds of hours they'll have to keep."

"Yeah, four a.m. deliveries don't appeal to a lot of people." Tya balanced her cup on her knee. "Once we get established, I'm sure we'll get more volunteers."

"We'll manage somehow," Jordan said, wondering if she could get by on yet less sleep and deliver their produce herself. She'd known it would take time to establish the community garden and draw in local volunteer help to supplement those she could pay.

"What are we going to do about the greenhouse?" Tya asked.

Jordan forced a smile she didn't feel. Tya needed this job desperately, and she didn't want to worry her with the financial concerns of keeping the project going. They'd become friends in the last three months, working side by side clearing the junk from the three-lot parcel just off Ninth Avenue the city had designated as a community garden project. They'd supervised the fence and coop construction and dug decades of rubble from the weed- and rock-infested ground. Now they had half a dozen raised beds, a space mapped out for the greenhouse, and plans to deliver their produce to local food pantries, restaurants, and hotels. But as much as they shared the dream and the labor, the responsibility of keeping the project afloat was hers, and she wasn't going to let Tya know how tenuous their situation really was.

"We don't need to worry about that until the end of the summer. We've got until frost to get the rest of the lot cleared and the greenhouse up. Then we'll be able to get our greens and tomatoes ready for the winter. We'll have plenty to do, don't worry."

"Another week we'll be past a late spring frost, don't you think?" Tya rose and dusted off the back of her khaki work pants.

"According to the almanac, but then you know how accurate that is."

"Well, we can't take any chances with our babies," Tya said, looking toward the three long rows of fabric-covered greens and seedlings.

"We won't." Jordan looked out over the small oasis of life in an otherwise abandoned stretch of windowless buildings, boarded-up stores, and trash-strewn streets. No, she wasn't going to let anything happen to this little glitter of hope in such a desolate land.

❖

The overhead light came on, signaling something—dawn, the changing of the guard, the morning meal? As Kip's fellow detainees stirred, the noise level in the cell block climbed with a jumbled chorus of coughs, curses, and surly snarls. Kip rose from her bunk where she'd been staring at the ceiling since Jeremy had left, and leaned against the bars, angling her head to see down the hall. Shadows writhed across the worn tile floor, shapeless, genderless forms that sent a twist of dread through her depths. How long did it take until the shadows crept beneath flesh and into bone, until all of them were reduced to ghosts, inside and out? *Them.* She was one of them now.

An officer approached her cell, his features coming into focus as he neared. Youngish, multiracial, close-cropped military-style dark hair. She held her breath as he fit a key to the lock on her cell.

"You're being released," he said amiably. "You'll get your belongings returned on your way out."

"Thanks," Kip said, her throat dry and scratchy. She hadn't had anything to eat and nothing to drink since the last cup of acidic coffee Carver had gotten for her. Her stomach was queasy and her head throbbed, but she'd never felt quite so exhilarated in her life. The taste of freedom would be enough to sustain her for a lifetime at this point.

After she'd been handed the manila envelope and told to check her belongings and sign where indicated to confirm everything was there, she was directed to a plain windowless door marked *Exit*.

Exit. Could it be that easy? She could walk out, but she would never forget the helplessness. She forced herself to walk slowly—she would not become a cornered animal and run. She expected Carver to be waiting for her, but Savannah jumped up and rushed to her with a sharp cry.

"Oh my God, are you all right?" Her cousin grasped her shoulders and pulled her into a tight hug.

"I'm okay, I'm okay." Kip jolted at the foreign sensation of arms holding her tight, and the rigid control she'd marshaled the last few hours to keep from screaming began to crumble. She took a breath and gently tried to extract herself from Savannah's embrace. "I must smell pretty bad, so you should probably let me go."

"Not too bad." Savannah laughed, her cheek against Kip's. "Believe me, both of us have looked and probably smelled a lot worse after some of those keg parties."

Kip tried to remember what it had been like to be younger and carefree, but at the moment, the specter of the bare cell and the stark bars was all she could envision. She finally pulled away. She missed the contact instantly but needed the distance. "Thanks for coming. You didn't need to."

"Of course I did."

"How did you know I was here?"

"Uncle Robert called and asked me to come. I would have been here sooner, if I'd known."

Desperate to get outside, Kip pushed through the revolving glass doors into a muggy Manhattan morning. The sights and smells of New York came rushing back, and she'd never found them so welcome. "I'm glad you didn't come sooner. There wasn't anything you could have done. Did Dad hear anything from my attorney?"

"Yes, you need to be at the courthouse at eleven. I've got the address—Uncle Robert is sending a car."

"What time is it?"

"A little after eight. I'm taking you to my place to get cleaned up and changed."

With her long blond hair loose and down to her shoulders, Savannah didn't look much different than when they'd started college. Kip imagined *she* must look like she'd aged a decade overnight. She felt as if she had. "You shouldn't be running around doing all this. I'll get an Uber."

Savannah clapped her hands on her hips, her baby bump barely perceptible beneath her white button-down shirt and black stretch pants. "You most certainly will not. I'm staying with you until this mess is cleaned up."

Kip shook her head. "No, you're not. You're not getting dragged around the city and sitting in the courthouse all day. I'll be fine."

"Don't be ridiculous. You're not going through this alone. And how the hell did this happen anyhow?" Savannah set her jaw in that way that reminded Kip of a tiny bulldog, stubborn and immovable and unexpectedly powerful.

Kip glanced around. With the usual obliviousness of New Yorkers, passersby skirted around them as if they weren't both standing in the middle of the sidewalk. She still didn't want to be overheard and barely registered the newfound paranoia. "I'll tell you when we get to your place. Let's get a cab."

She flagged one down and closed her eyes while the cabbie took them on the brief ride to Savannah's apartment on the West Side.

"I've got clothes that will fit you," Savannah said as she let them into her apartment.

The place was small but had a multi-million-dollar view of the park, which at any other time Kip would have paused to enjoy. "I really need a shower."

"Go ahead and I'll— Have you eaten? What do you want?"

"I'm not hungry."

"I don't care. You're eating something, so either choose or eat what I make."

Kip grinned, a little bit of normalcy filtering back into her world. Savannah had always been so bossy. Younger than her by only a few weeks, they were more sisters than cousins. They'd gone to the same schools since they were five, shared stories of boyfriends and girlfriends throughout high school, and applied to the same colleges so they could room together. That was where their lives had started to part ways a little. Savannah had managed to escape the tentacles of the Kensington family businesses that employed most of their parents' and their own generation, pursuing her career in art instead. But still, she was the sibling Randy might have been if things had been different. Randy. She'd failed him, and she still didn't know why. "Bagels?"

Savannah rolled her eyes. "Of course."

"That would be good."

Savannah made a shooing motion. "Get cleaned up and changed. Then you can tell me everything."

Kip stood for a long time in the shower, her head tilted back, hot needles stinging her face and chest. Even after her skin began to scald and hunger finally drove her from the shower, she couldn't shake the sense of being not quite clean. Tainted somehow, as if the air in the cell had permeated her pores.

She toweled off her hair, finger combed it, and dressed in the trousers and shirt Savannah had left for her. They were close enough in size that the fit was good, although the waist was a little tight for her. She avoided the mirror, afraid of what changes she might see there.

Settling at the small table tucked into the eating nook facing the park, she opened the window and breathed deeply. The air smelled faintly of blossoms and the ever-present undercurrent of New York—fumes, food, and the sweet musky scents of humanity, of life. "Thanks for everything."

Savannah slid a buttered bagel and a hot cup of coffee in front of her. "What can you tell me?"

Kip shook her head. "It's probably better if we let it go."

"Better for who?" Savannah snapped.

"The fact is I was driving a stolen car."

Savannah hissed. "Like you would steal a car."

Kip shrugged. "I made a stupid assumption, and I should have known better."

"Let me guess—Randy is part of all this."

"Look, I know you're not fond of Randy, and—"

"That's not true. I love him, but he's…" Savannah sighed. "That's not the point right now. Is he all right?"

"He's on his way to rehab. Maybe this time…"

"Maybe. I hope so." Savannah gripped her hand. "And maybe it's time you let him stand on his own."

Kip sighed. "I know, and you're right. But there's a difference between tough love and throwing him to the wolves."

"And what about you? What if—" Savannah swiped at the moisture in her eyes. "God, Kip. What if something bad happens, and you—this is ridiculous. You can't go to jail!"

"My father wouldn't have sent Carver if he wasn't a good attorney, so it's not going to come to that." Kip willed herself to believe her own words, but somewhere in the hours between the first click of the cuffs on her wrists and the clank of the cell gate opening, she'd lost the ability to trust, or hope.

CHAPTER FOUR

At ten thirty, Kip stepped out of the car in front of Manhattan Central Booking. At street level the five-story gray stone building looked like hundreds of others in the city. She'd probably passed it dozens of times and never noticed it. This morning, however, every arched window exuded a threatening aura, as if warning that once inside, there was no escape. She squared her shoulders.

"I wish you'd stayed home," Kip murmured to Savannah.

"And I wish you'd be quiet." Savannah clutched her hand.

Kip squeezed back. "I'm glad you're so stubborn. It helps."

"I know."

Kip let out a long sigh. She really did have to trust Carver. "Okay, let's get this done."

She and Savannah shuffled along in a line two and three people wide until they reached the metal detector. Kip hated removing her watch and wallet, instantly transported back to those moments when everything had been stripped away—her identity, her dignity, her power. Stepping through the barrier, she quickly retrieved her belongings, and they followed the sign to the courtrooms down a long marble-floored corridor. The carved wooden doors set back in alcoves were all closed. Their footsteps mingled with those of dozens of others, disappearing into the shadowy recesses of the cavernous ceilings. When they found Courtroom C with Judge Neville Aronson's name on a bronze plaque next to it, they squeezed onto a long bench with half a dozen other nervous-looking individuals ranging from teens in baggy jeans and unlaced sneakers with T-shirts sporting baseball and football insignias hanging over their belts, to elderly women with threadbare cardigans and shoes too small for their swollen feet.

Kip's stomach soured and a headache set up a steady pounding at the base of her skull. Yesterday at this time she'd been discussing engine performance with a design tech at the factory in Hoboken, her biggest concerns how well the bearings would wear at the projected speeds and where to take Julie for dinner. Julie, the theater, sex—hell, simple human pleasures—all seemed foreign to her now. Remote and inconsequential.

At a few minutes before eleven, Carver came striding down the hall, briefcase swinging, his step quick and confident. He'd changed his suit to a navy one with a monochrome shirt and thin pale green tie. Hip but not too hip, and not a single crease in his face to suggest he'd missed a night's sleep.

"Walk with me," he said, leading Kip to the far end of the hall.

"How are we doing?" Kip said when they were alone.

"I just finished talking to the ADA. They're willing to reduce the charges if you plead guilty. The judge has the final say, but there's a very good possibility you'll get some kind of probation."

Kip let out a long breath. "What's the charge, then?"

The corner of his mouth lifted. "Joyriding."

"Joyriding." Kip stared. He had to be joking. Carver quirked a brow. Okay, he wasn't. "All right, fine. What does that mean in terms of charges, exactly?"

"It's a misdemeanor rather than a felony, since the charge indicates you had no intention of depriving the rightful owner of his property and planned only temporary use of his vehicle."

"Well, that's actually fairly accurate, although not conscious on my part."

"Yes, well, we're not going to get into the specifics of how you came to be driving."

Meaning they weren't going to mention Randy having the keys. "I understand. And that's irrelevant now. So how does this work?"

"We still have to get through the arraignment, enter your plea, and hope that Judge Aronson is in a benevolent mood this afternoon."

"If he isn't?"

"Judges tend to go easy with the sentencing in this kind of crime, and considering your family profile, I expect he'll be lenient." Carver lifted a shoulder. "If for some reason he wants to make a statement of some kind, you could spend a little while in prison."

"How much time?"

"Usually a year—the max is three."

Kip's vision dimmed, and a swell of nausea filled her throat. The breath in her chest burned. She'd never been given to panic, but claustrophobia rode her hard. She couldn't go back into that cell. She'd almost drowned once, and last night had felt exactly the same. Airless and suffocating.

"Look, that's not likely to happen."

Carver's smooth voice edged into Kip's consciousness, and she forced herself to focus. No matter what came next, she'd find a way to handle it. She always had.

❖

Jordan coaxed the sputtering truck down the weed-choked alley between the stockade fence enclosing the acre of land that made up the Ninth Avenue Community Garden and the adjacent, abandoned three-story building. Even at midday the building blocked the sun from ever reaching the ground, and now, at a little after six, the passageway was nearly dark. By the time she approached the parking spot she'd cleared of broken bricks and glass shards, the engine had quit and she was coasting. The gas gauge indicated she had a quarter of a tank still, and she'd checked the oil just the day before. She was no mechanic and didn't have a clue what was wrong, but one thing she did know was she couldn't afford to lose this truck. Or fix it, for that matter.

After a long day spent preparing planting beds, making phone calls hunting up customers, and making a late pickup at the hardware store, she was too damn tired to sort out one more problem. She wanted to secure the flock and head home. She climbed out, locked the truck, and sorted her keys while heading for the gate. Heart stuttering, she stopped abruptly.

The padlock and part of the hasp lay on the ground, half hidden in the weeds. The gate stood open a few inches. She fumbled for her cell phone in her back pocket and with her thumb hovering over emergency, pictured the rows of greens waiting to be cut and packaged, the seedlings barely out of the ground, the helpless flock. Every important document and contact she had was in her office.

Damn it, she couldn't just stand out here and wait. She eased the gate open, thankful again she'd thought to oil the hinges, and grabbed a hoe from a large plastic barrel filled with spades and rakes and other garden implements just inside the gate. Brandishing it in two hands like a club, she started down the center aisle, blinking in the early evening gloom. She saw the intruder right away, peering into the chicken coop, one hand on the latch.

She hefted the hoe. Speed was probably more important than stealth. Racing forward with a loud cry, she aimed to strike at an arm holding a weapon or any other body part she could get to.

A woman swung around and jumped back from the coop with both hands out in front of her, eyes wide. "Whoa, whoa, whoa, whoa! Friend. Friend!"

Jordan jerked to a stop, the hoe still angled over her right shoulder for a strike. "Who the hell are you?"

"Ah..." Kip couldn't come up with anything intelligible while her stomach occupied her throat. The woman brandishing the hoe looked like an avenging angel, her long, dusty-blond hair swirling around a narrow, sculpted face, her wide green eyes piercing, her pose fierce and fearless. If she hadn't been about to brain her, Kip would've found her incredibly beautiful. Another time, another *life*time, sexy even. But not any longer. "I work here."

"You most certainly do not. What were you trying to steal? Fertilizer for meth or something?"

Kip couldn't help it, she laughed. "Right. Do I look like a meth head to you?"

Jordan narrowed her eyes, starting to feel just a little bit foolish. The stranger was just about her height, with clear blue eyes, collar-length dark hair that was a little shaggy but professionally styled in the recent past, a slightly wrinkled white shirt tucked into black trousers, and loafers that were definitely not meant for hard labor. No jewelry, but the end of an iPhone peeked out of her pants pocket. No vagrant, and likely no thief. Jordan lowered the hoe but kept it in both hands, just in case. "Why did you break in here?"

"I didn't," Kip said. "The gate was open and I thought I heard someone, some*thing*, screaming. I came in to take a look around."

"The padlock has been jimmied off the gate," Jordan said. "You're inside where you don't belong. Ergo, you're the most likely person to have broken in."

"Logical, but incorrect." Kip's insides dropped. "Please, please tell me you didn't call the police."

"Why not?"

Kip swallowed. "Did you?"

Her fear was palpable and Jordan didn't truly think she was dangerous. "No."

"I wasn't kidding," Kip said quickly, relief making her light-headed. "I work here. Or I'm supposed to, starting tomorrow."

"Since this is my place and I didn't hire you, that's a really bad lie."

Kip frowned. "This is the Ninth Avenue Community Garden project, right? I got the address right." She pulled a slip of paper out of her pocket and double-checked it. "I wasn't sure I could find it and I…I felt like walking. When I heard the scream, I came in. I didn't see anyone, and…well, here we are."

"Let me see that."

Wordlessly, Kip handed it over.

"What's your name?"

"Kip."

"I'm Jordan Rice." Jordan took the paper and, dividing her attention between Kip and the printed form, scanned it quickly. From what she could gather in a cursory glance, one Catherine Kensington had been sentenced to four hundred hours of community service to be fulfilled at…the Ninth Avenue Community Garden. She looked up into expectant eyes, surprised to see amusement there. "I don't think any of this is funny." She waved the paper. "I don't know anything about this, and I'll need to make some phone calls. I wasn't aware that we were being assigned…"

"Criminals?" Kip said flatly.

"Anyone," Jordan finished a little self-consciously. Picturing this woman as a criminal was very difficult to do, but she'd obviously committed some kind of crime since this paper was a court order. Community service. Didn't that usually mean drug offense or petty theft—shoplifting, forgery—God, she didn't really know. "If you're any kind of violent offender, you're not working here."

Kip paled and Jordan regretted her words, but she didn't apologize. She had Tya and, soon, the two kids to think of. She hadn't asked for this woman to be sent here, and no one had discussed it with her.

"I assure you, I am not a violent criminal or a sexual predator. That's what you're thinking, isn't it?"

Jordan held her gaze. Denying she at least had to rule those things out would be pointless. "Look, let me get some more information and we can sort this out."

Kip glanced at her watch. Seven p.m. "I don't think anyone is going to be available to answer your questions until tomorrow. What are you doing here now anyhow?"

"My place, remember?" Jordan gritted her teeth. Why did she keep answering this woman's questions? Why didn't she just tell her to leave? "Ordinarily I'd be getting ready to close up, but my truck has decided to die in the alley. So now, in addition to dealing with you, I have to get a mechanic and a tow truck out here. So my night is not exactly going according to plan."

"Well, it must be your lucky day," Kip said. "Or night, rather."

Jordan scoffed. "Believe me, I seriously doubt that."

"I'm a mechanic. Do you have any tools?"

"How fortunate," Jordan said, wondering if that was some kind of con.

"Believe me or don't, but if you want your truck fixed, cheap and now, you'll let me take a look at it."

The idea of saving some money and time was worth the risk. "We've got some basics in the garden shed. I don't know if they'll be what you need."

"Let me check and see."

Jordan gestured with the hoe toward the metal shed in the corner. "Over there. I'll get you the key in a second. I need to put the chickens up."

"I think one of them is dying," Kip said. "That's what I heard screeching, I think."

Jordan laughed. "She's just upset because she likes to lay her eggs in the straw pile over in the corner and I was late getting here and haven't let them in yet."

"I didn't think laying eggs was such a painful process. Aren't they supposed to do that naturally?"

"Well, you've seen the size of them. How would you like to push—"

Kip shot up a hand. "Never mind. I don't need that picture. I'll just grab those tools and see to the truck."

Jordan gave Kip the key and watched Kip stride to the shed, still irritated but intrigued despite herself. The woman was a mass of contradictions—confident one second, almost panicked the next; charming and funny, and guilty of some crime; polished and attractive and afoul of the law. Good looks and smooth manners meant nothing— anyone could be dangerous, no matter how innocent they appeared. Catherine Kensington had to have been involved in something criminal even if she had been only sentenced to community service, and that was enough reason to be careful. No matter how friendly or good-looking she happened to be.

CHAPTER FIVE

If she couldn't hear the faint clatter coming from the garden shed, Jordan might've thought she'd just imagined the whole interlude. Catherine—Kip—Kensington did not look like someone who ought to be sentenced to community service or act like someone who ought to be working in a community garden at all, for that matter. Except for those few moments when she'd been visibly anxious about the idea of police showing up, she'd been cool and confident and surprisingly engaging. If Jordan had met her at a social gathering, she would have pegged Kip as a businesswoman or attorney, going by her appearance and mannerisms—and that was still possible. Individuals convicted of white-collar crimes probably received reduced sentences all the time, with lip service to community service thrown in. Kip didn't look like any mechanic Jordan had ever seen either, but she supposed she didn't look like a farmer, even though at heart she was never far from the countryside she'd grown up in.

Jordan mentally ran some quick math. Four hundred hours was a long time. Regardless of who Kip appeared to be, she was apparently going to be spending quite a bit of the spring and summer at the project, as Jordan thought of the garden. She could use the help, no doubt about that, but she didn't look forward to overseeing someone who resented being there or in all likelihood was going to make more work for her instead of less. Surely she'd be required to keep some kind of record of Kip's hours—honestly, the idea sounded worse and worse by the second. Maybe there was some way to get her assigned somewhere else. After all, she hadn't requested or volunteered for this kind of court-appointed assistance. Just because Kip was friendly and effortlessly attractive and impossible to easily categorize didn't make one damn bit of difference.

Jordan shook her head. She wasn't given to finding strangers, particularly strangers who came with big red flashing warning signs, instantly fascinating. Now, there was a thought she didn't want to dwell on. She hadn't found a woman fascinating in ages—or maybe she just hadn't taken the time to really look at some of the interesting women she met. And there was something *else* she didn't want to look at too closely. Why she was so relentlessly single. She couldn't blame a broken heart or a string of failures—if anything, she could point to a series of enjoyable if less than earthshattering relationships that had slowly dwindled in length and frequency in the fifteen years since she'd finished college and taken a position with the Cornell Agricultural Extension. Sure, she worked a lot, but so did most people. But when she wasn't working, she spent her time in solitary pursuits—reading, watching late-night movies, biking in Central Park. Usually one weekend a month or so she'd have lunch out with Tya and the kids. She didn't go out clubbing, she avoided invitations from colleagues to social gatherings, and she hadn't initiated a personal connection with a woman in recent memory. So she was a little introverted. Considering the circumstances, just as well. She already knew enough about Kip to know she'd be wise not to want to know more. Stymied and annoyed by circumstances she couldn't change, at least not until morning, she did the sensible thing. She called the chickens.

"Come on, girls, time for bed."

Routine always served her well. A plan, a purpose, was the antidote to everything—kept her mind occupied, her body satisfied enough to make other satisfactions unnecessary, and most days, left her content if not exactly completely happy.

She latched the coop, turned to go, and jumped in surprise. "Oh!"

"Sorry," Kip said from right behind her.

"Hey," Jordan said as her heart rate settled back toward normal. "Find what you need?"

"Enough basic tools to check a few things, although I might need to bring some of my own if there's anything major amiss. But it occurred to me we ought to check the place out, make sure no one is hiding anywhere."

Kip stood with legs spread, one hand in her pocket, a wrench dangling loosely from the other. A faint smile lifted the corner of her mouth, and the sun, rapidly dropping behind the buildings, caught her in its last glancing rays, highlighting the sharp angles of her face and appealingly unkempt dark hair, giving her the careless look of a ruffian, or a pirate. Promptly squelching that image, Jordan swept her arm to take in the open lot. "Hiding where? Under a wheelbarrow?"

"I didn't see or hear anyone except the tortured hen when I walked in," Kip said, "but it'd probably be a good idea to check your trailer."

"I'll do that." Smothering her swift jolt of discomfort, Jordan started across the lot. "I was planning to see if anything had been disturbed, although I didn't think about anyone actually still being inside."

"I'll come with you." Kip's tone wasn't asking permission.

"All right." Jordan surprised herself by agreeing. She didn't need any kind of protection and hadn't relied on anyone for help except for Tya's friendship in a long time, but it just made sense for the two of them to check together. And she never argued with being sensible. She led the way to the trailer and frowned when she saw the door slightly ajar. Halting abruptly, she muttered, "Damn it."

Kip stepped in front of her, her body angled toward the trailer door, weight on her back leg, right arm raised, wrench at the ready. "What is it?"

"Someone's been in there. I know I left the door closed when I left."

"This is where we call the police, then."

"I thought you didn't want me to do that."

Kip kept her eyes on the door. "I'm not anxious to be in their sights again, but I don't want you in any danger either. Go ahead, call 9-1-1."

Jordan dragged her phone from her pocket and placed her thumb on *Emergency*, slipped around Kip, and yanked the trailer door open. Standing off to the side, she yelled, "All right, no one is going to hurt you. I want you to come out or I'm calling the police."

"That wasn't what I meant," Jordan said through clenched teeth. She stood on the other side of the door, ready to tackle someone if they jumped out, whack a weapon out of a hand with the wrench, do… whatever. A minute passed and nothing happened.

"I'm going to look inside," Jordan whispered, anger at being frightened in her own space making her impatient.

"Not just yet." Before Jordan plowed ahead into potential danger, Kip jumped the two steps up into the trailer and scanned it in one fast glance. It wasn't very big, and even in the rapidly deepening gloom, she saw it was empty. Several of the file drawers were open and a few papers littered the floor. "Come on in. I think someone's been i—"

"Damn it." Jordan was already at her elbow. "They must have been looking for money, and I don't keep any here. Thank God they didn't trash the place. You must have scared them away. I owe you for that."

"No, you don't. I just happened to walk in." Kip liked Jordan's praise, but she'd rather deserve it. All the same, a swell of pride caught her by surprise. Stupid of her. As if Jordan would ever think that highly of her, considering the circumstances. She'd probably never trust her, let alone respect her. The brief surge of pleasure gave way to the dark again. "Can you tell if anything is missing?"

"Not a lot at first glance." Jordan sighed. "I'll look more carefully in the morning. There was nothing here of any real value." She glanced around. "It looks like they took what they could carry—the coffeepot, damn it to hell, the portable speakers, and the adding machine. That's it, I think."

"I didn't see anyone come out past me, so they were either gone or they went out another way. Is there another door or gate out of this place?"

"No, but it wouldn't be hard to get over the fence in quite a few places. If they heard you coming in, they probably just took off."

"I did call out when I first saw the gate open—I just figured it was unlocked because someone was here. When no one answered and I heard noises, maybe a minute had passed."

"Long enough for someone to make it over the fence." Jordan picked up a loose pile of paper and stacked it on the desk, centering a mug filled with pencils on it to keep the papers from flying away.

"You sure you don't want to call the police?" Kip asked.

"Do you really think there's anything to be done?"

"Honestly, no. It's petty theft at most, and I doubt it would be high on anyone's list to search for those items you mentioned."

"And impossible to find them." Jordan grimaced. "I'm happy it wasn't worse. If they'd been intent on vandalizing instead of stealing, they could have destroyed a season's worth of work."

Kip took in the neat rows of covered green things and the chickens scratching in their enclosure and the flats of seedlings waiting to be planted. All neat and orderly and cared for. Cared about. This place mattered to Jordan, probably to a lot of people. But it was Jordan who spurred a wave of protectiveness. She pulled her gaze away from Jordan's worried eyes. "It might not be a bad idea to alert the local police, though, so they can keep an eye on the area during their patrols."

Nodding, Jordan leaned against the doorjamb inside. "Then I'll call them in the morning. It's not going to make any difference in the end result, and frankly, I don't want to spend a few more hours here."

"I don't suppose you've got any kind of portable light?"

Jordan glanced at the shelf above her desk. "I had a flashlight, but apparently I don't anymore."

"It's getting pretty dark. I'd better get a look at the truck or I won't be able to work on it until morning."

"I'll lock up here, then."

Worry etched little lines around Jordan's eyes, but she was beautiful all the same. Kip edged by her to get to the door, their shoulders brushing. She flinched, suddenly aware of how small it was inside the trailer, and how close Jordan was standing.

"Something wrong?"

"No," Kip said quickly. "Nothing at all."

"Well, damn." Jordan ran a hand through her hair. "I don't know how I'm going to secure the place if I don't have a lock on the gate anymore."

"Go ahead and close up here," Kip said, needing to feel useful after her nightmare day of being reduced to a nonentity, "and I'll go look at the broken lock. I can probably jury-rig something that will do for tonight."

"You really don't have to," Jordan said. "You must have more to do tonight than help me put this place back together. But if you could just look at the truck—"

"I don't have anything at all to do tonight." Kip jumped down from the trailer. "Or any night. Show me the lock."

"Ah, okay," Jordan said, wondering at Kip's sudden dark mood. "This way."

Jordan found the hasp with the lock still attached and handed it to Kip. "What do you think? Can you use it?"

"I ought to be able to replace it on the gate, but I'd recommend changing it to something a little more substantial tomorrow. This would be easy to pry off with a crowbar."

"All right, sure. Maybe you can make a suggestion."

"No problem." Kip dug out some of the screws and screwdriver she'd pocketed in the garden shed and reattached the hasp and lock mechanism.

"I'm afraid I'm putting you to work before you're officially assigned," Jordan said, leaning against the fender of the black Dodge pickup.

"That's okay," Kip said without turning around. "It helps."

Jordan stilled. "Helps what?"

The light was rapidly receding, and not much of the reflected glow from the avenue penetrated the alley, but she could still see the discomfort pass across Kip's face. She didn't like personal questions much herself and regretted probing. Business—keep it all about business. "Never mind. I appreciate the help. I'm glad you're here."

"So am I." Kip lifted the hood and leaned in. Just being surrounded by the smell of engine oil and metal made her feel like herself for a merciful moment.

Hearing the hollow note of resignation in Kip's voice, Jordan warmed with a wave of sympathy. She remembered all too well reaching the end of a horrible day, a series of horrible days, and wishing for one moment of normalcy. One instant when she recognized her own life. Maybe she was projecting, reading too much into the weary sag of Kip's shoulders and the dull flatness in her voice. Maybe. But she wasn't planning on doing anything beyond falling into bed with a book, and most likely being asleep before the end of the chapter. Like most nights.

"If you can at least figure out what's wrong, I'll buy you dinner," Jordan said before she could think herself out of the idea.

Kip searched Jordan's face for some sign dinner might be more than just dinner, and then chided herself for being an idiot. Clearly, Jordan wasn't the kind of woman who wanted to be in anyone's debt. That's all there was behind the invitation. "In that case, I'll get right on it."

Jordan moved as if to squeeze her shoulder and then pulled back. "Thanks."

"Hey. I'm the one who should be thanking you."

Kip turned quickly away, and Jordan was left studying her unawares for the second time in less than an hour. She'd never been all that drawn to the secretive, brooding type or in the habit of impulsively asking women to dinner, but Kip was apparently an exception to all her rules.

CHAPTER SIX

O w. Fu—"
"What's wrong?" Jordan asked.
"Nothing. Jammed my hand. Dark down here."

Jordan leaned close to Kip, her hip lightly pressed to hers, and held out her iPhone with the light on. "Does that help?"

"Yeah." Kip inched away, uncomfortably aware of the pressure against her side. Jordan's scent somehow eclipsed the familiar bite of engine oil with something far more earthy and alive. Kip couldn't put a name to it, but she sensed young green shoots stretching up through the earth, innocent and vital. The image wasn't quite right for Jordan, since there was something flinty in the depths of her eyes, a hard strength that belied innocence, but her vitality was impossible to ignore. The air around her practically vibrated.

"So what do you think?" Jordan asked.

"I think your truck would be far happier if you took it in for a tune-up every now and then."

Jordan huffed. "I'm sure you're right, but honestly, the emotional state of my truck hasn't been particularly high on my list lately."

Kip chuckled. "I think your air filter is shot."

"Is that bad?"

"Not as bad as it could be. It's pretty inexpensive to replace. I can pick one up easily enough and change it out tomorrow. But this truck really does need some serious maintenance, especially if you want it to last much longer."

Jordan sighed. "I need it to last until the next century."

Kip straightened and almost wiped her hands on her back pockets. Not a good idea since she was still wearing Savannah's trousers and not her work pants. Ordinarily, she'd have a cloth tucked into her pocket, but she wasn't exactly dressed for work this evening. She'd escaped the courthouse and couldn't face getting into an Uber and going back to her apartment as if it were any other day. Not when everything had changed. And she couldn't face another hour of Savannah's worried attention or field the phone call she expected from her father either. So she'd cut and run. Without a destination, she'd pulled the court order from her pocket and hunted down the address where she was to report the next morning. And here she was.

"Wait." Jordan rummaged in the front seat and came up with a wrinkled bandanna she used to blot condensation off the windshield in the morning. "Here."

"Thanks." Kip wiped her hands, tossed the cloth back into the truck, and shut the hood. "I ought to be able to tease a few thousand more miles out of this, if you don't mind me taking a look at it. If you have your own mechanic—"

"No." Jordan chuckled grimly. "I can't say that I keep a mechanic on call. Every bit of money we have is…well, that's no matter. So thank you for the offer. Just let me know what you need."

"No problem. How early do you need this thing running tomorrow?"

"I don't suppose four a.m. is possible?"

Kip laughed, then halted abruptly when she caught a flash of Jordan's face in the rising moonlight. "Something tells me you're serious."

Jordan nodded. "Markets, nurseries, fresh food stalls—everything opens before dawn. That's when the produce is freshest and the plantings are in best condition. Right now it's not as critical, but we're scheduled for plantings tomorrow, and we want to get them in before the heat of the day. So I'd like to get to the nursery and also check out some of the open-air markets before seven."

"I'm not sure I can get the parts by then, but as soon as I do, I'll get this running. Just temporarily," Kip warned. "I'll still need a day to really work on it."

"That would be wonderful. And honestly, I can't expect you to be here that early. You must have to go to work yourself."

"Six or as soon after that as I can."

"Great."

"It's getting pretty dark down here," Kip said, avoiding the topic of her schedule. "I think we've done everything we can tonight. How about I get us an Uber."

"My place isn't all that far, if you don't mind walking," Jordan said. "There's a little restaurant around the corner, good Italian. How does that sound?"

Kip realized she was famished and she hadn't had anything since the bagel that morning. "It sounds like heaven. And walking is fine with me."

Jordan didn't mention how skillfully Kip avoided talking about herself, and as curious as she was to know more about her, the privacy screen was welcome too. She wasn't interested in revealing any of her past, either.

When they reached the street, the sidewalks were busy as always, anytime of the day or night, anyplace in Manhattan. Threading their way through the evening throngs made conversation difficult, and they walked in companionable silence, their strides evenly matched.

"Here we are," Jordan said fifteen minutes later, stopping on a quiet side street in front of La Famiglia, one of the neighborhood restaurants still family owned—and one of Manhattan's best kept secrets. With only a dozen tables or so, they didn't take credit cards, took their time making your food, and didn't object if you lingered over espresso and dessert. It was one of her and Tya's favorite places, but she'd never eaten there with anyone else.

"Looks great," Kip said, peering through the plate-glass window into a cozy looking place where half the tables were occupied. The night before she'd had dinner with Julia at one of the current hot dining spots, with hovering waiters, a pricey menu, and ultimately forgettable conversation. Standing on the uneven pavement beneath a live maple tree with kitchen smells wafting out on a wisp of a breeze, she might as well have stepped into a different lifetime, or someone else's life. The thought of having dinner with Jordan in this unassuming place was unexpectedly comfortable, a welcome relief, and for an instant, she toyed with the idea of just walking out of her life altogether. Of course, she couldn't do that any longer, could she?

Now she had a sentence to fulfill and a probation officer to satisfy. The grim reality swamped the brief fantasy, as all dreams sooner or later surrendered.

"Are you okay?" Jordan asked. Kip had gone still, her expression distant and dark. "I'll understand if you'd rather call this off. After all, you probably have plan—"

"No," Kip said quickly. "That's the last thing I want to do. Sorry, my mood is not the best today."

Against her vow to steer clear of the personal, Kip's sadness moved Jordan to ask, "Any particular reason?"

Kip grimaced. "More than I can possibly explain, and absolutely more than you would want to know."

Jordan wasn't at all sure that was true, but Kip had made her boundaries clear. "Fair enough, then. Let's have dinner and talk about nothing of consequence."

Kip smiled, thinking that was exactly what her dinner the evening before had been like, and somehow she didn't think tonight would be a repeat. Eager to find out, she rested a hand on Jordan's lower back and pulled the door open, holding it wide for Jordan to pass. "Here's to no consequences." When Jordan's spine tightened beneath her palm, Kip pulled her hand away. "Sorry, automatic."

Jordan laughed softly. "So chivalry isn't dead. No need to apologize."

"Then I won't," Kip murmured as they stepped into a big open room with a high tin ceiling, cherry wainscoting, and the only illumination coming from tulip-shaped milk-glass wall sconces glowing amber. The small white-cloth covered tables were scattered at reasonable distances from one another, another unusual situation for a New York restaurant, allowing patrons some degree of privacy while they ate. A dark-haired, slender woman in her midfifties hurried forward, wiping her hands on a snowy white towel. "Ms. Rice, how good to see you. I've got a table open in the window for you and your friend."

"Mama Castellini. That's perfect. Thank you so much."

The restaurant's obvious matriarch gave Kip an unabashed once-over and held out her hand. "I am Sophia Castellini, but everyone calls me Mama."

Kip bowed her head slightly. "Very happy to meet you. It smells wonderful in here."

Mama gave Jordan an approving glance. "You picked one with taste. Good for you."

"Ah, yes. Red wine?" Jordan said to cover her embarrassment, afraid her ears were flaming. She'd never brought a date there, and ate either alone or with Ty. She couldn't imagine why Mama assumed Kip might be a date. That definitely wasn't the case, and wouldn't be even if it turned out Kip was inclined to date women. She quickly hushed the little voice that whispered *I certainly hope so*.

Grinning as if Jordan's thoughts were written all over her face for anyone to read, Kip followed Jordan to the table and settled across from her. "The perils of family restaurants. Once they get to know you, they treat you like family and embarrass you without mercy."

Jordan stiffened. "Yes, I suppose so."

"Sorry," Kip said, instantly aware she'd touched on something painful. So family was off-limits with Jordan, something they both shared. "Right, we're sticking to casual and impersonal. Sorry."

"That's okay." Jordan hid her discomfort by studying the menu she knew by heart. "Everything's good. I have a preference for the eggplant parm, but you can't go wrong with anything." She hesitated, uncertain of the limits. "I hope the red is okay—oh, I didn't check. Can you drink?"

Kip frowned. "I've never had a problem with…oh." She winced. "Right. Well, no one said I couldn't."

Her voice had gone completely flat, cold and hard.

"I'm very sorry," Jordan said. "I don't quite know the rules here."

Kip leaned back in her chair, ice trickling through her chest. Was this what her life was going to be like now? When it was over, when the slate was wiped clean as Carver suggested it might be when she'd fulfilled her community service, could she put this episode behind her, or would it follow her forever, something she needed to explain, something that raised question marks in a woman's eyes? Something that left doubt and uncertainty about her, between her and everyone else. "I don't actually know the answer to your question, but I intend to have a glass of wine, and I hope you don't mind."

"I certainly don't. And I'm sorry for bringing it up."

"You don't need to be. It's my problem, not yours."

Actually, Jordan didn't think that was entirely true. Kip Kensington and whatever shadow hung over her were going to be her problem too for as long as Kip worked on the project, and if Jordan couldn't stop thinking about her as anything other than that, she'd have more problems than she wanted. She smiled, hoping to lighten Kip's mood. "Back to the inconsequential, then."

"Hardly that, but tell me about the community garden." Kip figured that was a safe, neutral subject, and something Jordan would be happy discussing. She'd gotten very good at keeping conversations away from areas she didn't want to share, and that was going to become very handy in her future, it appeared. Besides that, she really wanted to know about the project, and especially about Jordan. How did someone who looked as urban and polished as Jordan, even in her plain cotton shirt and khaki pants, end up in one of the seediest parts of Manhattan trying to bring new life back to long-dead ground?

"It's just one in a multicity project," Jordan said, comfortable with the spiel she'd given dozens of time to potential contributors and supporters. "The idea is simple enough—there's an untold number of undeveloped acres scattered throughout the city lying fallow, what were once community parks and are now abandoned lots or overgrown plots where buildings have fallen or burned down. The community garden project is aimed at reversing urban blight by reclaiming these areas and making them productive parts of the ecosystem."

Kip leaned back as Mama appeared with a straw-wrapped wine bottle, expertly pulled the cork, and poured a little into Jordan's glass. Jordan smiled, tasted it, and nodded. Kip waited while Mama poured hers and sipped. A rich chianti, what else. She smiled and met Mama's expectant gaze.

"Perfect. I'll have the saltimbocca to go with it."

"Excellent choice." Mama glanced at Jordan. "Your usual?"

Jordan laughed. "I think I'll be adventurous tonight and have the cacciatore."

"Wonderful. Now you relax, enjoy the wine, and we'll bring your antipasto so you won't be hungry while we make you a perfect dinner."

"I'm moving to this neighborhood," Kip muttered.

Laughing, Mama retreated.

"So," Kip said, savoring the wine, amazed to feel the tension seeping from her shoulders, "in addition to putting these dead zones to some use, I imagine you're hoping to make some money from it?"

"The idea is for the garden to be sustainable, of course." Jordan blew out a breath. "Something like that takes time."

"I can imagine. There are quite a few locally sourced restaurants outside the city, and the whole locally grown movement is definitely becoming more popular in Manhattan, but these markets can't be easy to penetrate, either."

Jordan was surprised by Kip's insight and business savvy. "You're right."

Kip eyed her. "Not what you expected, considering my pedigree?"

Jordan flushed, but lifted her chin. "I don't know anything about you or your pedigree. Usually anyone I tell is shaking their heads at this point, that's all."

"Right. Sorry." Kip rubbed her eyes. "I seem to have lost a layer or two of skin somewhere in the last day."

"Is that how long it's been?"

Kip met her gaze. "No, it's been going on for years."

Jordan wasn't sure they were speaking of the same thing any longer, but she nodded, waiting for more. She didn't mind talking about the garden project—in fact, if she wasn't careful she'd go on and on about it until people's eyes glazed over. She wasn't even offended at having the conversation controlled. She was curious to find out why Kip was so good at it.

"How many people do you have working with you?" Kip asked, breaking a crust off the warm loaf of bread Mama had left.

"Presently, one." Jordan half smiled. Redirected again. Kip was very, very good at that.

Kip looked up. "One. Wow. I'm impressed. I thought the whole idea of the community garden was to have community workers."

Jordan laughed softly. "Well, that is the idea, but sometimes theory is more powerful than practice."

"Something along the line of if you build it, they will come?"

Jordan nodded. "That's the idea."

Kip saluted her with her wine. "Good luck, then."

"Thank you." Jordan sipped the wine. "And things are looking up, since I now have another pair of hands."

Kip's eyebrows rose. "I'm afraid that's a very uneducated pair of hands. What I know about gardening you could write on the head of a pin."

"That's no problem. I know quite a lot about it." Feeling playful and not stopping to ask why, Jordan added, "The question is, how well do you take direction?"

Kip swirled wine in her glass and regarded Jordan across the table. The green eyes looking back held just a little bit of tease, and she wondered if Jordan actually intended to flirt. Whether she did or she didn't, Kip liked it. "I think it's safe to say I'm trainable."

CHAPTER SEVEN

Y ou want dessert now?" Mama asked as she cleared the plates
herself from their table. No busboys for her favorites, apparently.

"I am too stuffed, as much as I wish I could." Jordan patted her
stomach and glanced to Kip. "How about you?"

Kip was almost too tired to answer. Halfway through the meal
the last of her energy drained away, leaving her muzzy-headed and
dull. The adrenaline surge from the stress of the last twenty-four-plus
hours had kept her going all day, but now the trauma of the night in a
cell without sleep and a day of waiting to find out her fate had worn
her thinner than just about anything she'd experienced in her life. Just
about. She smiled, hoping to cover the slowness of her brain and the
weariness of her flesh with the social mask she pulled out for occasions
when she really wanted to be elsewhere. That wasn't the case here, but
she did want to hide her precarious grip on her capacities. "I'm afraid
everything was so good I didn't leave room for another course."

"Hmm." Mama glanced from one to the other and nodded. "Then
next time, yes?"

Jordan laughed. "Promise."

Kip doubted there'd be another time, at least not for the two of
them together, and added another regret to a long list of them. She'd
enjoyed relaxing over the dinner and the casual conversation that flowed
easily from topic to topic once they had both come to the unspoken
arrangement not to tread on personal ground. Jordan had obviously *not*
asked her anything about her personal life—not even where she lived

or the barest of personal details like her age or where she'd grown up. That had to be intentional, and Kip appreciated the careful respect for her silence.

In turn, she'd held back all the questions she wanted to ask, things she hadn't even considered asking Julie the night before. Was it really just the night before? Could that have been *her* the night before, blissfully unaware of how quickly her life could be turned upside down, having dinner with a beautiful woman, having an offer of sex, and being too unaffected by the hours she'd spent with Julie to even want the superficial intimacy offered her? Apparently her life really had been going along without much intention or direction on her part until that moment when the flashing red lights in her rearview mirror signaled a sea change. Now, when she actively wanted to pursue getting to know an interesting, sexy, warm woman, a wall of secrets and silence stood between them.

"Sorry," Kip muttered, meaning so many things. She'd guessed from a few references Jordan had let slip, clues she hoarded like bread crumbs before a long siege, that Jordan was twelve or fifteen years older, putting her somewhere in her late thirties, and hadn't grown up in the city. That was just enough to make her want to know more—like everything. "I'm afraid I'm not the best company right now."

"You're perfect company," Jordan said softly, "and I hope you don't take this wrong…but you look beat. Are you all right?"

Embarrassed, Kip straightened and resisted the urge to rub both hands over her face to wake herself up. "I apologize. Believe me, it's not you. I've enjoyed this evening…more than anything in a long time. I was actually just thinking about that."

"Funny," Jordan said almost to herself, "I was thinking something along those lines myself."

"Really." A new surge of adrenaline, this time one spurred by pleasant interest rather than fear, brought Kip back to startling awareness. She hadn't realized how true her words were until she'd spoken them out loud. Despite her miserable, life-shattering day, she'd lost herself for a few hours in the company of an intriguing woman. Oh, she spent plenty of time with attractive, interesting women in business and social capacities, or when pushed by Savannah to date, but she'd rarely been as comfortable as she had been with Jordan. Her conversations with other women often seemed scripted, as if each knew their parts and played them. Often those conversations were filled with subtle probing about the private affairs of others, gossip masquerading as interest in her. Dinner with Jordan had been nothing like that. With Jordan she had no past. She only wished her present was different as well. "I don't think I've had a conversation about steampunk with anyone before."

Jordan grinned. "Well, obviously you haven't been talking to the right people. Because really, if they don't appreciate steampunk…" She waved a hand. "There must be something seriously wrong with them."

"You're absolutely right. Add that to a lack of taste for Westerns, and really, what would be the point."

"I agree with you completely. Not worth pursuing."

For an instant, a lighthearted wave of simple happiness lifted the clouds from Kip's shoulders. She wished she could hold on to the sensation for just a little while longer but she'd run out of excuses to prolong the evening.

"I wish I didn't have to admit this," Kip said, "but if I'm going to take a look at that truck first thing in the morning, I'm going to have to call it a night."

Jordan glanced around. "Wow, this is a first. I think we might actually be closing out the place."

"Can't say I've done that in a long time." Kip frowned. "Actually, maybe never."

"That makes two of us," Jordan said. Pleasure, warm and slow, settled inside her like glowing embers, a fire banked and just waiting for a single breath of air to flare into life. The sensation was thrilling and a little terrifying. She wasn't used to having that kind of reaction to anyone, even women with whom she shared intimacies. She and Kip had barely touched, and then just by accident, but the spark in Kip's eyes and the husky tone of her voice stirred someplace inside her, waiting to be stroked to life. The place she hadn't even known she had and wasn't sure she really wanted to awaken. Noticing she was turning her coffee cup in aimless circles, a nervous habit she had when uncertain of her next step, she forced herself to stop. She knew what she needed to do. "I should be getting home too. It's hard to believe, but I'm not really an early riser."

Kip laughed. "That's very sad, then."

Jordan laughed with her. "I know, ridiculous, isn't it? But once

I'm up, I'm so happy to see the dawn every morning and think about all the promise of the day to come."

"You're an optimist."

"I don't know about that."

"You are. Some people view the morning as just the beginning of a long series of hours to be gotten through."

"Is that what it's like for you?"

Kip hesitated, considering. She didn't exactly get up every day with the anticipation of excitement and promise. "Yes, maybe. I never really thought about it. I like my work, and that pretty much defines my day. The rest is mostly obligation."

"Maybe you're an optimist just waiting to be born."

"I suspect I'm not. I'm pretty well formed, and change is not likely."

"You never know." Jordan wanted to say Kip was young and had lots of time to discover what she wanted and needed to make life more than just work and obligation. She was far older and could still be taken by surprise. The whole evening with Kip was outside the norm for her, and considering the powerful desire she had to reach out and stroke Kip's arm, to somehow lighten the darkness she read in her eyes and heard in her voice, she'd already been changed by just the few hours they'd spent together. She only wished she knew what it meant. "I think you need some sleep. And I think you need to forget about fixing the truck in the morning. I'll call a mechanic when I get home."

"Absolutely not. I told you I would look at it, and that's what I'll do."

"Do you always do what you say?" Jordan asked softly.

"I don't know, I hope so. Right now, you might have to take it on faith," Kip said quietly, as if searching her memory for the truth.

"I can do that," Jordan said.

"Thanks." Kip hadn't realized until that moment just how much she wanted a chance to prove herself to Jordan. To show her that she was more than what Jordan must expect her to be—unreliable, unprincipled, even dangerous. She wasn't ever going to explain to anyone how her sentence had come about. When she'd taken the two of them out of the club and gotten behind the wheel of the car, she'd assumed responsibility for all of them. She wasn't going to implicate Randy when she'd already admitted to the crime and accepted the consequences. She was lucky to have gotten such a light sentence, something she could hopefully live through and live down. "I appreciate you giving me a chance, especially when you didn't ask for any of this."

"Honestly, I was thinking the same thing myself earlier. But we do need the help, and you've been helpful already."

Kip sighed. "I haven't done much of anything, but I'll try my best."

"I'm sure you will." Jordan's instincts said Kip could be trusted, even as her head recommended caution. She reached across the table and squeezed Kip's hand. She'd only meant to offer some friendly support when Kip was so obviously distressed, but as Kip's thumb curled over the top of her knuckles and brushed back and forth, she didn't let go. She should have, her brain told her to, but the contact was surprisingly mesmerizing. Kip's hand was warm and firm, her skin unexpectedly soft. A trickle of excitement escaped the confines of her control and raced along her spine. Her pulse stuttered and beat fast in her depths.

Kip glanced down at their joined hands and back up at Jordan. "I should go."

"Yes," Jordan said thickly, slowly extracting her fingers from Jordan's grasp. The pull of attraction lingered. "So should I."

"I'll see you in the morning, then."

"Let me give you my number, in case you can't make it."

Kip took out her cell phone and handed it to Jordan. "You can put your number in my contacts yourself. But I'll be there."

Kip said good night to Jordan in front of the restaurant and turned to walk south toward her apartment. Jordan went the other way. She could have summoned an Uber and been home in ten minutes, but even as tired as she was, she wasn't in any hurry to get there. Walking seemed to be the only thing that settled her, breathing in air that hadn't been recycled in an eight-by-ten box and shared with a dozen other hopeless souls. Walking felt like freedom, and she needed to be able to turn in any direction and go anywhere she wanted, even if she had nowhere to go. When she reached home, she went directly to the bathroom, stripped off Savannah's clothes, and stepped into the shower. She didn't even wait for the water to warm and gasped as the cold sluiced over the back of her neck and down her body. She shivered until the temperature rose and she finally washed her hair and scrubbed her body and wondered how long it would take, how many showers, until she felt clean. Her legs were shaking by the time she finished. She grabbed a towel, rubbed her hair and hastily blotted most of the water from her skin before stumbling into her bedroom, pushing back the sheets, and falling facedown. Naked, but blessedly free, the last thing she thought of was the touch of Jordan's hand in hers.

❖

Too restless to sleep, Jordan wandered around her apartment, a large one by Manhattan standards, and it still took her only a minute to traverse the whole place. Three times. Finally, she settled in front of the front bay windows with a book in a big old overstuffed chair a neighbor had donated when they'd moved out. The chair was in great shape, but apparently didn't match the color scheme of the new place. She loved the feeling of being enclosed in its deep seat and high, broad arms. She laughed to herself—betting a shrink would have something interesting to say about being embraced in her solitude by a safe inanimate object rather than the real thing. For some reason, her thoughts fled to Kip and she imagined herself in her arms.

"Whoa," Jordan muttered. "Time to squash that idea."

She leaned forward, searching for a distraction before her mental meanderings crossed a dangerous border. From where she sat on the third floor, she could look down onto the street and watch people setting out for the evening. Nighttime activities generally didn't start till eleven in the city, and she was always asleep by then. She ought to be in bed now, but she was too keyed up and didn't want to lie there staring at the ceiling. Her body vibrated with energy, and she had the strangest urge to go running. She didn't even like to run, although she did on a semi-regular basis because it was good for her. She did enough physical labor she wasn't worried about her strength, but she liked the loose, limber way her body felt when she finished running. What she hated were the first few minutes when the muscles in her legs and butt screamed at her to stop.

When she picked up the steampunk anthology she'd been reading in fits and starts, she instantly thought of Kip. Funny that they liked so many of the same things, especially when those things taken together were such an odd assortment. By rights, they shouldn't have anything in common—they were barely the same generation and she'd be willing to bet they came from totally different backgrounds. Kip had been as careful as her not to disclose her past. That made her instantly curious.

Kip was a cipher, a puzzle to be sorted and the pieces rearranged until they fit together. She liked puzzles, but this was one she had to avoid trying to solve. Kip was like a magnet, drawing her nearer, enticing her interest, inviting her to know more. It had to be because their meeting the way they had was just so unbelievable. Kip, a stranger arriving on her doorstep, stepping into her well-ordered life and disordering everything, had made a notable first impression. That was all—just a temporary, if pleasant, diversion. Now it was time to set the unwise fascination aside.

Jordan closed the book and set it aside. She was going to be Kip's boss and that was all, if only the rest of her would get the memo.

CHAPTER EIGHT

*D*on't *let go, Kip. Don't let go. That's my good girl.*
Randy's face, pinched and terrified, floated in the frothy gray sea. Her mother's voice, so strong and sure, faded slowly away.

I won't, I promise. I promise.

Of course she would never let go. Randy was her baby brother. She was supposed to look out for him. She reached for Randy's hand, gripped his small cold fingers.

Mom? Mom? Mom...

Kip jerked awake and opened her eyes in the dark. Cold sweat coated her bare skin. She sucked in a breath and forced herself to focus. In her bed, not on the *Virginia Beauty*. Almost twenty-five, not ten. Randy, all grown up, not in the water. Just a memory. Why did therapists always call them dreams? Bad dreams. Nightmares. If something really happened, it wasn't a dream, was it? Whatever she called it, she knew one thing with certainty. She couldn't change it.

She'd just usually been much better at keeping the past where it belonged.

Rolling onto her side, she squinted at the bedside clock. Four a.m. Why did that ring a bell? She grimaced. Jordan had mentioned needing to be at the project at four a.m. Maybe she wasn't serious. Right. As if Jordan was the type to joke about anything connected with her project. Nope, she meant it, although she had given Kip two hours' grace for her first day.

Groaning, Kip buried her face in the pillow and willed herself to go back to sleep. Ordinarily, she didn't really need much sleep, but like everything else in her life, that had been totally turned upside down since the arrest. She'd gotten almost six solid hours, but she felt like it had been a month since she'd had any sleep at all. Her nerves tangled and twitched, her stomach was doing some kind of jig, and her mind was racing with a jumble of incoherent thoughts she couldn't string together. She'd never been one for fooling around with drugs, even in college when it was pretty much what everyone did, but the few times she'd tried anything, she'd felt like this. Like she was coming out of her skin and if she didn't move, body parts would start flying off in all directions.

She was a mess, and wide awake.

"Crap."

She sat up and switched on the bedside light. She was officially up now, strung out, and feeling hungover. Which she wasn't. Perfect. The shower helped clear out the last of the memories that clung to her mind like torn scraps of paper blown in on the wind. By the time she finished, she'd resurrected her control and felt human, aside from a nagging headache. She considered making coffee and then decided she'd better wait an hour or two. She checked the refrigerator and found a protein drink, which would do for now. While she leaned against the counter finishing it, she considered the day ahead. She needed to call her father and check on Randy. Too early for that. She needed to look at that truck and get it running so Jordan could do whatever she did before the rest of the world got up. She checked her phone. Four thirty.

Late enough. She punched in a number.

"Yeah," a gravelly baritone responded almost instantly.

"Harv, it's Kip. Sorry I left you hanging yesterday. A few things came up and I didn't get a chance to call."

"No problem," the foreman at the Hoboken facility responded. "I got the message through channels." He paused. "Everything cool?"

"Yeah, thanks." Kip wondered how much of the whole story had gotten around. Carver wouldn't have mentioned it, neither would her father, but somehow, nothing ever stayed private in the business world. In any world, really. "I'm gonna be tied up off-site for a while. I'll work on the UAV-21 remotely and just come in for project meetings."

"Okay, sure. How long we talking?"

Kip hadn't really thought about it until that moment, but she swiftly made a decision that felt right even though no one would be happy about it. "Three, four months, probably."

He whistled. "Okay. We'll reshuffle some things if we have to." The silence was longer this time. "Does Michael know about this?"

Michael Phillips ran the Hoboken facility and reported directly to her father. He was ten years older than her, a distant cousin twice removed or thereabouts, and they'd never had much to do with each other growing up. She always got the impression Michael expected to be groomed for higher things, and maybe he would be. That didn't matter a bit to her. She didn't want anything more than what she had right now, and her father had finally accepted that. Randy was the one her father pushed now, and Randy wanted even less to do with the family business than she did. She would've liked to think the pressure to conform, to step in line with most of the other Kensington offspring, was part of the reason he rebelled, but she didn't really think that was true. *No* had been his first word, and after the accident, he'd just gotten worse.

"Kip?"

Kip rubbed her face. Hell, she'd been drifting. She really was more tired than she thought. "No, but I'll let him know later this morning. You know me and how much this project matters. I'll stay on top of it."

"Okay. Sure. I do."

"That's not why I'm calling, though."

"What do you need?"

"An air filter."

"Come again?"

"One compatible with an '09 Dodge truck. Can you have one of the guys down in maintenance run one over to my place?"

"Sure. When do you need it?"

"How about now?"

He laughed. "I'll send Ronnie. Anything else?"

"Yeah, can you have him put together a toolkit for me—general maintenance and construction."

"We'll take care of it."

"I appreciate it. I'll call Felicity later and go over whatever meetings I had scheduled. You just keep it all nice and shiny for me, will you?"

"Don't worry, it's a thing of beauty."

"We're still ready to go online first of September?"

"If it don't rain and the creek don't rise."

Kip was too tired to parse the image but she got the idea. "I'll take that as a yes."

"Say, ah, Kip," he said hesitantly, "you need anything, you call me, okay?"

"I will. I'm okay, Harv. Talk soon."

"You got it."

As crazy as things were, she was more than okay. She loved her work, but she wouldn't miss the office politics and one-upmanship that was endemic in the competitive industrial design world. Despite the mess her life had become, she hadn't looked forward to the coming day as much as she did right now in quite a long time. The buzz of anticipation she got when she imagined seeing Jordan again was new too.

❖

Jordan stopped at her favorite bakery and picked up scones, the most sinful cinnamon buns she'd ever eaten, and coffee. While she waited, she texted Tya. *I've got goodies. C U in a few.*

Tya wouldn't be in for another two hours, so Jordan skipped getting her coffee. Kip had said she'd be at the project at six, but Jordan wasn't convinced she'd actually make it that early. Just in case, it was only polite to bring her coffee.

"Sue," Jordan called.

The barista turned, her dreads swinging about her shoulders. She'd threaded colorful beads throughout, and the little bits of gleaming glass reflected in her dark eyes. "What do you need?"

"Add another black eye, would you?"

"You got it."

"Thanks."

A few minutes later, she loaded up her cardboard carry tray and set off. At five thirty, the streets were still almost empty. A few joggers with earbuds in and remote expressions passed her, maintenance workers hosed down the sidewalks in front of hotels, and cabs sped by ferrying early morning travelers. A clear sky promised another warm day. The spicy scent of spring, impossible to stifle even in the midst of concrete and fumes, stirred the excitement she always experienced this time of year. At home, trees would be in bud, the fields would be greening, and the birds would be nesting. Everywhere, life would be exploding. She still thought of the farm as home, even though she hadn't lived there in almost twenty years. Even though the house was gone, and all the land with it. Still, the old saying was true. Home is where the heart is, and her heart would always reside in the valley with those fields and the creek and the life she'd thought she would have.

A police car shot by, siren blaring, and shocked her out of her reverie.

She didn't often do that, drift back. She couldn't afford to do it now. She had a full day's work ahead, and a life of her own to tend to. She turned down the alley and stopped, letting her eyes adjust to the gloom while taking in the scene. The hood of the truck was up. The engine revved steadily. Glad she'd thought to get another coffee, she walked the rest of the way down and stopped by the open hood.

Kip, in jeans and a plain gray T-shirt that hugged every line of a nicely muscled torso, leaned with one arm on the grille, a screwdriver dangling from her other hand, staring intently into the guts of the truck. Jordan looked too. She could tell it was running smoothly and sounding better than she'd ever heard it. The rest was alien. "It's alive."

"Hi." Kip grinned. A smudge of dirt marred her right cheek. Her dark hair was tousled and she looked mighty pleased with herself. Pleased looked good on her.

"How'd you get it running?"

"Keys in the magnet box under the right fender. You might want to rethink where you keep the extras."

Jordan pursed her lips. Couldn't argue that. "Uh-huh. What have you done to it?"

"Just a little sweet talk and a few minor adjustments."

"You've obviously got a very polished line."

"Oh, I do. You probably noticed that last night."

Jordan laughed. Kip was young and good-looking and undoubtedly knew it. All the same, her easy confidence was disarming. Maybe a little too disarming. Jordan pulled her gaze away from the subtle curve of Kip's breasts and the very nice way her butt filled out her jeans. "Can't say I did."

"I'll have to work on my delivery, then." Kip grinned again, completely unfazed. She closed the hood, turned off the engine, and stowed her tools. She picked up the big shiny black box and put it in the truck bed.

Jordan frowned. "That's not ours."

"Nope. It's mine. I can work with most anything, but I'd rather have my own tools."

"You just happened to have them hanging around your apartment?"

"I got them from the shop."

"That was fast." *Whatever, wherever the shop is.* "I thought you couldn't get an air filter until later today?"

"Got lucky and had one hanging around."

"Oh. Well, don't we all."

Kip glanced meaningfully at the two cups of coffee and the bag balanced between them on Jordan's carryout tray. "Is there any chance one of those is for me?"

"Oh, gosh, I'm really sorry. I didn't know you'd be here."

"Hey, no problem."

Kip looked so pitiful, Jordan laughed. "Yes, one of them is for you. Tya won't be in until after she gets her kids to school around seven thirty. I thought you might want coffee."

"You have no idea."

"Come on, then." Jordan headed around to the driver's side. "It's time to go to market."

"Where are we going?" Kip jumped in the passenger side, and Jordan handed her the carryout tray.

"Hunts Point." Jordan slid behind the wheel, started the truck, and backed down the alley.

"The Bronx? Why?"

"Because it's the biggest wholesale produce terminal in the world and we need to get a contract with them." Jordan headed for the FDR Drive. "You can put two creams in mine. And the apple fritter has my name on it. Hands off."

"Anything else reserved?" Kip rummaged in the bag. "Man, do these look good."

"Nope. Tya isn't fussy, we just need to leave her something."

"Then I've got dibs on the blueberry scone." Kip put Jordan's coffee cup in the pullout dash holder closest to her and fished out the scone. "Thanks for thinking of me."

"I really appreciate you getting this truck running," Jordan said.

"No problem. I'm here to work, remember? Since I'm not a farmer, I should do what I do best, right?"

Jordan glanced at her. "What is that, exactly? You said you're a mechanic. Does that mean you work in a garage or an auto shop repairing cars?"

Kip stared out the window. "I have done plenty of car repair. Restorations too. My grandfather was a whiz with cars, and he had a thing about restoring old trucks and cars. He taught me."

"That's pretty special." Jordan pushed aside the lightning-fast flash of riding beside her father on a tractor when she was four or five, long before her feet could reach the gears.

"Yeah, it was."

Kip looked at her as if she'd read something in her face. Maybe she had. "So that's what you do now?"

"Not exactly." Kip shifted in the seat and watched Jordan as she drove. "I sorta quit my job this morning."

Jordan shot her a quick surprised look and stared back at the road. "Really. Okay. That sounds drastic."

"It was kind of spur of the moment, true. It didn't make any sense to me to try to work these hours that I owe you—"

"It's not me you owe, you know that, right?" Jordan wasn't comfortable being in the position of supervising Kip. She supposed she should get over it. After all, she was Kip's boss, in practical terms. That distinction was a bit murky too. And it shouldn't be. Black and white. Wasn't that what she'd told herself the night before? Business only. So why was she pushing Kip again to tell her about her personal life? "Sorry. Not my concern."

"No, you're right. I owe the court, not you." Kip sighed. "But if I'm going to be working at the project fulfilling my sentence, then the best way for me to really contribute is to show up every day. Otherwise I won't be good for anything except cleanup duty."

"What do you want to be?" Jordan said softly.

"I don't know. Useful."

The way she said it made Jordan think Kip needed more than to be useful. Whatever she was looking for, or looking to make up for, left the undercurrent of pain in her voice. "All right. We can work with that. But you realize you're not getting paid."

"Right. That's what *volunteer* means."

"So—was it really a good idea to quit your job?"

Kip grinned. "Well, that might be a slight exaggeration."

Jordan frowned. "Explain."

"I haven't actually quit—I'll be working on a few things on and off."

"I'm not going to ask you what. Your private life is your own business."

"You already know one of the worst things about me," Kip said.

Jordan glanced at her. "You broke the law?"

"That's right."

"I can't imagine it was a terrible crime."

"Actually, it was a stupid one, but a crime nevertheless." Kip's eyes took on a distant look. "Sometimes the worst secrets are not crimes at all."

"Then maybe they're best left that way," Jordan said softly.

"I know."

CHAPTER NINE

Kip leaned forward to peer through the windshield as Jordan turned through the gate in an endless length of ten-foot cyclone fence. Tractor-trailers and gigantic metal sheds like the buildings she'd often seen at port terminals along any busy waterfront crowded the sprawling lot. A sign spanned the gateway. Hunts Point Terminal Market.

"Whoa, this isn't quite what I expected. This place is huge."

"One hundred thirteen acres, actually," Jordan muttered as she maneuvered down narrow, twisting aisles between parked trucks, commercial shipping containers with their back doors open to reveal stacks of crates, and swarms of workers off-loading pallets of cartons onto dollies and forklifts. ATVs marked with yellow caution triangles front and rear and packed with equipment swooped in and out with the reckless abandon of bicycle messengers in Midtown.

"Every day it's like this?" Kip craned her neck to see down the row and still couldn't see the end.

"All day, every day, Sundays included. New York has to eat." Jordan made a sharp turn and pulled the truck into a narrow space between several others. "Fresh produce arrives every morning by boat or rail or truck. Buyers from wholesale markets all the way to upscale restaurants show up to get the best deals on fresh produce."

"How much of it is locally sourced?"

"Not the majority, not yet." Jordan turned off the engine, reached behind the seat, and grabbed a butter-yellow ball cap. Pulling her hair into a ponytail and securing it with a stretchy tie, she threaded it through the back and quick-looked in the rearview mirror. Apparently satisfied, she pushed open her door and held it wide with her foot. A breeze ripe with sea salt and warm fruit aromas wafted in along with a faint scent of diesel. "A lot of it is big-name consortiums like Dole and Driscoll's. All of them have organic divisions, which is mostly what people are looking for here. It's tough for smaller enterprises to compete, but it would be a terrific outlet for us."

"I'm surprised the city hasn't negotiated for their community gardens as a unit to get a place here." Kip climbed out and joined Jordan at a brisk trot toward one of the nearest sheds. Jordan slung a canvas bag embroidered with fruits and vegetables over her shoulder. Somehow it looked chic with her skinny tan pants and long-sleeved scoop-necked mint green tee.

"Supposedly they are in negotiation," Jordan said, "but you know bureaucracy. I'm hoping we can come to some agreement for a small space here. If we could get it, it would handle a lot of what we're going to produce."

"But you'd need to deliver every day."

Jordan winced. "Yes, and of course, we don't have a driver."

"You do now," Kip said.

Jordan raised an eyebrow and gave her an appraising look. "Four a.m., remember?"

"I don't sleep a lot—I'm one of those people that sleeps in shifts. Three or four hours and then I'm up again. I get a lot of work done in the middle of the night. Then I might grab another couple hours and get up. I can handle it."

"I appreciate the offer, believe me. But let's see what happens here." What she didn't say was, *Let's see how things work out once you start at the project.* Kip was, after all, a forced volunteer, and she hadn't any idea what the work would be like. She might very well change her mind about how involved she wanted to be and just put in her hours when convenient, to work off her sentence. Jordan hated the word *sentence*—it sounded so wrong when applied to Kip. She was profiling, and couldn't deny it. Just because Kip was the kind of woman she might want to know better—okay, know personally—under other circumstances didn't mean she knew anything about her at all. Kip was obviously intelligent and her easy confidence and charm made it hard to think of her as nefarious, but a great smile and appealing manner were hardly enough to make an assessment of someone. Physical magnetism and undeniable chemistry were totally untrustworthy guideposts, because she'd found her appealing from the start. Okay, more than appealing, attractive. Oh for God's sake. Hot. She could admit that at least to herself. There was nothing wrong with acknowledging she still had a normal level of functioning hormones and found a young, magnetic woman hot.

"I guess we'll find out," Kip said quietly.

"Sorry?" Jordan chastised herself for letting her thoughts wander down paths she had no intention of traveling. Kip's look, grave and searching, gave Jordan the feeling her thoughts were visible on her face again. "Find out what?"

"How well things work out at the project."

"Yes. We will." Jordan dodged a forklift ferrying crates of bananas. "Let's win this battle first."

Kip shoved her hands in the pockets of her jeans and surveyed the big building in front of them. "So what is this place?"

"It's called the food barn. It's where vendors set up stalls and sell their produce."

"How tough is it to get one of the stalls?"

"There's a waiting list for the big ones, but we wouldn't need much space, and that helps."

"Pricey?"

Jordan sighed. "Demand is high, so yes, but this is something I'm willing to stretch for."

"Who controls your budget?" Kip said.

"The city semi-officially, but it's a grant, really."

"You don't actually work for the city?"

"Not officially. I'm the grant administrator, which I suppose puts me under some bureaucratic umbrella somewhere, but there's not a lot of oversight."

"That's handy."

Jordan laughed. "I can see you've got some experience with organizational hierarchy."

"Everybody answers to someone, usually, but the looser the reins, the better, in my opinion."

"The biggest problem is the more autonomy you have, the less you can pull on official connections to help. And that's why we're here begging."

They walked through the open industrial overhead doors into controlled chaos. Three aisles ran the length of an enormous space that had to be three stories high, a couple of football fields in length, and about as wide. Stalls with big numbers next to their vendor names packed either side of the aisles, separated from their neighbors by wooden counters and filled with bins of fruits and vegetables.

Kip halted abruptly. "This is a madhouse. How do customers decide what to buy or who to buy from?"

"A daily bulletin comes out every morning around three thirty with prices, descriptions, and bargain status, like the stock market."

"It looks about as incomprehensible to me." Kip laughed, the energy of the place contagious. She couldn't wait to explore.

"Once buyers make connections with vendors, they'll keep coming back, even if your prices fluctuate a little bit higher than your competitors'. The key is the relationship, and the quality of the goods, of course." Jordan surveyed the room as if assessing a battlefield. "This is just the beginning. We have to start networking with local bodegas and restaurants and street-side retailers to buy from us here by direct delivery."

"You need a marketing team."

Jordan pointed to her chest. "That would be me."

Kip shook her head. "So far by my count you're CEO, COO, head of sales and marketing, and apparently research and development too."

"At least I'm no longer repairs and maintenance."

Kip gave a little bow. "At your service."

"I can't tell you what a relief that is."

Kip relished a swell of satisfaction. She liked providing something Jordan needed, even if that was only something as simple as keeping the truck running and taking care of the relatively straightforward construction repairs needed at the project. "I don't know how you wear so many hats without your head exploding, but I admire your energy and your determination. I'm sure you'll make it all work. All the same, a couple more hands will help."

"True, and we'll be reaching out to the community soon too." Jordan smiled. "And thanks for the pep talk."

"Anytime." Kip envied Jordan the chance to build something from the ground up, even if the effort was enormous. She'd more or less walked into her position at the factory, even though she'd studied, trained, and earned it. Still, the infrastructure was there waiting for her. The enormous corporation, actually many of them now, had been chugging along for generations, and she didn't have to worry about how it would survive from month to month. She liked that about her job. She'd never wanted to be a manager. She was a hands-on engineer and extremely lucky that what she really loved to do was something she could contribute to the family enterprise. She was happy to at least fulfill some of her father's ambitions for her, even if she'd disappointed him by refusing a career path to a corner office. He'd finally begrudgingly accepted she wasn't headed for the boardroom, and they'd come to peace over their slightly disparate visions. The Ninth Avenue Garden Project was something entirely different from the safe, stable, and unchangeable world of Kensington Corp, and Kip looked forward to contributing whatever she could. Besides the project being a worthy one, the chance to help Jordan held powerful appeal.

"I'm going to find someone in the business office," Jordan said, "and see if I can sweet-talk them into putting us on a list that will get us in here as soon as possible."

"What do you want me to do while you're begging?" Kip asked.

"Why don't you take a walk around and see what the layout looks like. I'm open to suggestions as to the best way to take advantage of whatever space we can find. Convincing buyers to try our produce is the first step. Once we get in the door, I know we can build the sales channels."

The spark in Jordan's eyes suggested she was ready to go to battle. Kip liked that about her too. She liked her confidence and drive and, well, pretty much everything else about her. Just being with her was a little dizzying, in an altogether new and enjoyable way. "No problem. You can text me when you're done. And good luck."

"Thanks. I'll see you soon." Impulsively, Jordan squeezed Kip's hand before turning away. "Have fun."

Kip watched her go, thrown off stride by the contact. A touch from Jordan, however brief, struck her as a lot more intimate than the kind of casual caresses she was used to from the women she went out with, women who often breached personal space with a kind of ferocious aggression that struck her as slightly predatory. She wasn't averse to being hunted, metaphorically speaking, particularly when the hunt led to the bedroom. She liked being chased as much as she liked chasing, but she usually preferred that the game have some basis in mutual attraction. And now she was reading far too much into that brief contact. Jordan was a warm and friendly woman. That's all there was to it.

Still, as she walked away she had the urge to whistle. She closed her hand around the tingling in her palm, just to hold in the strange and welcome pleasure a few more minutes.

❖

Kip's phone buzzed forty minutes later.

All done. Meet me by the entrance. J

She headed that way although she could have used another hour to explore. She'd barely completed a circuit through half of the enormous warehouse, stopping often to talk to the uniformly friendly vendors, casually asking them what she hoped were intelligent questions about their produce and how things were moving. She took mental notes on which stalls and displays had the most traffic. For the first few minutes everything looked pretty much like a free-for-all, and she couldn't make a lot of sense of it, but as she began to follow the traffic, she got a better feel for what kinds of things were drawing the biggest crowds, not just in terms of the products themselves, but accessibility and patterns of flow. In her mind, she superimposed the mechanics of a well-oiled, high-efficiency machine on the human interactions and physical space. In her view, everything in the environment, man-made or natural, contained intrinsic patterns of movement that could be analyzed in terms of efficiency and economy of design. When she looked at the world, she often saw an invisible grid made up of iridescent paths crisscrossing and intersecting into one huge tapestry of movement.

"How was it?" Jordan asked when Kip found her in the crowd by the entrance.

"Fascinating."

Jordan raised a brow. "Really? How so?"

"I'll tell you in a bit. First, what did you find out?"

"There're half a dozen stalls coming open, and since the market has a mission to support community efforts, I shamelessly pushed our community connection as one of the reasons we needed to be here. The terminal actually gives away everything that's unsold at the end of every day to charitable outlets and food kitchens, so we fit right into their social agenda."

"Good move," Kip said.

"I hope so. They're going to prioritize our application. By the time we have our first harvest in six weeks or so, we may have a stall here." The excitement in Jordan's voice caught Kip in its wake and pulled her along. "Do you think you'll have a choice of location?"

"I can certainly push for one. Why?"

"I'd like to get a map of the layout here. There's an interesting pattern to the way buyers frequent some stalls and not others, and I think we might want to optimize our position if possible." Only after she spoke did she hear herself. *Our.* She had to remind herself her role at the project was only temporary. In a few months she'd be gone, back to her normal life. The idea rang hollow.

"Really?" Jordan tilted her head, expression intent. "You found that out just from walking around for half an hour?"

"It's kind of what I do—well, it's more like how I see the world. In patterns."

"Tell me."

Kip knew she was blushing. She never talked about this with anyone other than Randy, who never laughed at her excitement when describing how she saw things. "It's probably gonna sound crazy."

"I bet it doesn't."

"Think about the satellite images of the city or the park—everyone is familiar with them, right?"

"Sure."

"Well, with some of the new laser satellite techniques, even in dense forest you can penetrate the canopy to trace deer paths and other animal trails at ground level. The patterns are very similar to the most efficient traffic flow patterns in a city—what we spend millions designing, animals do naturally. Same right here in this building. People gravitate to natural pathways."

Jordan gave her a long look. "And you can…see them."

"Yeah, pretty much."

"Wait right here, I'll get a diagram of the stall layout."

"I won't move." As Jordan spun around, Kip couldn't decide what was better—the rush of pleasure at being understood or the view of Jordan from the rear. Jordan had a *really* nice rear. And since no one was watching her watching, Kip allowed herself the pleasure. Jordan had almost melted into the crowd when she paused and looked back. She caught Kip looking and narrowed her eyes with just a trace of a smile. Kip lifted a shoulder as if to say *guilty*. Jordan laughed and was swallowed up by the milling crowd.

CHAPTER TEN

"Next stop, New Jersey." Jordan climbed back into the truck, checked her watch, and pulled out her phone. "Let me just text Tya with an update. It'll be almost noon by the time we get back."

"What's in Jersey?" Kip shivered as Jordan pulled out onto the highway. Between heartbeats, the cab of the truck, stuffy from the heat that had built up in the shadeless lot, was suddenly way too small, squeezing in around her.

"The nursery," Jordan said, sounding far away. "I've got a half dozen pallets of tomato seedlings and some other plantings to pick up."

"Right...I remember now." Fog dimmed Kip's vision. Dank walls, prison walls, closed her in. Icy sweat pooled in the middle of her back. Fighting for air, she fumbled for the window control. As soon as the acrid scent of hot concrete and spilled fuel assaulted her nose, the image of the cramped cell fractured and slid away. Breathing deeply, she instantly missed the lush fragrances of fresh produce and ripe fruit, but at least now she was back in the present.

"Sorry there's no AC," Jordan said, eyes on the road.

"No problem." Grateful Jordan had missed her mini-panic attack, Kip searched the limited information in her memory banks about gardening, which, having grown up in the city, was nil to less than that. Her mother had kept a garden at the summer house with vegetables and a few herbs, but Kip had always been more interested in games and swimming and hadn't paid much attention. Her father had sold their summer house after everything, so then, even her summer forays into the countryside had stopped. "I thought you never planted tomato plants until after Mother's Day."

"Ordinarily, that's true, if you're a backyard kitchen gardener, but we need to bring our harvests in as quickly as we can for as long as we can. So we'll cover the seedlings with protective mesh against drops in temperature. We should be past frost by now, which is the only real concern." Jordan sighed. "Of course, if we had the greenhouse, we wouldn't even have to worry about that, but that's something a bit down the road."

"I noticed a lot of construction materials in the back part of the lot. Is that for the greenhouse?"

"Yes, but we still need plans and…" Jordan laughed. "Well, money and a construction crew and that kind of thing."

"If you tell me what you need, I can design it for you. I can probably get a lot of the framing done too, if I had maybe one more pair of hands."

"That's a big job. You really think you could?"

"Sure." Kip busily assembled plans in her head, the buzz of a new undertaking bubbling through her. After what had just happened, the chance to work outside was exactly what she wanted. More than that, she really wanted to do something, anything really, to lend Jordan a hand. Jordan's gratitude that morning when she'd fixed the air filter, something she'd done a thousand times and never given it a thought, made her feel as if she'd conquered an army. Jordan's pleasure gave her a high that was so addicting she could probably live off the heat in her eyes. "I can have the plans ready for you to look at in a day or so."

"Excellent." Jordan shot Kip a piercing glance that heated her skin. "You're proving to be awfully handy."

Kip grinned. "A woman of many talents."

"Ha. I think that's a line from some old TV show or something."

"It's only a line if it isn't true, right?" Kip couldn't stop herself from teasing. Maybe she'd inspire another one of those hot stares.

Jordan rolled her eyes. "Nothing wrong with your ego, I see."

"Maybe you just make me want to brag a little."

Jordan stilled, the tightening in her midsection signaling the conversation had just taken an unexpected and disconcertingly tantalizing turn. "Do I."

"Apparently," Kip said, her voice low and husky. "Before you know it, I'm going to ask if you want to see my frog."

"Really? Your frog. Is that a euphemism?"

"No, I'm serious. Really. I love frogs. Don't you?"

Jordan forced her attention to stay on the road, despite the urge to see if Kip was feeling the pull too. She didn't really want to know. Then what would she do? Best to ignore it, whatever *it* was. "Neutral on that score. Actually, I love toads."

"You're not just saying that to make me feel better? Because you know, you already make me feel pretty terrific."

"Stop. I'm driving, and you're killing me." Jordan tried sounding casual, bored even, anything but enchanted. She didn't need to be sending mixed signals, not when she didn't even understand them.

"Need a time-out?" Kip's voice had dropped even lower.

"I wish," Jordan said, purposefully not understanding. She pulled onto the interstate and groaned. "Look out there. This is going to take forever."

Kip stretched an arm out along the seat back. Her fingers were inches from Jordan's shoulder. If she leaned just a little closer, she'd touch her. She wondered if she did what Jordan would do. The urge to find out almost cut the chains on her good sense. Almost. Jordan hadn't invited that, hadn't even signaled she was interested. She usually didn't mind going slow, but right now slow felt a lot like starving. "Take the next exit, and I'll get you there in twenty minutes."

"Now you're really trying to impress me."

"Maybe, but it's true. I know this area. I work over here."

"Where's that?"

"So why do you like toads?"

"They're great for controlling garden pests. Is there some reason you don't want me to know where you work, because I get wanting privacy, I really do. I'm just not sure where the lines are with you."

Kip hesitated. Jordan was the first woman she'd been interested in who didn't know all about her, or *think* she did, in forever. She liked shedding the family mystique, even though she was tarnished by the community service sentence. That was real, at least. And she didn't want to get into why she couldn't actually talk about her work. "I work in a plant right outside Hoboken."

"A factory you mean, not a garage?"

"That's right. We make things."

Jordan laughed. "Aha. Well, that's clear."

"Engines. That kind of thing."

"Okay. I get that. That's what you work on, putting engines together?"

"Pretty much. I like working with my hands as much as I can. Sometimes I do a little design." All true, but she squirmed a little inside anyhow. She'd gotten good at half-truths without even thinking about it, and that wasn't where she wanted to go with Jordan.

"That must be pretty exciting, seeing something you've created actually take shape."

"Isn't that a lot like what you do? You plant something and you watch it grow?"

"Well, it's the first time I've ever thought of an engine quite like a tomato plant, but you're right. Do you love what you make—not love making it, but when it's done?"

"Yeah," Kip said softly. "I do. I love the parts and the way they work together, the way it shines, I even love it when it gets dirty."

"And you're sad if it's ailing."

"I don't like things not to work. I have a need to fix things, so they do what they're supposed to do." Kip shifted to keep Jordan in sight. Looking at her took the edge off wanting to touch her. "It must be hard for you, to watch them die."

Jordan shrugged, her expression pensive. "You'd think so, but you know, nature provides. We save the seeds of our best plants to use the next year. I don't so much anymore, but I used to."

"Before?" Kip heard the unspoken and couldn't let it go. Jordan was even more cautious than her, and as much as she understood secrets, she wanted to know more. Wanted to know everything.

"Yes," Jordan said, a distant note in her voice. "Before I started working for the agricultural extension. I thought I was going to develop new hybrids, crosses between heirlooms and something more hardy. Plants we could grow organically that would give us the size and robustness of some of the more modern varieties."

"It didn't work?"

"I don't know, I didn't have time to finish it." Her voice carried the wistfulness of an interrupted dream, one Kip wished she could somehow make come true.

"Well, maybe you will, one day."

"Maybe."

Kip pointed to the left. "Take that fork over there."

"You mean that little tiny road that looks like it doesn't go anywhere?"

"That's the one. Remember, patterns. Sometimes you want the path that doesn't look like it goes anywhere."

"The road not taken?"

"Yeah. Believe me, I'm in the know."

Jordan shook her head and made the left turn. Fifteen minutes later, she pulled into the lot of a rambling one-story weathered building surrounded by racks of flowers, rows of freestanding plants, and clumps of trees balanced on hemp-covered root balls. She shut off the engine and looked at her phone. "All right, you get a gold star for saving us an hour."

"Good, I might need one. Probably a lot of them when I start messing up with all the rest of the things you need me to do, especially if it has to do with gardening."

"Don't worry. I won't let you mess up." Jordan opened the door and jumped out. When Kip didn't follow, she leaned on the side of the open cab. "Okay?"

"Yeah." Kip swallowed around the tightness in her chest. "It's just...I'm not exactly used to that, so you might have to be obvious about what you want."

"All right," Jordan said softly, her voice as intense as a caress, "I'll be sure to be very clear."

❖

Two hours later, Jordan pulled up in the alley next to the garden. "How do you feel about a little manual labor before lunch?"

"I love it." Kip pushed open her door. She did most of her design work at night so she could be on the plant floor or outside watching the prototypes in action as often as she could sneak away. Getting a workout while she worked sounded like heaven. "Point me to it."

"You don't have to pretend enthusiasm, you know."

"I'm serious. I'd rather be outside doing this than almost anything."

Jordan laughed. "Then I'll take shameless advantage. Let's get these pallets unloaded. Oh, hey—hi, Tya."

A small pretty woman in sleeveless tan coveralls and a white tank top ambled out to join them. She looked at Kip, then to Jordan, a question on her face.

"Tya," Jordan said, "this is Kip, a volunteer."

Tya held out her hand. "Great. You live in the neighborhood?"

"Not too far away," Kip said.

"Oh. Well, I'm glad you're here. We can definitely use the help."

"Thanks," Kip said. Tya was clearly confused but apparently wasn't going to question Jordan in front of Kip, for which Kip was grateful. The last thing she wanted was to talk about the details of why she was there. She supposed it would all come out, and she'd probably have to go through it any number of times in the future. The idea was humiliating. "I'll get started on those pallets. I don't suppose you have a forklift, do you?"

"Afraid not," Jordan said as she came around the truck to help her. "We'll have to carry the flats by hand."

"No problem." Kip slid the first slatted wooden pallet onto the tailgate. "I'll drag these back to the greenhouse once we've emptied them. They might come in handy."

"What greenhouse?" Tya lifted a flat of tomato seedlings and started toward the gate.

"The one we're going to build," Kip said, following her in with another flat. "Where do you want these?"

Tya propped hers on the edge of a raised garden bed. "Just put them down at about six-foot intervals along this row."

"Are they all going in today?" Kip asked, straightening as Jordan edged down the narrow aisle.

"That's the plan," Jordan said.

Jordan's hip brushed Kip's for an instant as she passed. Kip froze, savoring the contact. Damn if she didn't get a kick like she hadn't gotten in recent memory. She probably needed a date if the slightest inconsequential and unintended contact was enough to jack her up. Funny, she hadn't thought of finding herself a date in months, content to let Savannah set her up and then never calling the women again. Easy to avoid connecting that way.

Jordan paused beside her. "There's water in the fridge in the trailer if you need it."

"What? Oh, right. I'm good." Kip headed back to the truck. Just great, if she didn't count the low burn driving her crazy.

Between the three of them, they unloaded the truck in under twenty minutes.

"I'll get these stowed." Kip hoisted the first pallet to drag it back to the far corner of the lot.

Tya joined Jordan by the trailer. "Are you sure we shouldn't be helping her?"

"She said it was just as easy to do it herself," Jordan murmured, studying the muscles in Kip's shoulders and arms flexing as she maneuvered the square wooden platforms through the aisle between the raised beds.

"Where did she come from?"

"She was volunteered." Jordan wished she didn't have to explain, knowing she should.

"What aren't you telling me?"

"Apparently, the court sentenced her here for community service."

Tya gasped. "Are you kidding me? She's some kind of criminal?"

"God, that sounds terrible."

"But it's true?"

Jordan's patience almost frayed, and she never lost her temper with Tya. She took a breath, waited while the urge to defend Kip cooled. "All I know is she's working off a court-ordered community service sentence. So, yes, she must've done something illegal. Obviously, something minor or she wouldn't have received such a light sentence."

"But you don't know what?"

"No. I didn't ask."

"Why not? Don't you think it's important to know? What if it's something—I don't know, threatening." Tya made an exasperated sound. "You know the sentence doesn't always fit the crime."

"Does she look threatening to you?" Ty was making sense, but Jordan still wanted to protect Kip. There wasn't a single thing about Kip that seemed threatening or dangerous, unless it was the way Kip made her feel. And wasn't that a thought. Losing perspective, maybe? The last of the heat evaporated, leaving Jordan tired. "Whatever happened, I can tell she's bothered by it. I didn't want to make her feel worse by probing."

Ty squinted at her. "Okay, I'm missing something here. She just showed up out of the blue, right? You don't know her or anything about her other than the fact she's broken the law. And that's it? That's all you need to know?"

"Are you worried about the kids?"

"No. I'm worried about you. The kids are street-smart, and we'll be here to keep an eye on things. It just seems to me if you're going to be riding around with her in the truck, off alone with her, you'd want to know something more about her."

"I know a lot about her. We talked a lot over dinner and—"

Tya took a step back, crossed her arms, and set her hip that way she did when she was about to scold one of her kids. "You had dinner with her already?"

"Yes, she was here late last night, and we were working on the truck until it got dark and—"

"Okay, why do I think I've missed an entire month. I'm pretty sure I was here yesterday and none of this was happening."

Jordan laughed. "All right, I know. But I'm telling you, she's a lot more complicated than you might imagine, and there's nothing about her that gives me danger vibes."

She didn't mention the personal danger vibes she got every time she looked in Kip's direction. At that moment, Kip tossed a pallet onto a pile and lifted the bottom of her T-shirt to wipe the sweat from her face. Jordan's heart stopped in her chest. Kip was seriously built, her waist muscled, and even from a distance, etched in a tight column down the middle.

"I don't suppose your opinion has anything to do with the fact she is righteously hot," Tya muttered.

"Since when do you find women hot?"

"I can be objective, you know. And she's built."

"Yeah, she is. And that has nothing to do with anything."

"Sure, uh-huh. Just promise me you'll be careful."

"Of course I will be."

"And you're going to call somebody in authority and find out what's going on, right? Because this seems all kinds of unusual."

Jordan blew out a breath. "I did plan on checking this morning, I just haven't gotten around to it."

"So how about now."

Jordan couldn't keep pretending Kip was an ordinary volunteer, just because she liked her. Just because they'd connected so easily. Nothing about Kip showing up was ordinary, and, okay, maybe her judgment was a tad swayed by how much she was drawn to her. She owed it to Ty at the very least to find out the truth.

"All right, I'll make the call."

CHAPTER ELEVEN

Jordan retrieved the folded piece of paper she'd slipped into the back pocket of her khakis that morning and smoothed it out on the makeshift desk in the trailer. She read it again. It didn't say anything it hadn't said before and still didn't tell her much. Catherine Kensington was remanded to four hundred hours of community service to be fulfilled at the Ninth Avenue Community Garden project. A form signature at the bottom, illegible of course. Fortunately, a printed name appeared under that. Jorge Garcia, clerk.

Jorge was probably someone at the courthouse or the justice center or wherever these things were generated. She really didn't know. The one and only time she'd been in court was to protest a traffic ticket, and that was at least fifteen years ago. Now she just paid them. Time was more important than money, especially the way things were going now.

And she was procrastinating. Letting her mind wander and skip like the stones she'd tossed into the pond as a kid, challenging her friends to see who could skip them the most times. But she wasn't a kid and it wasn't endless summer and her days didn't stretch forever, filled with hope and promise. Tya was right. She needed at least some information about the person who was going to be working with them and exactly what her responsibilities might be. Hopefully, she wasn't going to be forced into a position of making Kip accountable to her. She didn't even especially like the idea of being her boss, let alone her de facto warden. She wasn't twitchy about workplace romances, not when they were between adults and no one was abusing power.

It was simplistic to assume everyone in a position of power actually abused it or that those who weren't would silently submit. But Kip's situation blurred the boundaries even more than usual for workplace relationships. The secrets surrounding her would have been intriguing under other circumstances. Still were, if she was honest about it. But they were barriers too, making any kind of personal association difficult to navigate. And why was she thinking about that. This wasn't about romance. Discovering why Kip was here was just about common sense and safety. Simple precaution.

Procrastinating again.

She found the number printed under the official header on the form letter and dialed it. She expected to be put on hold and braced herself for the Muzak that would undoubtedly follow. To her surprise, a human answered.

"Division of Criminal Justice. Can I help you?"

Criminal Justice. Well, that was a little like stepping into an ice-cold shower. Hard to pretend Kip was just another volunteer. Jordan explained the situation.

"What's your question?"

"I'm confused because I didn't even realize our project was part of this kind of program. I have no idea what we are supposed to do."

The woman sighed. "Didn't they explain all of that to you when they did the site visit?"

"Ah—that would be a no. Like, no site visit."

"Let me check something. Please hold."

The line went to static. Jordan fidgeted. Maybe it really *was* all a mistake. Would that mean Kip would be sent somewhere else? Jordan's breath shortened. She didn't want her to disappear.

"All right," the exceptionally helpful woman said, "I've checked the list of assignment sites. Your organization is listed."

"Is there any way I can find out the details?"

"I'll transfer you to the community resources section."

After a fair amount of phone tag and more waiting, Jordan was finally connected to someone who identified himself as a community service director.

"I wanted some information about Catherine Kensington. She's been assigned to community service at a project I oversee. Can you tell me anything?"

"I'm sorry," responded the pleasant-sounding man whose name she'd immediately forgotten. "Those files are not available to me."

Jordan blew out a breath. "Well, how would I find out what the circumstances are? Shouldn't we be informed of the details if we're responsible for overseeing their involvement here?"

"I can connect you to the probation office. They may be able to direct you to the case officer."

Jordan resisted the urge to bang her head on the desk. "Can the case officer tell me—"

"I think I can probably save you some time," Kip said from behind her.

Jordan's heart leapt into her throat. Her face heated. She felt like the guilty party. She looked over her shoulder, and the rest of the officer's words were lost on her. Kip's face was set, blank as a statue someone had begun to carve and forgot to finish. Nothing behind her eyes, the sensuous lips closed tightly, no lines of anger or accusation. If she hadn't talked to Kip, hadn't seen her laughing, hadn't caught the spark in her eyes when she teased, she would've thought the woman facing her to be cold and remote. That wasn't what she read behind Kip's stoic façade now, though. She'd heard the resignation in her voice, sensed the withdrawal and the closing of whatever door had opened between them.

"Thank you, you've been helpful. I'll try back later." Jordan disconnected the call, pushed her phone aside, and swung around to face Kip. What could she say? She wanted to apologize, but she wasn't even sure what she would say she was sorry for. "This is all new to me. Your showing up here is…unexpected."

"I know. I'm sorry."

"I don't want you to be sorry, damn it. I just—" Jordan pushed a hand through her hair. Words deserted her. Or at least the only ones she thought of weren't the ones she wanted. Why was it so difficult to just come out and say it? She'd never had problems before making herself clear.

"Why don't you just say it, Jordan? It'll probably be easier for both of us."

"How do you do that? Know what I'm thinking practically before I do?"

Kip finally smiled, a small one, one tinged with what might've been sadness, and then it was gone. Jordan missed it instantly.

"Your face is expressive, and your eyes even more so. You're frustrated, maybe a little angry at yourself. Definitely pissed off at me."

Jordan pointed a finger. "You're wrong there. I'm not angry at you. It's not your fault that you're here."

Kip scoffed. "Of course it is. Have you forgotten exactly why I'm here?"

"You know, you're doing a good job of punishing yourself—I'm not sure the community service is even needed. I get that you did some—"

"Let's not sugarcoat it. I broke the law." Kip leaned her back against the side of the open doorway and folded her arms across her chest, almost daring Jordan to disagree.

"Yes, fine," Jordan snapped. God, Kip was aggravating at times. "You broke the law and you're being punished. But you didn't choose to be *here*."

"Well, apparently I'm supposed to be suffering in some way. That's the whole point of being sentenced."

"What exactly bothers you the most—what you did or the sentence?"

"Being here is not a punishment. I'm half afraid someone will figure that out and tell me it's a mistake." Kip's eyes, dark and wounded, found Jordan's for an instant. "The sentence doesn't bother me."

When the brief connection broke, Jordan tried to recapture Kip's gaze and failed. Disappointed, irrationally feeling abandoned, she said, "Don't you think that says something about you?"

"Yeah, I do. It says my judgment sucks and you should probably know that. It undoubtedly says a lot of other things I'd rather not think about, if it's all the same to you."

Jordan hesitated. She should let it go, try going through official channels again, but that seemed the coward's way out. She needed to reach Kip, face-to-face, not call around behind her back. "Can you tell me what you did, or is that something you don't want to talk about either?"

Silence stretched for an interminable moment. Kip sighed.

"I was arrested for driving a stolen car."

Jordan heard the words, but couldn't quite decipher them. She stared at Kip. "I'm sorry. Are you telling me you stole a car? Why on earth would you do that?"

"I didn't exactly say that, but it amounts to the same thing."

Jordan tried to work out what exactly Kip was saying. That she hadn't stolen it, or she had stolen it? Obviously she was driving it. And whatever the circumstances, she didn't want to talk about them. And probably that was fair. Kip had answered her question. What more could she really expect. "All right. Fair enough. Is that something you make a habit of doing?"

Kip winced, but a smiled flickered too. "Actually, no, and I don't habitually have a problem with lifting things that don't belong to me."

"So I don't have to worry about the rakes going missing?"

"Your tools are safe." Kip's gaze darkened for an instant. "And so is everything else. Including you."

Kip's tone had grown darker along with her gaze, a slow, sensuous heaviness that made Jordan's throat tighten. "I never doubted that. You must know that."

"I'll bet you thought about it, about me being a threat. It's only natural. No hard feelings."

Again the shift in tone. This time a cold, hard edge crept into Kip's words. The heat was gone, the distance between them visible. Ice crystals settled on Jordan's skin. What did she expect? That they'd be able to go back to teasing and flirting after she'd basically forced Kip to confess? Right. They'd be lucky to salvage a working relationship that wasn't horribly awkward. But she had to at least try to do that. "Can we start from here, then?"

Kip pushed away from the door. The sun was behind her, her face in shadow. "Sure. What do you need me to do out here?"

Jordan stood. So that's the way it was going to be. Just what she'd told herself it should be. Business, and just that. A friendly distance. She could do that, had always known she should do that. "We're planting this afternoon. You should grab some lunch and then I'll show you what to do."

"Right. Half an hour okay?"

"Kip, your service is voluntary, remember? Take what time you need."

"You should probably keep track, because I don't think anyone is going to believe me on that score."

"All right, yes. Until I hear otherwise, I'll do that."

"Thanks." Kip turned, jumped down to the ground without bothering with the steps, and disappeared.

"Well, that sucked," Jordan muttered. She stared through the open door, replaying everything she'd said and wishing she could take it back and start over, somewhere that didn't begin with her forcing Kip to talk about things that hurt her.

"Everything all right?" Tya climbed into the trailer. "I just saw Kip leave. She looked a little grim."

"I'm not surprised."

Tya raised a brow. "Is it that bad?"

"Do you trust me?"

"Of course."

"All right. I know what she did, and it isn't anything that would impact us or the kids or her working here. Is that good enough?"

"I won't say I'm not curious, but I get that it's private." Tya shrugged. "I've done a few things I'd prefer to leave buried. And of course I trust you. I'm sorry if I ever made you feel that I didn't."

Jordan closed her eyes for an instant. "No, you didn't. You were right about me asking questions, and I know it. It's just so damn awkward."

"Especially when you really like her."

Jordan let that pass. Liking her wasn't the issue. Liking her too much was. "We'll all be spending time together this summer, and I hope that it won't make anyone uncomfortable."

"Hey, it'll be fine."

"Right. You're right." Jordan determined to believe what she was saying, even when nothing felt right at all.

❖

Kip headed in the general direction of Central Park, just walking, just wanting to put distance between her and her humiliation. At least she was getting plenty of exercise. Threading her way through midday crowds, she bought a bag of roasted nuts from a street cart and ate them without tasting them. The sun was on her back, and before long sweat trickled between her shoulder blades. She'd need more than a walk to purge the embarrassment of explaining to Jordan what she'd done. She was no stranger to shame, along with guilt and self-recrimination, or how long the foul taste lingered in the back of her throat. She hadn't always known the words, but then she'd only been ten, after all. The feelings were exactly the same, though, the wanting to hide, to be invisible, to erase what she had done. Or failed to do.

She dropped the bag of nuts into an open barrel, crossed the street to the park, and found a bench in a shady corner by Turtle Pond along with the homeless who stretched out on most of the available benches. A few pensioners threw peanuts to the birds, but she was already far away, bouncing on what remained of their sailboat with her fingers clenched around Randy's arm and no one else in sight. No one else at all.

She should have reached her, should have held on to her too, like she held on to Randy and the sharp edge of the boat that made cuts in her hand. Their fingers had barely grazed before she was just…gone. And when the men came in the big boat with the orange vests and the loud voices shouting over and over, all she could do was point to where her mother had been. But she wasn't there anymore.

She knew shame then. And fear.

Spots danced before Kip's eyes and her stomach turned over. She lowered her head and laced her fingers behind her neck. She hadn't felt anything like it in years. It would pass. Even the cold, clammy sweat of being locked in the cell was nothing like this. It would pass soon. When she was certain she wouldn't vomit, she straightened and blinked sweat from her eyes. An elderly woman with stockings rolled down to her blue-veined ankles, shapeless house slippers, and an even more faded, shapeless dress stood a few feet away. She held two plastic shopping bags over her right arm and a drugstore cane in her left hand. "Are you feeling all right, dearie?"

"Actually, I feel terrible."

"Something you ate?"

Kip grimaced. "No. Nightmare."

"Oh." The old woman nodded as if Kip had actually explained anything. "I've got a bottle of water if that would help."

"Will you let me pay for it?"

The woman cocked her head, her tight gray curls barely moving. "That seems fair."

Kip fished a twenty out of her wallet and held it out. "Here you go."

"That's quite a lot for a bottle of water."

"Not when you need it as much as I do. It's an even exchange."

"Hmm. You would know best, then." The woman searched in a bag and came up with a plastic bottle of water. She passed it to Kip, took the twenty, and carefully slipped it into a voluminous black pocketbook that resided with the grocery bags. "I hope you get to bury your ghosts someday."

"How did you know I had them?"

"I've had a few myself. Recognized the look." She nodded, her gaze on something far away, and turned to go. "Good luck, dearie."

"How did you get rid of them?" Kip called after her.

"I learned to forgive."

"Who?"

"Myself."

Kip watched her shuffle away. Too bad that wasn't going to work for her.

CHAPTER TWELVE

I think we're going to need a new spigot over here." Tya danced around in a fountain of water spewing from the hose connection. "I can't get it to turn off."

"Of course not," Jordan muttered, because why should anything actually work around here. She took a breath. "See if you can find the shutoff valve inside the shed. I'll look at it as soon as I can."

"Okay." Tya raced away as a rainbow glittered in the arcing spray.

Pretty, at least. Jordan went back to transplanting the tomato seedlings, cradling their delicate roots in cardboard sleeves to help keep the slugs away. Not that there were any just yet, but there would be once it warmed up a little bit more.

She'd look at the incontinent hose later. She'd gotten fairly handy at fixing things out of pure necessity, but she didn't enjoy working with tools. Invariably she jammed her finger, cut herself, or managed to make the problem worse. If Kip had been there, she would've asked her to check it. But the afternoon had dragged on, and Kip hadn't come back. Kip wasn't under any obligation to come back, and Jordan had said as much to her. Practically told her in so many words not to return if she didn't want to. Maybe Kip had had enough of people poking into her business.

She probably got a lot of that, or she would if whatever had happened followed her around. And it would. Jordan shook her head, no stranger to the unwanted attention that came from the curious and even the well-meaning. She'd fled as quickly as she could from unwanted scrutiny and told herself that wasn't the reason she avoided going home.

But it was, partly, avoiding the curious stares or the sympathetic ones, or the ones that still held the acid edge of condemnation. As if somehow she was at fault, if she'd only been around, seen the signs, chipped in to help the way she should have instead of staying away at school. Sighing, chasing away the ghost of a time she had soundly put into the past, she straightened and pressed a hand to the small of her back. As much as she loved gardening, sometimes the work was a chore.

"What do you think?" Tya joined her by the raised bed where she was digging.

"About what?" She had too many thoughts about too many things, things she wished she didn't need to think about. The hurt in Kip's eyes, the shame she felt for putting it there, the gnawing worry that Kip was gone for good.

"Think she's coming back?"

"Yes," Jordan said with more certainty than she felt. "Kip doesn't strike me as a quitter, and nothing that we talked about was really all that terrible. Embarrassing, I guess—"

Ty snorted. "I imagine anything you get arrested for is embarrassing, unless you're some kind of real career criminal or sociopath or just an idiot." Tya pulled a water bottle from the pocket of her coveralls and sipped. "She doesn't strike me as any of those things. She doesn't look like she belongs here or anywhere else serving any kind of sentence. Something's really weird, don't you think?"

"I can't say I'm an expert on people who break the law, but you're right, something feels terribly off."

"Just be careful, will you?"

"Course. There's nothing to worry about."

Tya gave her a look, shook her head, and went back to snipping the young lettuce shoots, placing them into plastic containers to weigh and price before the afternoon delivery to their restaurant clients. Jordan reached for another flat and moved it down a few feet, squatted on aching thighs, and dug another hole in the soil. There wasn't anything to worry about, other than her peace of mind, and she could handle that.

The creak of the gate brought her upright and spinning around a minute later. Kip came through, her face pale and her hair disheveled, as if she'd been running. Jordan forced herself to stay still, even though every other part of her wanted to hurry over to greet her.

"Sorry, I lost track of time," Kip said.

"There's no problem. Like I said, you're not on the clock."

"Not exactly true, but I appreciate the latitude. I got…caught up."

Jordan wanted to know in what, but kept from asking. Not her business. That was going to have to become her mantra. Not her business where Kip went or who she went with or what she did when she got there. Not her business if Kip looked upset, or if she was the cause of Kip's unhappiness. If she was, she hadn't a clue how to make things right. She couldn't very well undo Kip's sentence or pretend she didn't know. She didn't even know how to comfort her, as if Kip had asked, which she hadn't. And now she was getting close to making herself crazy. "We've got a few hours of daylight left. How do you feel about planting?"

"About the same as I feel about bungee jumping. Looks interesting from a distance." Kip grinned weakly. "Just give me the step-by-step, and I'll give it a go."

Jordan laughed. "I think you'll find this substantially easier, and safer, than extreme sports. The most important thing is to be gentle with the roots. They're very fragile, and until they get established in their new location, the seedling is essentially starving. All the nutrients come up from the soil, of course."

"Okay. Don't squeeze the root ball. Got it."

"Don't squeeze, don't shake the dirt off, don't crush them when you put it in the hole."

Kip regarded the ten-inch-high plants skeptically. "Maybe there's something else I could do. I don't want to be the cause of many little seedling deaths."

"Trust me, I'll keep an eye on you. The first few times."

"All right, if you say so."

Smiling, relieved to have Kip back, Jordan pointed to the garden shed. "Why don't you go around to the other side of the bed, and we'll work down the line together. There're gloves in the shed and a trowel in there too."

"Be right back."

Heart tripping, Jordan watched her go. The heavy sense of unease lifted, and she would absolutely swear the day was brighter. That couldn't possibly be true. She ought to be nervous, on guard, suspicious of the way she felt, but she couldn't pretend she didn't like the excitement of having Kip near. She very much did. When

Kip emerged, gloves in one hand and trowel in the other, and saw her watching, she grinned. Getting caught looking was becoming a habit, but Jordan didn't mind. Kip didn't seem to either, and her self-satisfied smile said so. Just seeing the return of Kip's smile chased away the last of Jordan's tension and worry.

Kip settled across from her, resting back on her heels, her muscled forearms surprisingly pale. Whatever she did as a mechanic, she did inside. Jordan's hands, in contrast, were several shades darker, already tanned after just a few weeks of early spring sunlight. "Ready?"

"Always."

Jordan didn't look up, pretending she didn't hear the slight husky note in Kip's voice. "Okay, first, before you take the seedling out, make a hole in the topsoil about this wide and this deep." She demonstrated. "Drop in a handful of the fertilizer pellets, a little layer of peat moss, and then lift the seedling from the pot by tilting it at about thirty degrees and squeezing until the root ball pops free."

"I'm not sure about the squeezing part. I can hear the little root thingies screaming," Kip said as she tried it the first time.

Jordan chuckled. "All right, I might've exaggerated their fragility just a little. These are hardy specimens from a very good nursery. They'll be fine."

Kip's jaw was set as she carefully deposited the seedling into the hole she made. "Now what?"

"Use both hands to kind of flatten and press the soil down around the root ball. You want to get rid of air pockets where water can collect and either drown the roots or prevent them from reaching the soil where the nutrients are."

"Okay. I've got it."

"Good. That's all there is to it. Now you'll be able to handle anything. In a few weeks we'll teach you how to weed."

Kip shot her a look. "I think I'm gonna be very busy constructing a greenhouse by then."

"I can't believe you're running from the garden chores," Jordan teased. "Where exactly is your green thumb?"

"I don't have one. My mother was the gardener."

Jordan caught the past tense as well as the flat tone of Kip's voice. She wondered, but she'd already pressed Kip for enough personal information in one day. "Well, you're catching on just fine."

She kept an eye on Kip as they worked their way down the long, four-foot-wide raised garden bed. Kip was careful, but not tentative, and confident the way she appeared to be about most everything. They finished the row and started another.

"How many tomatoes do you expect?" Kip asked.

"If these produce the way I expect, and we don't have problems with the weather or pests, several dozen from each plant."

"Wow." Kip turned, looking down the row. "That's a hell of a lot of tomatoes."

"Tomatoes are one of the biggest sellers. The season is so short, especially in the Northeast. Plus, the fruit is central to all kinds of seasonal dishes. Restaurants and wholesalers are clamoring for more than we can provide most of the time."

"So tell me about the tomato you wanted to make."

Jordan frowned. "Sorry?"

"The heirloom thing—the hybrid. What were you going for?"

"Oh." Jordan laughed, self-conscious. "Well, I wanted an oversized fruit, like a beefsteak, but one that was a little more on the juicy side as opposed to the meaty side like most beefsteaks. Some of the heirloom varieties have incredible flavor and delicate meat, but they tend to be smaller and not as robust. I had several crosses I was planning to work on."

"So what happened?"

Jordan hesitated. Where to start. Places she didn't want to go. Maybe another day she would've changed the subject like she so often did when her past came up, but she'd asked Kip to bare a difficult secret and she had. She hadn't wanted to, and even though the circumstances weren't the same, Kip had been more than honest. She'd shown her self-recriminations and her vulnerability. Now it only seemed fair for Jordan to answer. More than that, she wanted to answer. She wanted Kip to know something about her. "I had big plans, like I already told you. My family were farmers, just ordinary farmers, for several generations back. We had a small dairy herd, the usual crops, and our produce was popular in area restaurants and farmers' markets even fifteen years ago, before local sourcing really caught on."

"Where did you grow up?" Kip asked, reaching for another seedling.

"A couple hundred miles upstate. I went to school at Cornell—it's a big Ag place."

"I don't think I knew that. They have a really good aeronautic engineering department too."

"See," Jordan said lightly, "I didn't know that, either."

"We're obviously a good team." Kip walked to the cooler at the end of the row and pulled out two bottles of water and brought one back to Jordan. "So you were saying about the farm?"

"Yes, right. Well, I planned to take it over, one day, in the far future." Jordan shook her head, remembering her naïve aspirations. "But the economy went into a tailspin and most farmers were overextended—easy credit let them purchase more land than they could afford and equipment they couldn't pay for and a lot of small farms went under."

Kip set her water bottle down and crouched across from Jordan, watching her intently with the tomato seedlings nodding between them. A frown line marked the space between her dark brows. "I guess I knew that, but I never knew anyone that actually had to deal with it."

"I didn't know I needed to either. My father didn't say anything to my mother or to me about exactly how bad things were. Not until…" Jordan swallowed and wiped away the sweat that had accumulated on her forehead and was slowly trickling down toward her eyes with the back of her hand. "Not until the morning he drove out into the field on his tractor and shot himself."

"I'm so sorry." Kip winced. "If I'd known, I never would have brought that up—I'm sorry."

"None of it was your doing," Jordan said, ignoring the lead ball dragging at her insides. "I don't know if I'd suspected what he was planning that I could have made any difference at all, but I didn't have any idea. My father was a proud man, and I doubt he would have asked for help, anyone's help, even if we'd been able to give it. Maybe I should've known, probably should've been paying more attention, but—" She blew out a breath. "I can't really blame it on youth. After a certain point, we know what we're doing or not doing, don't we? I just wasn't thinking about them."

Kip caught her lower lip between her teeth, nodded sharply. "I don't know what the circumstances were for you then, but I'm guessing if you'd had any clue, you would've tried to help. In fact, I'm sure of it."

Jordan raised her eyes, searched Kip's, found understanding and compassion and certainty. Grateful, but not convinced, she said softly, "Why? I mean, what makes you think I wasn't like most twenty-three-year-olds—self-absorbed, still expecting someone else to solve the problems, blissfully unaware of other people's suffering."

"Because if you had been, I don't think you'd be suffering now, and I know that you are."

Jordan went back to planting, her refuge from the memories. "Well, I appreciate your kind opinion of me. After that, my mother sold the farm, had to, to cover the bills." She busied herself making a new hole and settling a seedling gently into place. "She went to live with her sister and died suddenly less than a year later. I finished my master's and have been more or less working around the fringes of agriculture ever since."

"So you've given up on the idea of farming?"

"Since I don't have a farm, it's rather moot." Jordan patted the earth down around the seedling, carefully compacting the soil to hug the hairlike rootlets. "Let's just say I've traded in dreams for reality."

CHAPTER THIRTEEN

H ey, Ty, what time are the kids coming home?" Jordan called. Kip glanced at her watch. Somehow four hours had slipped by. While they'd planted, she and Jordan had fallen into an easy rhythm, moving down the rows in tandem, talking as they had at dinner about news and books and sports. Like her, Jordan had high hopes for the home baseball team that season. And they'd talked about Jordan's plan for community outreach, expanding the project's merchant base, and creating a self-sustaining enterprise. Tya floated in and out of the conversation, sharp and funny and still a little wary of Kip but too cool to really let it show. Kip might have missed it if she hadn't developed a sixth sense for what people weren't saying from dealing with bureaucrats and spooks. She didn't blame Tya for her caution.

She and Jordan carefully avoided talk of family and past, but she kept thinking about Jordan's story. Unlike Jordan, who had lost her family and her home in one tragic moment, she still had her father and Randy. She still had the security of the family enterprise. She'd always had a place. Jordan had rebuilt her life, and thinking about that made Kip wonder if she would have been as strong.

Tya coiled the hose under the spigot Kip had repaired with a new gasket. "They have band tonight, but I ought to get going soon."

"Go ahead home, then. We're good over here." Jordan straightened with a slight groan and turned to Kip. "That's the last of them for today. You get another star."

"That's two already."

Jordan smiled and shook her head.

Kip grabbed the empty flat and tossed it onto a pile next to the shed. "You need a dumpster."

"I need a vacation house in the Bahamas too," Jordan said, massaging her back.

"Sore?"

"Mmm. Occupational hazard. How do you feel?"

"Like my knees are frozen in a permanently flexed position." Kip grinned and rubbed her thighs. "I'll feel it tomorrow."

"We got twice as much done—no, even more than that—with your help." Jordan squinted toward the sky. "And we won't get much more done today. It looks like the rain that was forecast is coming."

"Should we cover these guys up or something?" Kip was already worried she might have shocked the little guys. A drenching rain couldn't be good for them. "They've already had a hard day."

Jordan laughed. "They'll be fine. Temperatures are supposed to stay in the midforties tonight. We ought to put the fabric over the beds, though. That will protect them from getting beat up."

"Is that the rolls of white stuff I saw in the shed?"

"Yeah, do you mind getting it?"

"No problem. How many?"

"Three."

Kip collected them and returned just as Tya was heading toward the gate. "'Night."

"See you," Tya called briskly and disappeared out the gate.

Kip sighed. "I don't think she's too happy about me being here. Is that causing problems for you?"

"No. Ty just needs a chance to get to know you."

"Maybe she thinks she already knows enough."

"You're not being very fair to either one of you if you don't give her a chance."

"You're right. It's just, I can see you two are close, and I don't want to cause friction." Kip stacked the rolls by the bed.

"I think I'm a pretty good judge of character, and I'm not worried. Ty will be fine."

"Then I'll stop worrying. Now what?"

"I can get the rest of this," Jordan said. "You don't need to stay."

"That's okay. Let me give you a hand. It'll go faster." Kip was in no hurry to leave. All she had to look forward to was her silent apartment, her empty refrigerator, and another call to her father. She needed to find out how Randy was doing and to get a number for him, if she could. Beyond that, she had nothing to do except wait for the next round of testing results to come in on the new engine. That would be at least a week.

"Okay, sure. I won't turn down good help." Jordan handed her a couple dozen wire hoops. "Stick these in the ground about every four feet. Then we'll run the fabric over them and stake it all down."

"Got it." Kip set the hoops in silence for a minute. "So what did she say?"

"Who?"

"Ty."

"About what?"

"About why I'm here."

"Nothing. I didn't tell her the details."

Kip stopped and stared. "Why not?"

Jordan met her gaze, a little challenge in her eyes. "Because she didn't need to know. All she needed to know was you aren't an ax murderer."

"That's not what I meant. Why didn't you just tell her? She must have been curious."

"I didn't want to," Jordan said softly. "I practically forced you to tell me. It's your private business."

"Thank you." Kip took a minute to savor the heat that pooled in her belly. She wasn't used to being defended. She'd always been the one doing the shielding, ever since Randy was old enough to get into trouble. "I don't think I have the right to privacy where this is concerned, but I appreciate it. This is…pretty humiliating."

"I'm sorry."

"You shouldn't be. I was driving the damn car, after all. No contest there."

"Who actually stole it?"

Kip shook her head. The responsibility had become hers the minute she got behind the wheel. And she'd already accepted the consequences in court. Randy had been guilty, but so had she. "Put it down to a string of bad decisions, and I ended up making the last one."

"All right," Jordan said slowly. She unraveled the first roll. "Grab one side of this fabric."

Together they walked the long sheet of six-foot-wide thin white mesh from one end of the raised bed to the other and staked it down. The seedlings looked like little tent poles underneath it.

"How long do you keep this stuff on there?" Kip asked.

"Probably the better part of a month. It not only protects them from wind and rain, it helps concentrate the heat, and tomato plants like heat."

"So, what's next?"

Jordan collected the leftover stakes, dropped them into a canvas bag she'd slung over her shoulder, and shooed a chicken out of the shed before storing her tools. "Peppers and eggplants. Everything else we'll start from seed. If I had a greenhouse, I'd have started my own seedlings by now."

"Do you have money enough in the budget to buy materials for the construction?"

"I can probably scare some up, depending on the amount. Will you be able to give me some idea on that?"

"I'll be able to tell you exactly what you'll need for materials. I use a program that will calculate all the specs once I put the designs in. Then I'll get you quotes."

Jordan studied her. "You're not exactly a mechanic, are you?"

Sometimes a little truth was enough. "Mechanical engineer. A hands-on engineer."

"Which is not exactly what I understood you to be at first," Jordan said.

"I might have let you misunderstand."

"I see." Jordan waited a beat. "Is there some reason you don't want to be more specific?"

"Yes."

"Is it me or everyone in general you don't trust?"

Kip winced. "It's complicated."

"What isn't?" Jordan shrugged. "Since we're avoiding the personal, let me show you what I had in mind for the greenhouse."

"Thanks." The ball of tension between Kip's shoulders loosened when Jordan didn't press her. Jordan was good that way. No matter what came up, Jordan seemed to handle it, seemed willing to give Kip space. She was glad for that and wished she didn't need it. Ever since her mother died, she'd felt as if an invisible barrier stood between her and almost everyone else, everyone except Randy, and the necessary secrecy of the job didn't help. Her father seemed comfortable with a kind of remote affection, and eventually she'd gotten comfortable with it too. She'd tried so many times to remember what he'd been like when they'd all been together as a family. He'd always been something of a shadow, the man who came home at night, sometimes after they were already in bed, and was gone in the morning before they woke up. And after her mother was gone, he was absent even more. Then there were nannies and, when they got older, housekeepers and other people who stood in for her parents. He'd been there, but never very close. After a while, she'd gotten used to the distance and found it harder and harder to be any other way with anyone else. Maybe that was why she didn't date very much.

Being around Jordan was the first time she'd wanted less space instead of more.

"I was hoping," Jordan said, stopping in the far corner of the lot, "we could do something back here. It doesn't get enough direct sun to be great for most outdoor planting, but we'll augment that with grow lights inside. Over the winter we'd have to do that anyhow. I was thinking forty by sixty?"

Kip put her hands on her hips and studied the space, checking the pitch of the ground, the fence on two sides, the likely shade from nearby buildings. "Where do you want your access gate?"

"What about the one in the alley?"

Kip shook her head. "Too far away. You don't want to carry all your supplies all the way down here. Plus, you want a double gate wide enough so you can back the truck in. I'd put it over there." Kip pointed to the street side of the lot. "That way you can come right down…what is it…Tenth?…yeah, Tenth…and directly into here. You'll need a good security fence, at least ten feet tall. Motion detector lights too. What kind of alarm system do you have for the trailer?"

"Um, telephone?"

"Not exactly what I was thinking. I know you don't keep anything valuable in there, but you still ought to have some kind of security."

"How about a padlock?"

"How about we at least get it wired to a local alarm and put some motion detectors at strategic points around the perimeter. This is too important a place to have it vandalized."

"I don't see how we can afford that," Jordan said.

"Let me work something up, and then we can talk about it."

"I can't even pay you for that, especially since I don't think it's something—"

"It's not a problem. I don't expect you to pay me."

Jordan tilted her head. "Why are you doing it, then?"

Kip thought about giving her some easy answer. She could always say she wanted to contribute to the community effort, and she did. She felt good doing something as simple as planting tomatoes and knowing someone would benefit from it. But that wasn't the entire truth, and she was tired of giving Jordan half-truths. "I like it when you smile at me."

"Oh." Jordan took a slow breath. The late afternoon sun was suddenly much warmer on her bare arms. The breeze ruffled the tiny hairs on the back of her neck. Her vision tunneled until the garden disappeared and only Kip remained. "Well. I'm not sure how to take that."

"Don't you?"

"All right, maybe I do." She didn't have much time to think, shouldn't think. No…no, should most *definitely* think. "And if I do take it the way I think you mean it, I'd have to say—"

"You're not interested."

"That's right."

Kip's insides quivered for an instant, as if Jordan had actually landed the punch. She shouldn't have been surprised. She already knew Jordan didn't play games. She'd liked that about her from the start, although right now, she might've appreciated just a little bit of game playing. "Well, you said you'd be clear about what you wanted."

"I did, didn't I." Jordan considered that. "So I should be clear. I *ought* to say I'm not interested, because we're not in any kind of position to do anything about anything else. But I didn't actually say that, seeing how it's not one hundred percent accurate."

"I'm trying to translate that," Kip said, taking a step closer, "since I'm all for accuracy. But the only thing I'm hearing is that you didn't say no."

Jordan braced her hand in the center of Kip's chest. Kip was less than an arm's length away now. Her heart beat quickly against Jordan's palm, strong and sturdy and fast. As fast as Jordan's heart tripped beneath her breast. The sun had somehow gotten behind them when she wasn't paying attention to anything except Kip, just low enough to paint Kip's face a shimmering gold and make her tousled hair glow like polished onyx. Kip's skin gleamed with a bit of sweat from the work they'd done all afternoon. She couldn't have been more handsome if she'd been plucked from one of Jordan's fantasies. "I didn't say no, but in case you were thinking of kissing me—"

"I was. I am. To be accurate." Kip cupped Jordan's waist just above her hip, played her thumb up and down Jordan's stomach.

"This is where I say no," Jordan whispered. Kip's thumb teased at her stomach through her thin cotton shirt and her muscles twitched, sending a jolt down the inside of her thighs that jellied her knees. "It's got nothing to do with wanting, exactly. Except I don't want to go there with you. I'm sort of your boss—"

"That's bullshit," Kip muttered, but she didn't move any closer. Not without an invitation.

"And more importantly, maybe, I'm not in the habit of getting involved with much younger women."

"Calling bullshit again," Kip said, every muscle vibrating. Holding still took more effort than she'd ever had to exercise doing anything in her life. She'd rather be lifting a five-hundred-pound engine with her bare hands than stand her ground right now.

"Neither is bullshit," Jordan said, "and even if they were, I'm not quite ready to kiss a woman I barely know."

"Would you kiss me if you knew me better?"

Jordan laughed. The woman was persistent, and she liked that even if she shouldn't. Kip was also too damn persuasive for anybody's good. Especially hers. "How can I know?"

"I think you already do. Know, that is. Because I do."

"We're not the same. I am the cautious type."

"And what am I?"

Jordan smiled, lightly fanning her fingers over Kip's chest before stepping back out of touching range. The safety zone was comforting, and a little disappointing. "I suspect you like adventure a little bit more than I do, and I'm not in the market for an adventurous woman. Or a complicated one."

"Is that what you think I am?"

"Oh, I'm certain of that." Jordan wished for the briefest instant she didn't have to think about tomorrow, but she'd learned that lesson the hard way. Every action had consequences, sometimes ones that haunted forever. "I want to keep things uncomplicated between us."

"I'm not sure that's possible, but if that's what you want." Kip grinned wryly. "You're the boss."

Jordan didn't argue, absolutely certain she'd made the right decision despite every instinct clamoring for her to call out, to call Kip back, when she walked away.

Chapter Fourteen

Half an hour later, Kip let herself into her apartment. She was right, the place felt empty and sterile, the refrigerator was a sad comment on her absent state of domesticity, and a long shower didn't do much to drive away the logy haze in her head or the steady churn of unrequited desire in the pit of her stomach. She was in that overtired, amped-up state that made falling asleep a remote possibility, and the memory of the almost-kiss pretty much guaranteed she'd lie awake tossing and turning. The insistent urgency in her loins would have subsided by now if she hadn't glimpsed the swift flame of hunger in Jordan's eyes when they'd touched. Brief and quickly extinguished, but definitely there. Her brain got the back-off message loud and clear, but her body hadn't read the memo. To hell with it. Distraction was what she needed to cure the annoying thrum of arousal, and she had a list of antidotes at hand. She toweled off, pulled on sweats, and made the call she'd been avoiding all day. Her father answered his cell almost immediately.

"Hello, Catherine."

"Hi, Dad. Have you had any word on Randy?"

"No, and I don't expect to. The director made it very clear. Their admission policy requires no outside contact while the residents"—he made a slight snorting noise, as if finding the term *resident* ridiculous—"get accustomed to the routine and show progress."

"What does that mean—how long?"

"As I understand it, the length of time varies with each individual. They're big on customized programs." His tone suggested the whole topic was distasteful. "I was given to believe at least four weeks, perhaps a little longer."

"What about his medical evaluation and his psych assessment? Have any of the staff called? I understand the rehab rules, but he's got to be having a tough time withdrawing from the substances he uses."

"I have no doubt he is." Her father's voice was laced with scorn. "But that's what I'm paying them to monitor. Fortunately, as I understand it, the worst physical effects will be over fairly soon, and he'll be properly medicated. Although I should think a little discomfort might be a good lesson."

Kip winced. She doubted tough love was really going to work with Randy, but arguing the point with her father would get her nowhere. "Do you have a number for the physician in charge of his care?"

"No, and I didn't ask for one. Whoever it is will contact us when it's the proper time, I'm sure."

Kip closed her eyes. She had to believe her father loved Randy and the ice in his voice was from frustration rather than disregard. "I know you're probably right, and he's being well taken care of. It's just hard to know he's going through something this difficult without any support."

"Really, Catherine, it's the best thing for him. He's had altogether too much support during his life."

"What's the alternative? We can't abandon him just because he acts out when he's unhappy or in pain. Everyone has their coping mechanisms, and his just aren't very functional."

"I won't argue with you about your brother's situation," her father said, sounding weary for the first time. "But it's time he dealt with whatever his issues are and started thinking about the rest of his life. He's not a teenager any longer, and he needs to shoulder his responsibilities."

"He's still got a couple more years of college, and even then he might not be ready to just step into your shoes."

Her father laughed. "I have no doubt of that, nor do I plan for that to happen immediately. But he'll need to step up sooner than expected."

Kip's stomach tightened. "Why? Are you okay? Is anything wrong?"

"No, just the opposite. In fact," her father said slowly, "I've been intending to tell you, but with these most recent events, there hasn't been a good time."

"Tell me what?"

"I'm getting married again, fairly soon, and I'm planning on cutting back on my business responsibilities."

Kip reached behind her for the kitchen chair, pulled it over, and sank down. "You're getting married."

"We'll be married at the beginning of the summer," her father went on as if discussing a corporate merger. "I'll necessarily be absent more than usual around that time."

"Who?" Kip ran through the list of women in her father's circle but couldn't ever remember him showing any particular interest in anyone beyond the usual business or social interactions. She'd never once in all these years considered he would replace her mother. Replace all of them. And how ridiculous was that on about a million levels? He was hardly replacing anyone, but it felt that way all the same. A new wife, a baby at some point probably, a new family. Theirs had fractured, and he was finally going to have one that was whole again that wasn't going to include her and Randy. "Who is she?"

"You wouldn't know her. Barbara Fischer. She's not local."

"How..." She cleared her throat. "Where did you meet her?"

"On a flight back from LA, of all things. She flies with United."

"She's a flight attendant?"

"No, actually she's a pilot. We met in the VIP lounge."

Kip had no trouble picturing it. Her father radiated power and assurance, and women probably found him attractive. "Well. I don't know what to say except congratulations. I look forward to meeting her."

"Thank you," her father said a little stiffly. "As to the other matter, I'm sure you'll hear from your brother before I do. Please do whatever you can to keep him in there. It's time he took charge of his life."

"Right, yes. I will. Good night."

"Good night, Catherine."

Kip set her phone aside and stared blankly across her kitchen. Her father was getting married and starting a new life. Why not? He'd been a widower now for almost fifteen years. He wasn't as old as a lot of men who started second families. She'd just never imagined he'd actually want anything like that. But then, she really didn't know what he wanted, other than dominating the business field. She shook her head. He had every right to be happy, and it was her problem if the idea left her feeling oddly disoriented and displaced. She could only imagine how Randy would take the news. What lousy timing. A surge of embarrassment followed quickly on that thought. As if her father should have to forgo happiness because Randy was unhappy. Because she was a bit at loose ends, settled professionally, but adrift in every other way.

Tired of her own mental whining, Kip grabbed her leather jacket from the closet. What she needed was to get out of her apartment and shed her self-pity for a few hours. She was sitting in a neighborhood tavern watching a baseball game with no sound, nursing a draft long gone flat, when her phone rang. She checked it, saw Savannah's number, and answered.

"Hi."

"Why are you avoiding me?"

"I'm not. Did I miss a call or something?"

Savannah harrumphed. "I haven't heard anything from you since we left the courthouse. I think that qualifies as avoiding. I don't have any idea what's going on with you. You could be in jail for all I know."

Kip shuddered. "Hey, be careful what you say. You don't want to jinx me."

"Where are you right now?"

"Riley's."

"It's a bar!" Savannah sounded aghast.

"It has been for the last twenty years."

"I don't think you're supposed to be there. And you never go out to bars. Who is there with you?"

Kip looked around the single large room with its scarred wood bar running down one side, a cloudy glass mirror fronted by shelves of faintly dusty liquor bottles, and a scattering of mostly mismatched tables and chairs. "About a dozen regulars and a couple of college kids."

"That's not what I mean, and you know it. Who's keeping you company—do you have a designated driver?"

"First of all, I'm fifteen minutes from my apartment, so I definitely don't need a driver. Second of all, I'm not drinking much. And thirdly,

I don't need a babysitter." As she said it she thought of Jordan, whose company she definitely would have preferred to…anyone's. The hungry longing she'd managed to ignore beneath the drone of bar voices and mindless TV came roaring back.

"I'm not so sure about that."

"Gee, Savannah, thanks. First you try to find me girlfriends, now you're trying to find me a chaperone?"

"You shouldn't be alone after everything that's happened," Savannah went on, completely undeterred by Kip's sarcasm. "I'm coming over."

"Savannah." Kip sat up sharply. "It's after ten and pouring outside. You're not coming out to a bar."

"I'm putting my coat on right now and requesting an Uber. I'll be there in…wait…twelve minutes. Don't leave."

"You're pushy and annoying, you know that, right?"

"But you love me," Savannah said in a slightly singsong voice and disconnected.

"Hell." Half amused, half aggravated, Kip slid her phone back into her pocket. Maybe company wouldn't be a bad thing. She wasn't doing a great job not worrying about Randy, and she couldn't go more than a few minutes without replaying every second of the last few minutes with Jordan. She didn't usually come on to women, content to let things happen—or not. Jordan turned a key inside her, opened the door on a need she hadn't realized was shut.

Savannah appeared right on time, saving her from any more torturous recollections, and Kip waved her over. As Savannah pulled off her raincoat and plopped into a chair, Kip stood. "I'll get you a seltzer water. Lime?"

Puffing slightly, Savannah nodded. "That would be good. I feel like I've run a marathon, and I just walked fifty feet."

"That's because you're ridiculously pregnant and probably going to deliver any day and shouldn't be here."

"Oh, be quiet and get me my sparkly."

Exasperated and ambushed by affection, Kip flagged the bartender and ordered a repeat of her beer and a seltzer for Savannah. She sat opposite her cousin and handed her the soda. "There's no reason for you to be here."

"How about I love you, I'm worried about you, and I'm a nosy parker and I want to know what's going on with Randy and that whole business."

"That business," Kip said dryly, "is going along swimmingly. Randy's incommunicado for another week and a half in some rehab center upstate, and I'll be spending the summer working off my penance."

"He really checked himself in?" Savannah stretched and turned an empty chair to face her. She propped her feet up with a grunt. "Better."

"He's there." And hopefully he'd stay this time. His first two times in rehab, he'd lasted less than forty-eight hours.

"What about you?"

"I'll be spending the summer working in a garden."

"Sorry? A garden, what does that mean?"

Kip explained to her about the Ninth Avenue Community Garden project.

"Huh." Savannah scrunched up her nose. "I guess a few hours a week won't be so bad."

"Actually, I'm taking some time off and working there more or less full-time. I'm in the finishing stages of a project, and I don't really need to be on-site all the time. I figure the more time I spent there, the faster I'll reduce my sentence."

"Wow, that sounds boring."

Kip pictured planting the tomato seedlings and exploring Hunts Point Terminal and Jordan's plans for setting up a distribution network. "There's a lot more to it than you think. I planted about four dozen tomato plants this afternoon. Pretty good at it too."

Savannah gaped. "You were literally digging in the dirt."

"I was. Next up is building a greenhouse."

"What did they say to you?"

"Who?"

"The people at the garden place."

"About what?" Kip said quietly.

"You know, how is their attitude about you being placed there."

Kip tried not to prickle over discussing her least favorite subject. "Pretty damn good considering Jordan had no idea she'd even be getting someone like me. She's been more than decent. Supportive, even."

"Who's Jordan?"

"She runs the project. It's pretty much her baby. The concept is pretty amazing, really, and her plans are—"

"Amazing," Savannah said, sipping daintily from her straw. "I see. And she's not concerned or anything—not giving you a hard time?"

Kip frowned. "No, she's been great. Easy to talk to and hasn't had any kind of attitude, and she certainly has a right to one."

"How old is she?"

"What difference does that make?"

"Just trying to get a sense of her. She younger or older than you, married?"

"She's in her late thirties, I guess, maybe forty." Kip frowned. Was Jordan single? What if she wasn't? What did it matter? It mattered. "Not married."

"And…" Savannah said, her voice rising in question.

"What? Come on, Savannah. Give me a break with the questions."

"Your very reluctance is telling. She's hot, isn't she."

Kip instantly had an image of Jordan kneeling across the garden bed from her, sunlight gilding her hair, face faintly flushed, damp locks tangled on her neck, laughing at something Kip had said. "She's nice to look at, sure."

"And is she, you know, into girls?"

Kip blew out a breath. "Where are you going with this?"

"Just wondering, simply curious, since you seem to be taken with her."

"I'm not taken with her. I like her. She's smart and capable and ambitious. Admirable."

"Admirable. Is that another word for hot?"

Kip laughed. "All right, I really like her, all right? A lot. And that's all there is to it."

"It's early days yet. Things could change."

Maybe, but then in Kip's experience, it didn't take a lot of time to know when you clicked with someone, when you wanted more of a connection, when things just felt right. She hadn't experienced that undeniable pull very often, in fact, rarely, but she didn't have any doubts about what she was feeling for Jordan. Unfortunately, Jordan had made it crystal clear the attraction wasn't mutual.

"Afraid not," Kip said.

"Well, in the meantime, I have this friend from my birthing class who has a sister—"

"No. Absolutely not." Kip rose and held out her hand. "I'm taking you home."

Savannah didn't protest, and forty minutes later Kip was home in bed staring at the shifting patches of reflected street light on her ceiling. She often thought up new design innovations when she was ready to fall asleep, but that night the only thing on her mind was Jordan.

Chapter Fifteen

Jordan shook the hand of the owner of Plum Blossom, a thin Asian man in a pressed white shirt and black pants belted at his narrow waist. He might have been sixty or ninety, but whatever the age, he was a shrewd businessman. Landing this account was a coup for her, and satisfaction settled like warm brandy in her middle. "Thank you so much, Mr. Liu. We should have your first delivery later this week. Broccoli, brussels sprouts, cauliflower, and baby spinach."

"Good. What about the tomatoes? And the eggplants." He raised a finger at her, dark eyes narrowed in challenge. "Must have the Chinese variety—sweeter, more tender."

Tomatoes and eggplants. Everybody wanted them. Those and peppers. For an instant, she recalled telling Kip the same thing the day before, and as she had a dozen times during her restless evening at home and the first instant after waking, she thought of the kiss. Well, it wasn't a *kiss* kiss, but might have been. Kip *wanted* it to be a kiss, there was no question about that. And if she was totally honest, which she damn well hoped she could be, she'd wanted it too. And since she was being honest, she could admit she'd wanted it for more reasons than Kip being an incredibly attractive woman. Kip was also bright and charming and the right kind of mysterious. And she looked like she could really kiss.

Eggplants and tomatoes. Right, her new customer, the one who'd just promised her to talk to some of his other restaurant friends about joining the farm-to-table project, was waiting. If she could develop a network in Chinatown, she'd sell locally a third of what she planned to grow. Exactly what her community garden should be doing.

"We've got them in the ground, Mr. Liu," she said, fudging just a little on the eggplant situation. But they would be in the ground in another week. "You know we're still a couple of months early for fresh tomatoes."

He smiled. "I know you'll figure out a way to get them for us. Leeks too. And when can we expect the bok choy?"

"You tell me what you and your friends want, and I promise I'll plant it."

His eyes sparkled. "Then I will talk to them, and you will give us good prices. And fresh delivery every day. The customers, they like it fresh, and now…" He waggled a hand. "Local is good."

"Local is great." She shook his hand again when he held it out. "You ask for it, I'll grow it."

Leaving with a head full of slogans, she decided she'd have to get a logo and put some kind of tag line on the side of the truck. Kip would probably know how to get that done. As she climbed in, she considered how Kip had already become part of her thinking. Probably not a good idea from a business point of view. Kip was temporary help, after all, and probably very temporary. She'd said she was a mechanical engineer. She wasn't going to be satisfied weeding garden beds for long. And personally? Definitely a bad idea to assume she'd stick around for long.

All the same, she was looking forward to seeing her. Nothing wrong with indulging in short-term pleasures, after all.

She made her usual stop for coffee and pastries and arrived back at the garden project at five thirty. As soon as she turned down the alley, she slowed. The gate was unlocked. Creeping quietly the rest of the way, she parked, shut off the engine, and sat in the truck staring at the dangling hasp. Call the police? That didn't seem like any better an idea than it had last time. Call Kip? No, that was a crazy idea. What was Kip going to do, race twenty minutes uptown to rescue her?

She grimaced. Really, she'd never needed rescuing, and just because Kip had the look of a knight errant about her, wasn't going to start depending on her now. Investigate on her own it was, then. She took inventory of what she had in the truck. Flashlight. A big one, a reasonable weapon. A tire iron, better weapon but buried under crates in the back, and besides, she probably couldn't wield it with enough efficiency to do anything more than hand it over to a would-be assailant. Her cell phone was probably still her best weapon.

With a sigh, she eased out and leaned against the door to click it shut without making too much of a noise. She hoped. Flashlight in one hand, cell phone in the other, she took two careful steps toward the back gate when it opened, and Kip walked through.

"I thought I heard you," Kip said. "Morning."

"I'm glad I didn't have the tire iron," Jordan said, half laughing. "I have to remember you tend to show up unexpectedly."

Kip eyed the flashlight. "Sorry. I didn't think you'd mind if I let myself in."

"No, that's fine. I'll get used to you being here early."

"Good."

Kip made it sound as if Jordan had done something particularly pleasing, and she felt the heat rush to her face. Great. Now she was blushing and pretending she wasn't. "It is pretty early—what have you been doing?"

"I couldn't sleep and I wanted to take some measurements for the greenhouse and check out security options. I'm really sorry about not asking first."

"You're free to come over whenever you want. As early as you want," Jordan repeated. She returned to the truck, stowed her flashlight, and lifted out the cardboard carry tray with two coffees and the bag of pastries. "The cranberry scones looked good today. I got your blueberry too, but you've got a choice."

"Do I have to choose? I forgot dinner last night." Kip smiled wryly. "And breakfast today too."

"Did you at least have lunch yesterday?"

"Half a bag of hot nuts?"

"That's just sad." Jordan handed Kip a cup of coffee and put the pastries back in the truck. "Come on. We're going to breakfast."

"Hey, do you have time? I'll be fine with the scone, really."

"Woman does not live by baked goods alone, and we've got a busy day ahead of us. There's a great diner a couple blocks away. We'll be back before Ty gets here."

"I'm sold."

Kip latched the lock on the gate, and Jordan led the way out to Ninth. The early mornings were still cool enough to require a light jacket, and Kip wore a faded denim one over a black T-shirt and black jeans. The jacket wasn't one of those fake designer ones, but one that looked like it had seen years of use. The fabric molded to her shoulders and lay softly against her neck. Her jeans were torn just above her left knee, and Jordan caught herself staring at the tiny peek of flesh that flashed every time Kip took a step. She couldn't possibly be so desperate for a little physical contact that a tiny inch of skin could fascinate her so. But apparently she was. Wrenching her gaze up and forward, she ignored the spicy aroma drifting from Kip's direction.

Shampoo? Lotion? Cologne? Obsessed a little, anyone?

Enough people were out and about that she and Kip were forced to walk close together to stay side by side, and her shoulder brushed Kip's with every step. Every time it happened, she felt a tingle despite the double layers of her dark green canvas work jacket and Kip's denim sleeve. Her nerve endings were raw from the constant stimulation. She was jumpy as the orange tabby who frequented the alley most days looking for scraps. She'd never given much thought to pheromones before, but Kip Kensington sure had something that lit her up.

"I would've come earlier to help with deliveries," Kip said, "but I wasn't sure of your schedule."

"I told you, you don't need to do that."

"I know, but I'm usually awake. Four a.m., right?"

"We don't actually have deliveries to make every day, but I've been cold-calling some of the local restaurants and markets, hoping to interest them in our project."

"That's a tough way to build a distribution market."

"Maybe, but it's also the best way. Face-to-face is really important for small business development."

"I can see that," Kip said, although nothing about her experience with business was anything like Jordan's. Even though she'd always been clear she didn't plan to follow in her father's corporate footsteps, the corporation had always been there, the door had always been open, a safety net slung beneath her from before she was even aware anything like that was needed. "It must be like that with farming too—a lot of face-to-face cooperation, right?"

Usually when Jordan thought about the farm, which wasn't often if she could help it, the memories were accompanied by pain. This time what she remembered was riding with her father to a neighboring farm during lambing season to lend a hand with the birthing, and off-loading hundreds of bales of hay into the barn loft for the winter. "There tends to be a lot more teamwork, maybe, than you see in other areas, probably because the rural population is so low and almost everyone depends on someone else for some kind of work. Every farmer is a bit of a jack-of-all-trades—I can drive a tractor, dig a ditch, and run a commercial thresher."

"Okay, I'm impressed."

Jordan laughed. "I didn't say I actually *wanted* to do those things. I kind of had a vision of someone else doing a lot of that."

Of course, none of her visions had been realistic or possible.

"I kinda like the image of you on a tractor, though," Kip said, and she meant it. Something about Jordan with her sleeves rolled up like they'd been yesterday afternoon, the taut muscles beneath the smooth, tanned skin of her forearms flexing as she worked, was a turn-on. Imagining her pushing a ten-ton machine around the field conjured up images of strength and power and capability, all the things she already associated with Jordan only in an earthy, unleashed way. Yeah, she liked that picture a lot.

"You have a very strange idea of attractiveness, then."

Kip turned her head, caught Jordan's gaze. "Oh, I don't think so."

Jordan couldn't misinterpret the husky note in Kip's voice or the teasing flirtation. She couldn't ignore the swell of heat that started low down in her midsection and climbed into her chest, either. Damn, she liked knowing Kip found her attractive. "Well, I'm afraid we won't have much call for a tractor at the project."

"That's okay, you're pretty outstanding with the hoe too."

Shaking her head and smothering a smile that would only encourage Kip, Jordan pointed the way into the restaurant. They were early enough to snag a booth toward the back.

"What do you recommend?" Kip asked.

"Anything is fabulous, but their hash browns are about the best in the world."

"Sold."

The waitress appeared, and waving away menus, they ordered.

"How long is your grant?" Kip asked as they waited for breakfast.

"Two years," Jordan said. "Hopefully, I can turn it over to Tya well before that. We'll have to get a renewal, of course, but once it's self-sustaining she'll be the perfect administrator. She's local, she has strong ties to the community, and she's a good gardener."

"What about you, then?"

Jordan lifted a shoulder. "I'm kind of used to being itinerant. I may move on to another one or look into doing some kind of Ag research."

"In a lab?" Kip shook her head. "I can't see you working inside."

"No, neither can I, but fortunately, most Ag research is at least partly fieldwork."

Kip leaned back as the waitress slid their plates onto the table. "Have you given any thought to your own farm?"

Jordan busied herself with her silverware.

"Sorry, sensitive question?" Kip said gently.

"I suppose," Jordan said softly. Not a question she ever let herself ponder.

Kip reached across the table, stroked a finger across the top of her hand, a gentle, comforting touch. "I'm sorry."

"Hey, you don't need to be. It's hard to think of being anywhere except the farm. You know, home."

"I think I can imagine."

Jordan knew Kip meant it, believed she understood the hole she'd never been able to fill in her heart, in her dreams. Maybe that understanding was what made it easier to talk about it. "Tillable land is getting to be a premium now, and the banks are a little suspect about lending for small farms. Too many hobby farmers borrowed money and couldn't make a go of it, so I'm not even sure I could find a place."

"How much land would you need?"

"Well, some people are doing incredible work with as little as an acre, which is probably a lot less than some McMansions have in their backyard, but ideally I'd want fifty. That would give me room for silage crops—"

"Um?"

"Hay, corn, soy—food crops for the animals, a small dairy herd, and enough acreage for produce."

"What about goats?"

"Sorry?"

"I read somewhere that goats are actually really good investments. Milk, cheese, yogurt—it's a biggie now, right?"

"That's true. I suppose I have the prejudice of being raised a dairy farmer, but I like goats. They're funny and cute and smart. Goats are a possibility."

Kip forked some hash browns into her mouth and pointed her fork at Jordan as she swallowed. "I think definitely goats."

Jordan didn't see goats, cows, or crops in her future, but for the first time in a very long time, it didn't hurt to dream.

CHAPTER SIXTEEN

Kip proved good to her word and showed up every morning for the next week at four a.m. to ride along with Jordan on her predawn rounds. Jordan shouldn't have been surprised that Kip followed through on what she said she would do, but she still experienced a jolt of pleasure every morning when she arrived and Kip was there. They worked easily together, loading the flats of baby lettuce, spinach, and arugula that Tya had harvested, washed, and packed the day before; stacking boxes of spring broccoli, cauliflower, and brussels sprouts in the truck for Mr. Liu and several other of his restaurant friends; sharing coffee and discussing news in the truck as their breath steamed the windshield. Spending the first hours of the day in the close confines of the truck, cocooned from the world while wending her way through the still-quiet streets of New York, or at least as quiet as New York ever got, was as natural as anything she'd done since growing up on the farm where chores were chores, but every one brought some small moment of pleasure too. Her childhood chores had never been as exciting as her mornings with Kip, though.

This morning Kip wasn't waiting when Jordan turned down the alley, and the lock on the gate was closed. Kip wasn't inside, then, measuring for some construction plan or wiring a security light. Inwardly chiding herself for getting used to Kip meeting her, Jordan swept aside a sharp pang of disappointment. She'd more than gotten used to their morning routine—she looked forward to it. Often, her last thoughts before falling asleep at night were of seeing Kip in a few hours. And wasn't that a bad habit to get into. Kip wasn't likely to be thinking about her or the project once she left for the night.

Expecting Kip to keep her hours was unreasonable too. Kip had earned a little time off. She'd been pulling her share, more than her share, every day at the project when all she had to do was show up and put in the minimum of effort. Instead, she worked nonstop at whatever Jordan needed her to do, and seemed to enjoy it. Lunch breaks had gotten to be shared events, with Jordan and Kip and Tya lounging on a bench in the sun or sheltering in the trailer when it rained, spending a companionable hour over sandwiches and carefully avoiding personal topics. They always found plenty of other things to talk about. Jordan couldn't quite figure out why Ty was still so reticent, not just reticent, but a little bit suspicious of Kip. She would've liked Ty to see what she saw in Kip—a sensitive woman who listened and offered support without asking for anything in return and without probing her silences. But then, Ty couldn't know Kip the way she did, hadn't spent hours sharing bits of herself as Jordan had, even the parts she usually didn't want to face herself.

Jordan glanced at the take-out black eye she'd gotten for Kip, sitting in the tray next to the stupid scones she'd so carefully chosen. She knew she shouldn't start to count on her, but it was hard not to. It was even harder not to look forward to seeing her during the private hours of the early morning, before Ty arrived and the demands of the day intruded on their personal moments. She could name a million reasons she shouldn't get attached, even if the circumstances had been different. If they'd met anywhere else, she still would've been smart to remember they came from different worlds, practically from different generations, and that mattered.

Damn it. When had she gotten so careless, when exactly had she started letting Kip in? Smiling despite herself, she thought of their first meeting and Kip's almost irresistible way of charming her way past Jordan's defenses. She'd been on shaky ground with Kip from the beginning, and maybe it was time to admit she was getting seduced by Kip's undeniable sexual magnetism. Jordan sighed. Hell, she hadn't had that kind of energy even when she'd been twenty-five. She never thought she'd find a younger woman attractive and ought to remember passion ran hot and fast—for a while. Time to come down to earth.

"Hey, thought I'd missed you," Kip called.

Jordan spun around, every argument she'd so carefully constructed against giving in to her attraction fleeing at the sight of Kip jogging through the dark morning toward her, a cardboard tube of some kind tucked under her arm.

"I thought you'd probably come to your senses and decided to sleep in," Jordan said, holding out Kip's cup of coffee.

"No way. Had to go back for the plans—I thought we could go over them later." Kip took the coffee and leaned against the side of the truck, the security light she'd installed at the top of the gate shining on her face. She grinned. "No way would I miss our morning date, especially when you bring me coffee and…what's in the bag today?"

Jordan hesitated, tripped up by the word *date*. Their morning rendezvous weren't dates. Dates were something you got dressed up for and went to some special place and most of the time didn't have a chance to talk to the woman you hardly knew, or worse, ran out of things to say. They weren't hours spent working side by side as conversation flowed nonstop from one topic to another, punctuated by laughs and sometimes even a sad memory or two, memories that, once placed back in storage, felt just a little bit less painful than they had before. Dates were sometimes awkward moments after a kiss or two when you fumbled for a way to say you really didn't feel anything deep inside and trying to connect wasn't worth the effort, and it definitely wasn't fair to suggest you wanted to step outside your nice safe life for the sake of a night's company. Dates absolutely weren't moments when you glanced over at the woman beside you and forgot what you were about to say, captured by the sunlight on her face, mesmerized by the intensity in her eyes or the quicksilver flash of her teasing smile.

Moments like that had nothing to do with dating and happened more than she wanted to admit when she was with Kip.

"Don't tell me you didn't stop at the bakery." Kip pressed a hand to the center of her gray T-shirt, a wounded look on her face.

Jordan banished images of dating and kissing and Kip. "No, no, no, I did. Sorry, though. No scones."

"Oh."

Kip's pained expression almost made Jordan laugh, and she couldn't keep up the ruse. Laughing, she squeezed Kip's shoulder and reached into the truck. "Maple walnut just came out of the oven. And your usual blueberry."

Kip let out a sigh and slid the cardboard tube into the backseat. "That was cruel."

Jordan handed her the bakery bag. "I'm sorry. I'm just glad to see you."

"So that's how you treat me?" Kip shook her head and peered into the bag. "You're not kidding. These look great. But it was still cruel."

"My version of frogs, I guess."

Kip looked up. "Oh yeah? You wanted to get my attention?"

"Maybe." Jordan shrugged a little sheepishly at her own foolishness. "I thought for a minute you weren't coming, even though I told you about a hundred times you didn't need to."

"I like starting the day with you," Kip said quietly.

"So do I, but you know you don't have—"

"Yeah, Jordan," Kip said with a little heat. "I do."

Before Jordan could move, Kip leaned forward and kissed her lightly on the mouth. "Thanks for the scones. I would miss them first thing in the morning, almost as much as you."

Jordan froze. Even the breath stopped in her throat. Her heart thudded erratically behind her breast. A buzz saw of arousal erupted in her midsection, hungry and threatening to devour everything in its path—which at the moment was her sanity.

Kip set the bakery bag back inside the truck. When she turned back, her eyes were dark and blazing. "I've been wanting to do that for quite a while now. I won't do it again if you don't want me to."

"I…" Jordan swept a hand through her hair. "I'm not sure how I feel about it. For now, I think I'd just like to not talk about it."

"Okay." Kip framed Jordan's face, happy with action instead of words. She didn't feel like talking either. She felt like doing what she'd been thinking about nonstop for what felt like forever. "No talking, then."

When Jordan closed her eyes, Kip kissed her closed lids, then the corner of her mouth. She'd never seen Jordan off balance before, but she was now. She didn't look unhappy, or angry, but her eyes were filled with questions. It took everything Kip had not to kiss her for real again. Not to answer those questions with the truth of how certain she felt, of how much she wanted her. She shuddered and brushed her thumb over Jordan's slightly parted lips. Her voice shook. "I just need one more little kiss."

Kip expected Jordan to pull away, but she tilted her head ever so slightly, and Kip kissed her, as slowly and gently as she could. Jordan tasted of sugar and a hint of coffee and, beneath it all, of wild heat.

"There now," Kip gasped. "We should go. Mr. Liu will be looking for his vegetables."

Jordan touched her fingertips to her mouth, her gaze fixed on Kip. "That was a very little kiss."

"I can do better."

Jordan laughed, a bit shakily, and caught her lip between her teeth. "Oh, I'm absolutely certain you can." She held up a hand when Kip clasped her hips to pull her closer. "And I don't want a demonstration. Trust me, you don't have to prove it."

"I planned on waiting," Kip said, "but I just couldn't help myself."

"It's the scones, isn't it?" Jordan asked breathlessly.

"I'll admit, they undo me." Kip brushed her fingers through Jordan's hair, let her hand drop when she felt Jordan stiffen. "But not as much as you. You keep me awake at night, you know that?"

Jordan swallowed. "That's not a good thing?"

"I don't mind losing sleep, when I'm thinking about you. The only problem is it makes me a little crazy." Kip lifted a shoulder. "It'd be a hell of a lot more satisfying if you were there for real."

Jordan's breath was coming faster and faster. She tried very hard not to think about Kip lying in the dark thinking about her, tried not to imagine Kip tossing and turning like she did until the ache between her thighs could only be quieted with her own hand. Tried not to think how much she'd like to be the one driving Kip to the edge. "I know what you mean."

"Do you?" Kip said slowly, her voice growing deeper, husky and slow. "Do you think about me at night?"

"Yes."

"Does it keep you awake?" Kip stroked one finger down Jordan's neck.

"Yes."

"Do you think about kissing me too? Because I think about kissing you a lot."

"Don't." Jordan leaned back, her throat tight, her skin ablaze. "Don't make me tell you things I don't want you to know."

Kip stepped closer. "Is that what you do? Keep secrets so I won't know you want me?"

"I have a hard time keeping secrets from you." Jordan closed her eyes. "Kip, we can't…"

"Yes, we can." Kip skimmed her hand beneath Jordan's hair and cupped the back of her neck. Her thumb stroked up and down Jordan's neck, turning the muscles in her legs weak. "You don't have to tell me your secrets if you don't want to. But I want to hear them."

"Why?" Jordan didn't recognize her own voice, so wispy and wanting and so damn needy. This was insane and she couldn't stop herself. She slid her hand inside Kip's denim jacket, pressed the tips of her fingers to the center of Kip's abdomen. Kip's muscles were as hard as she'd imagined them to be. She hadn't expected the heat that poured from Kip's body like a furnace. "You're so hot."

Kip grinned. "Somehow I don't think you mean that the way I want you to."

"Take it any way you want, it would be true."

"If you don't want me to kiss you, you need to move your hand."

Kip's voice was low and gravelly, barely recognizable. Her eyes glowed golden and hot with a kind of wild fury Jordan had never seen before, like those of an animal caught in her flashlight beam in the absolute darkness of the countryside. "I can't. I can't say no just this moment."

"Good."

Kip's mouth covered hers, hot and firm and surprisingly gentle. Jordan slipped both arms around Kip's waist, pressing into her, desperate to feel all of her. Kip's hand tightened on the back of her neck. Her lips slipped silkily over Jordan's, teasing and tugging in a request to enter. Jordan opened for her as thirstily as a parched field drank in the rain. She heard a moan, felt it in her throat before she knew she'd made a sound. Her breasts tightened and her nipples chafed against the inside of her soft flannel shirt, so sensitive she wanted to cry. She angled her head, caught Kip's lower lip between her teeth, and sucked slowly.

The sound Kip made, a barely restrained growl, detonated a need to possess, to demand, to claim. Jordan dug her fingers into the rigid columns of muscle along Kip's spine and pressed her thigh between Kip's legs. Kip jerked, cursed under her breath, and drove her tongue into Jordan's mouth, no longer teasing. Jordan bit down, a taunting challenge. She would make Kip as hungry for her as she was for Kip.

Kip groaned, holding her fast with a hand on her nape, her free hand fumbling with the zipper on Jordan's old farm jacket. She tugged it down, pushed her hand inside. She cupped Jordan's breast and Jordan shuddered.

"God, wait," Jordan gasped, her legs shaking.

"Sorry." Kip rested her forehead against Jordan's. "Sorry. I'm going too fast."

"No need for sorry. Just…I'm…" Jordan shook her head. Not ready? Oh, she was ready. Ready for Kip's hands all over her, ready for her mouth to take her. Ready for…too much. Too crazy much. "No time. Not…time. God, I can't even talk."

"I want to keep kissing you all day."

Kip's chest heaved. Her gaze was unfocused, and the muscles under Jordan's fingers quivered. Jordan loved feeling Kip's need, wanted to make her as crazy as she was. Wanted her to ache the way she ached. She clutched at the last little bit of reason and lightly gripped Kip's hips, moving back.

"Sooner or later we probably have to stop."

"Why?" Kip kissed her throat. "I think we're just getting started."

"Mr. Liu will undoubtedly send someone out looking for his vegetables."

Kip laughed and kissed the underside of her jaw. "I want you."

"Kip," Jordan said with a small shake of her head.

"Can't you feel how much I want you?" Kip raised her head, let Jordan see the need in her eyes.

Jordan caressed her face. "You're making me all kinds of crazy, but can we just slow this down?"

"Only if you promise not to think yourself out of wanting me."

Jordan started to protest, but couldn't lie to her. "I can't. Promise, that is."

"Why? I want you. You want me." Kip frowned. "It's right."

"That makes no sense."

"Oh yeah, it does." Kip stepped back. "And not saying it doesn't make it not true."

Jordan didn't argue. Not acknowledging what seethed between them might not make the wanting go away, but it might stop her from heading right into heartbreak.

CHAPTER SEVENTEEN

I'd say that was a successful morning all around," Kip said as they walked back to the truck from the Plum Blossom restaurant.

"Uh-huh." Jordan had a feeling Kip meant a lot more than just the outcome of their restaurant visits, and she was trying very hard to keep her mind on business. The task wasn't made any easier by being shut up in the truck with Kip, where the slightest hint of her scent or a brief glimpse of her tousled hair and cocky grin could set her blood raging again.

She tossed her clipboard into the backseat of the truck and started the engine. She probably should get into the habit of taking notes on her iPad, but she just couldn't give up the pen-and-paper lists she'd been using all her life. There was something comforting about being able to hold the page that displayed the evidence of her morning's achievements. She'd get it all into a spreadsheet as soon as she got back to the trailer. Five more names of local businesses. Five accounts that would go a long way toward building their presence in the community and bringing in some much-needed revenue.

Kip pulled her seat belt down and hooked it. "I'm pretty sure Mr. Liu has a crush on you."

Jordan laughed and pulled out into traffic. "I doubt that very much."

"Oh, I don't know, he seemed pretty frisky there."

Nothing could be further from the truth. At first she'd had trouble reading Mr. Liu's stoic baseline expression, but she was getting used to his fake orders, which were really requests cloaked in the form of finger-pointing commands.

You will bring me broccoli.

"He's been a huge help with his referrals, and I enjoy seeing him every day," Jordan said. "We're really making progress."

"You mean *you're* making progress," Kip said.

"Not just me. None of these accounts would make any difference if we didn't have anything to bring them. Ty deserves most of the credit for keeping watch over the gardens. And it wouldn't help much if we didn't have any way to get the produce delivered." She patted the steering wheel. "For which we have you to thank."

"So far, my contribution hasn't amounted to much." Kip stretched her legs out into the wheel well, never finding a comfortable position to ride in the cab of the truck unless she was driving. "When we get back and you have a chance to look at the plans, maybe I can get started on something that will matter."

Jordan sighed. "I don't know, Kip. I'm not sure we can budget for what it would take to do something like that."

"Well, let's start with the plans and see where we go. And Mr. Liu does so totally have a crush on you."

"No comment."

"Okay, maybe I'm projecting."

Jordan shot her a look. Kip was turned sideways in the seat, watching her as she drove. Kip often watched her. She could feel Kip's eyes on her when she worked, when she talked to the restaurant owners, when she drove. In fact, whenever she was around Kip, she felt as if she was the center of Kip's focus, and she liked that. She liked it way too much. She averted her gaze, focused on the traffic. "You're incorrigible."

"Not really. Maybe a little determined." Kip stretched across the space between them and stroked Jordan's arm. "I'm still thinking about the kiss. Aren't you?"

"I am very definitely and determinedly and purposefully not thinking about it."

Kip chuckled. "Why do I think the lady doth protest too much?"

"Because your ego is the size of the planet?"

"That aside. Oh, I know. It must be because you kissed me back."

"Reflex." Jordan wished she didn't have any reflexes at the moment. Kip's light strokes up and down her forearm shot straight to places she didn't want to think about while driving, or doing anything else at all in public.

"Uh-huh. Try again," Kip said, her voice slow and teasing.

"Self-preservation, then."

Kip leaned a little closer. Now her fingers found the back of Jordan's neck, and Jordan shivered.

"What were you saving yourself from?" Kip toyed with the lobe of Jordan's ear.

Jordan hunched her shoulder to pull away. "Stop that."

"I can't help myself."

"You're a pest."

"Mm-hmm. And a nuisance." Kip sighed. "I hate this seat belt. If I could just get a little closer—"

"You"—Jordan took one hand off the wheel and poked a finger into Kip's chest—"stay over there and keep your hands to yourself."

"Spoilsport."

"Adult."

"Killjoy."

"Working."

"Chicken."

Jordan risked a two-second glance. Kip was grinning, her eyes glinting with that fire again, and a faint flush colored her neck. Jordan had no trouble imagining what would happen if Kip wasn't held down by the seat belt. Kip's hands would be all over her. The insides of her thighs tingled, and she pushed back in the seat. "You're going to get us killed."

"I thought you were being responsible and unaffected by my charms?"

"I'm working on it."

"It was a five-star kiss, though. Don't you think?"

Jordan merely smiled.

Undeterred, Kip traced the shell of Jordan's ear. "I don't suppose we could take a long lunch hour."

Jordan threw back her head and laughed. "Absolutely not. There is no way I'm having a nooner with you or anyone else."

"Well, I'm very glad to hear that. Because if you disappear for two or three hours in the middle of the afternoon, I'm going to get awfully worried. And mighty jealous."

"You have nothing to be jealous about," Jordan murmured.

"No special woman in your life?" Kip asked, her voice all serious now.

"No. No one."

"I'm glad, but it doesn't seem right. I know you're not a hermit, and any woman with half a brain who's anywhere near you would be attracted."

"Your flattery is blatant," Jordan said, but her heart skipped a beat all the same. She was in so much trouble here. She was even willing to be flattered.

"I mean every word. So why isn't there anyone?"

Jordan could have used any of a dozen stock responses. She'd been asked that question a lot in the last dozen or so years. She could have, but hiding from Kip was hard to do. Something she didn't want to do. "Since my dad died and then my mother not so long after, and the farm went too, I've been pretty rootless. I've moved a lot, and…" She blew out a breath. "I'm not cut out for casual. I had this picture of my life, one I had for as long as I can remember, and then the picture disappeared."

"A farm with a wife, two kids, and a white picket fence?" Kip asked softly.

Jordan nodded. "Something along those lines."

"And what do you see now?"

"I make it a point not to look too far ahead. I'd rather spend my energy on today."

"Then I'm glad I'm here today." Kip tugged Jordan's hand off the wheel and kissed her palm. "The first thing I saw—well, after the hoe you were about to brain me with, that is—was how beautiful you looked all fired up and ready to take me down."

"I thought you were pretty amazing for a burglar myself," Jordan murmured, retrieving her hand while she still had a brain left, and headed up Tenth toward the project. She almost wished they weren't going back, that she could take an hour or two out of the day. She wanted to take Kip to her apartment, to sit beside her on the sofa, alone in the sunlight, and finish the kiss. If she did, she knew where they would end up, and as hard as that was to fathom, that was exactly what she wanted. She wanted Kip. She shivered.

"Cold?" Kip murmured, continuing to stroke Jordan's neck inside the collar of her cotton shirt.

"No, just the opposite. Could you move your hand?"

"You don't like it?"

"You know I do."

"I know *I* do. Anytime I'm near you, even if I'm not touching you, I'm happy. When I'm touching you, I can't describe how I feel except— feeling like the whole world opens up and anything is possible. That's what it's like to be with you. Every minute is like a new dawn."

"I'd rather you didn't say things like that."

"Why?"

"Because they'll be hard to forget."

"I don't want you to forget. I want you to believe me."

"Kip, why do you force me to say things you don't want to hear." Jordan gripped the wheel harder, channeling her frustration. "Everything else aside—"

"Everything? You mean me being a criminal, don't you?"

"That's the last time I want to hear you say that, all right?" Angry at herself for being pushed into a corner and angry at Kip for continuing to beat herself up, Jordan forgot to be careful. "If you were a criminal, you wouldn't be working off your punishment at a community garden center, you'd be in jail. You're guilty of being stupid and maybe irresponsible, you said that yourself. We've all been there. Sometimes, most of the time, no laws were broken, except maybe the laws of common decency and responsibility. Someday maybe you'll even tell me *why* you did what you did, but that's not what matters now."

"And what does matter?"

"We're not suited, Kip—just because we've got chemistry doesn't mean we've got anything else. How long do you think you'd be satisfied dating me, or whatever you want to call what we'd be doing? After the sex cools off, you'd discover that I'm far too old and probably too staid and boring for you."

Kip's mouth fell open. "You can't be serious. You're trying to use age as an excuse not to get involved with me?"

"You're not listening. Sex is one thing. A relationship is something else, and I'm not really interested in a quick toss with you."

"Well, that's good then, because I'm not interested in it either. But I wouldn't mind starting with the kiss, someplace private, where we wouldn't have to stop and you wouldn't have a chance to find an excuse."

"That's not going to happen today, so this conversation is pointless."

"We're going to have it again, Jordan. Because I'm not going to stop wanting you, and you're not going to stop thinking about me wanting you, and wanting me back."

"You seem very sure of yourself."

"I'm not always, but I am this time. I'm not going anywhere." Kip eased back in her seat. "And neither is the constant urge to put my hands on you."

Jordan was not about to let herself believe any of that. Kip would leave, and she just had to decide how close she was going to let her come before she had to let her go. "We're planting peppers today. That should take your mind off your unrequited lust."

Kip laughed. "I don't think so, but if you'll be planting too, I wouldn't mind so much. I can at least watch you and fantasize."

"Great." Jordan muttered. "Just try to behave. I know that's difficult for you, but I believe you might be able to, if you really try."

Kip pressed her hand to her heart. "Anything for you."

Jordan rolled her eyes, pulled up next to the garden gate, and hopped out. They'd almost reached the gate when a black SUV turned down the alley and parked in the narrow space between the truck and the neighboring building, completely blocking any access to the street.

"That's an asinine place to park." Jordan turned around to tell them to pull in behind the truck when Kip gripped her arm.

"I think you should wait."

"What? Why? They can't block the alley like this. We're supposed to be getting a delivery of mulch, remember?"

"I don't think they're gonna be here that long," Kip said.

Kip's flat, emotionless tone made Jordan stop and study the two men who stepped out of the vehicle. Both were in their thirties with trim waists and broad shoulders, dark suits and ties, matching close-cut haircuts, and sunglasses. The hairs on the back of her arms stood up. "You know them?"

"Not exactly. You should go inside."

"What? Why?"

"Just go, Jordan," Kip said quietly.

"Ms. Kensington, Ms. Rice. A word with you, please."

Jordan stiffened and jammed her hands on her hips. She didn't like being ordered around by strangers. "Do I know you?"

Both men reached into their matching suit jackets and extracted slim leather folders. The first let his fall open and the second followed suit. Some kind of official seal, photos, and bright shiny badges. Jordan's stomach clenched. Kip was still as a statue beside her.

"Agents Davis and Carmichael," the sandy-haired one said as he quickly flipped the wallet closed and his companion did the same.

"Agents from where?" Jordan raised her voice to hide the tremor. The sun was out, people passed by thirty yards from them at the mouth of the alley, and she could hear Ty's radio on the other side of the garden fence, but something about these men made her feel as if she was caught in a trap. Some atavistic sense buried deep in her animal brain screamed danger as fight-or-flight hormones flooded her system.

"If you'd both get into the vehicle, please. This won't take long."

"No." Kip stepped quickly in front of Jordan. "You know why I'm here. Ms. Rice has absolutely nothing to do with what you're interested in, and you both must know that. I'll go with you."

Jordan grabbed the back of her shirt. "You're not going anywhere with these men until I get an explanation. What do they want?"

"It's okay," Kip said. "I work for them—sort of."

Jordan didn't lessen her grip on Kip's shirt. "I don't believe it."

"They just want to talk, but they don't have very good manners." Kip looked at the men. "Look, let's not complicate this. I'll come, but Jordan stays here."

The men exchanged glances and one nodded.

"Kip, come inside." Jordan couldn't have felt more exposed if she'd been standing in the alley naked. "We'll call an attorney or...or something."

Kip turned her back to the men, putting herself between Jordan and them. "They're not going away, and they tend to be short on patience. Just go inside before these guys start throwing their weight around."

"What about you?"

Kip lifted a shoulder. "I'll be fine. Don't worry."

"Call me, will you call me when you're done?" Jordan had the feeling if she let Kip go now, she wouldn't see her again. She wasn't ready to let her go. "After all, there's still that small matter of the kiss."

"Now you decide you want it?" Kip gave her a crooked smile.

"Never said I didn't. Be careful?"

"Trying."

Jordan stood rooted to the spot as Kip joined the two men, who pivoted in formation and walked her, one on each side, to the SUV. One opened the door, Kip climbed in without looking back, and he slid in beside her. The other got behind the wheel. The blacked-out windows blocked any sign of the passengers. The doors closed, and an instant later, the big black SUV backed down the alley and disappeared.

Jordan waited five minutes for Kip to walk back down, but she didn't.

CHAPTER EIGHTEEN

Morning!" Ty dumped a bag full of cullings into the to-be-burned pile and waved. Her radio—a real radio, not an iPhone or iPod connected wirelessly to miniature speakers somewhere—played an upbeat reggae mix. She moved between the beds with an unconscious rhythm that matched the energy of the music.

Jordan let the fence gate swing shut behind her, looking numbly out over the gardens. What had just happened? Did people really just get whisked off the streets like that, with no warning, with no explanation? Who were those men and what were they doing here? Were there really agents, and *agencies*, with that kind of power? She supposed she'd always known somewhere in her mind that such people, such organizations, existed, but, like most people, had no reason to think about it, so she didn't. She didn't want to think about it now, didn't want to experience the helplessness and fear she'd felt out there in the alley again, but Kip was gone and she couldn't not think about that.

She tried to remember everything she could about the bizarre encounter. God, she hadn't even thought to get the license plate number. Think. What had Kip said? She'd said she worked for them, but what did that mean? It certainly didn't look like any work relationship Jordan had ever seen. It looked like Kip was going with them against her will. All that was missing was the handcuffs. Was that what she had just witnessed? An arrest? If it was, where had they taken Kip, and what should she do about it?

She should call someone—report what had happened. Find out what the hell was going on.

Who should she call? She didn't even know where to start. Wait, yes, she did. Kip's family should be notified.

What had Kip said about her family? Nothing, or almost nothing. Her mother was dead, Jordan knew that. But Kip hadn't said anything about the rest of her family, nothing Jordan could recall—no names, no childhood anecdotes, no mention of recent phone calls or visits. Now that she thought about it, she knew nothing of Kip's life outside the confines of their relationship here. She'd never been to her apartment, never met any of her family, never even heard her talk about her friends. Could Kip really be that alone, or was she hiding something?

Jordan shook her head. Of course Kip was hiding something. She very obviously avoided talking about her personal life and even more obviously obfuscated the details of her job. And Jordan hadn't pushed. She'd rationalized her willingness to accept Kip's secrecy because *she* had such an intense need for privacy, because *she* had always avoided talking about old pains that couldn't be changed, because she'd stopped short of anything truly personal with anyone she wasn't forced to be open with herself. Her life wasn't any different than what she knew of Kip's. Except for Ty, she didn't have friends. After her mother died, she'd lost touch with the rest of her family and friends. By choice, yes, but also out of fear. She just didn't want reminders that hurt.

"Where's Kip?" Ty dumped the empty bucket and strolled over. "And, more importantly, where are the pastries?"

"Oh—I left them in the truck."

"I'll get them. For a second I was afraid you two had polished them all off." Ty paused and cocked her head. "Jordan? What's wrong? Where's Kip? Isn't she with you, or is she taking the day off?"

"No, she was with me. But she's…" Jordan paused out of habit, but there was no reason for secrecy at this point. Maybe there never had been any reason, at least not one that was fair to everyone involved. "Two men just picked her up. I don't know when she'll be back."

"Two men." Ty frowned. "That's sort of vague. Are you all right? You look…I don't know, a little stunned."

Jordan grimaced and ran a hand through her hair. "Shell-shocked, I think. I don't know who they were. They had badges and they wanted to talk to Kip. She went with them."

"Police, you mean? From the probation office or something?"

Jordan shook her head. "I don't think so. They were driving a big SUV and didn't look like any of the police I've ever seen. Their credentials looked federal, at least how I imagine federal credentials would look."

Ty took an abrupt step back, her eyes widening. "You're sure? Federal agents?"

The fear in her voice was unmistakable. Jordan blinked away the fog in her brain and focused on Ty. "I think so, why? Does that mean something?"

Ty licked her lips, glancing around the garden as if she expected the two men to jump out from behind the trailer. Of course they were alone. Aside from the rare visitor, they were always alone here.

"Ty?"

"I don't think you should keep Kip on here any longer."

"Why? Because she might be in trouble? She hasn't done anything wrong."

"Obviously she did, that's why she's here. And maybe it's not over, whatever it is."

Jordan scoffed. "For heaven's sake. She was driving a car that didn't belong to her—hardly an international crime."

"She stole a car?"

"Yes, well, I'm not sure exactly. I don't know the details."

"That's my point!" Ty closed her eyes briefly and sighed. "Listen, I know that you like her. Maybe more than like her, but what do you really know about her? And now, she's bringing trouble around."

"Trouble for who, Ty?" Jordan couldn't argue about Kip and secrets, since Ty had only said what she'd just been thinking. All the same, she had a feeling the two of them were talking about very different things.

Ty wrapped her arms around her body. "Did they ask any questions about…us?"

"You and me?" Jordan frowned. "No. They knew my name, which I thought was strange, but they only seemed intent on taking Kip. They didn't bother me at all."

"What about me?"

"No. Why would they even know you're here?"

"No reason," Ty said quickly.

"Look, we're friends, right? If there's something going on, we should deal with it together." Jordan squeezed Ty's arm. Her body was rigid as steel. "Let me help."

"I'm not legal," Ty said quickly.

"You're not…" Jordan struggled to assimilate that news. "But you've got a Social Security number and you pay taxes. I know, I file them for you."

"Nothing like paying taxes right on time to make you just another number in the system, as long as the taxes aren't too high or too low." Ty smiled wryly. "Anyone can get a Social Security number if you know the right people."

Jordan leaned back against the fence. "Okay, I'm not all that up on this…I mean, what about your kids? Your mother?"

"My children are United States citizens. They were born here. But I wasn't, and neither was my mother." Ty sighed. "And we didn't get here legally."

"And isn't there any way to…get legal status?"

"None that are easy or guaranteed." Ty's eyes filled. "We have a life, the kids and my mother and I. I haven't wanted to take the chance of announcing my undocumented status and then finding out I'd have to leave in order to try to immigrate legally."

"God, what a mess. And the kids?"

"What would I do? Leave them here? With who? Or take them back to a world they don't know?"

"Living like this has to be so scary."

Ty grimaced. "You never really forget about it, but after a while, life just goes on. If I had to leave, what would I do?"

"Look, there's no reason to think whatever's going on with Kip has anything to do with us."

"But what if they start looking into the project, into us, because she's here? I have to quit right now."

"What? No!" Jordan gripped Ty's shoulders, afraid she'd bolt and disappear. "Let me find out what's going on. As soon as I've talked to her, I promise you, I'll get all the information."

"Can you trust her to tell you the truth?"

Jordan didn't hesitate. "Yes."

Ty studied her, worry aging her smooth features. "All right. I trust you, and if you trust her, I'll wait. If it's all right with you, I'd rather not come to work for a while."

Jordan hugged her. "Oh, Ty, I'm so sorry this is happening. Of course. Do what you need to do."

"I'm sorry I'm leaving you with all this work right now."

Jordan waved her off. "It doesn't matter. I can take care of things here. And maybe Kip will be back today, and we can straighten all this out. I'll call you, all right?"

Tie nodded. "I'm taking the kids and their grandmother to a friend's. Just in case."

"Keep your cell on, okay? I'll call you as soon as I know anything."

"I'm really sorry about this, Jordan. I never meant to deceive you."

"I know that, and it doesn't change anything between us." Jordan squeezed her tight. "Be safe and take care of your family. I'll talk to you soon."

As soon as Ty left, Jordan went directly to the trailer and booted up her computer. It was time to find out who Kip Kensington really was. She stared at the blank screen, willing herself to type in Kip's name. She'd never looked up herself or anyone she knew. She hated the idea of searching for pieces of someone's life on the internet. The invasion of privacy was unbearable, but there was more at stake now than her own discomfort or even Kip's privacy.

Deliberately, she typed Kip's name.

Nothing popped up. Of course.

Catherine Kensington brought up pages of entries.

Catherine Wells Kensington. The birth date listed checked out. Jordan smiled inwardly. As she'd guessed, almost fifteen years to the day younger than her, as if that mattered now. She scanned various other names and news items, found a few with photos of Kip. No mistaking her identity. The Kensington family was a large and apparently famous one. Kip's ancestors had been part of the early industrialization of the country and had manufactured everything from steam engines to air conditioners. The present Kensington Corporation was a vast international conglomerate involved in all kinds of global enterprises. Nothing came up regarding Kip's official status at the company, but Jordan imagined she held some kind of position, since all the Kensington family apparently did.

Items referencing a brother, Randolph, were mostly social entries and entertainment articles. A series of archived news reports also detailed the death of Kip's mother. Jordan took a breath and clicked through them.

Carolyn Kensington, age thirty-five, had drowned in a sailing accident after her skiff capsized in rough waters off Long Island Sound during a freak storm. Her two children managed to cling to the overturned boat until they were rescued. Kip had been ten years old.

"Oh, Kip," Jordan murmured. She closed her eyes, trying not to visualize a young Kip suffering such terror after having lost her mother so horribly. Jordan understood the ravages of loss. There was no way to quantify or compare the losses of loved ones, but at least she'd been an adult when her father died, and she hadn't witnessed his death.

Jordan closed the browser and spun around in her chair, needing to see the beginnings of life and the late morning sun through the open trailer door. Needing the warmth when she was so cold inside. She willed Kip to walk back through the garden gate. Nothing seemed right without her.

Kip knew better than to ask for an explanation from her companions and wasn't surprised when the agent beside her was silent as stone while the one driving maneuvered them through Manhattan traffic. She didn't bother asking where they were going. He wouldn't tell her that either. When they pulled into an underground garage, she waited for him or his partner to open her door. Her door handle would not be functional from the inside, the childproof lock concept repurposed for prisoners. Whatever name they put to what was happening—questioning, briefing, interview—she was still a prisoner. There were all kinds of cages, and this nameless concrete building was just another version. When she stepped out, she couldn't place their location. Rows of official-looking vehicles filled the spaces along the wall adjacent to an elevator.

"This way, please," the sandy-haired agent said politely.

She followed along into the elevator and watched the numbers as it climbed to the sixth floor. They directed her down a bland, featureless corridor carpeted in trendy gray, an agent on either side of her, until they reached one of a dozen identically unmarked doors and the taller agent knocked.

He touched his ear, nodded, and said, "You may go in."

He held the door open and Kip stepped inside. Three men in suits sat on the opposite side of a long, modern-looking conference table facing her. They ranged in age from midforties to early sixties, all with similar neutral expressions. The man in the middle, a dark-haired, fit-looking fifty, indicated a chair across from them. "Ms. Kensington, please have a seat."

Kip remained standing. "If you'd told me you wanted to talk to me, I would have been happy to oblige. However, considering the circumstances, I prefer not to speak with you without my attorney present."

"Given the sensitive nature of our discussion, I'm afraid your right to an attorney does not apply. Please have a seat."

Ice slithered down Kip's spine. Were they really citing the Patriot Act? No one knew where she was. Theoretically, they could keep her here or incarcerate her for as long as they wanted. Memories of the cell, the isolation, the depersonalization flooded through her. For an instant, the magnitude of her powerlessness left her weak.

But she wasn't weak. She'd faced far greater threats than these men could present. She'd watched death claim the most important person in her world and refused to let go when death came for her. Nothing could ever threaten her as much as that morning when the skies had turned black, the wind had come up out of nowhere, the sails had torn from the mast, and waves taller than her house carried her mother away.

"What exactly am I doing here?"

"Your recent arrest calls your position with us into question."

"Why is that?" Kip said, refusing to buy into their paranoia.

"Considering the nature of the project," the younger agent, a redhead with an incongruous sunburn he probably got from spending time on the golf course and not paying attention to the spring sun, said flatly, "we want to ensure there hasn't been a breach of security."

"What, you think I was discussing engine design with my fellow cellmates in county lockup?"

"We're actually more interested in what your brother might have discussed."

Kip gritted her teeth. What the hell? "Randy isn't involved with the project, you all know that."

The third man shrugged. "Not directly, perhaps. But he is your brother, and he is potentially privy to the company's projects through any number of avenues. His recent…activities…of which you were a part clearly constitute a security risk."

"Look, I don't discuss high-security projects with anyone, especially not Randy. Neither does anyone else. Your department spent a year looking at me before I got my clearance."

"While your previous evaluations suggested no problem areas, your arrest requires examination."

Kip shook her head. No way were they going to keep her here indefinitely, and she wasn't going to tell them a damn thing about Randy. "Not without a lawyer."

Check.

The one doing most of the talking, the friendly good-cop player, nodded as if he agreed. "We're trying to be reasonable, so you have a choice. You can either explain the circumstances concerning your conviction, or we can interrupt your brother's stay at the Glendale Center. I'm sure if we offer to arrange his permanent release, he'll be happy to cooperate."

Checkmate. Kip sat down.

CHAPTER NINETEEN

Five o'clock came and went, and no word from Kip. Jordan left two messages on her phone and couldn't think of anything else to do after that. She sat in the trailer, more alone than she'd felt in a long time. Ty was gone, Kip was gone, and the garden had never seemed so quiet. Try as she might, she couldn't make sense of the day.

She'd started the morning with a kiss she could no longer pretend she hadn't wanted, and for a few brief moments, she'd imagined more. Another kiss, a whole series of kisses, and touches that went beyond the surface to a place she'd kept hidden from everyone, even herself, for so long she'd forgotten the exhilaration of true connection. She'd been ready, almost, if she didn't think about the long term too much, to open those doors for Kip. For a few hours, she'd been ready to dream. Now Kip had disappeared as quickly and mysteriously as she'd appeared, and Jordan had no way of knowing if she'd ever return. After all, Kip was only here on hiatus from a life Jordan knew nothing about. A life where the sudden appearance of stone-faced men with badges was normal.

And now that world, Kip's other life, had spilled over into her world here at the garden—her world and Ty's.

God, Ty. How horrible to have to live with the fear of losing everything at any moment. And not just Ty's way of life was at risk, but her children's future and her mother's security as well. Ty would have worked within the system if there'd been a way for her to do it without risking everything, if the odds hadn't been so unfairly against her. But once she exposed herself and admitted her secret, she'd be vulnerable and powerless and at the mercy of an unfriendly, antiquated, and sadly biased system. No wonder she was terrified.

Jordan had experienced firsthand the devastation wrought by a system that left human beings out of the equation. She couldn't think of Ty without thinking of her father. He must have felt so much the same when faced with losing the farm, knowing his wife's security and his daughter's future would be altered forever. His very identity had been tied to that land and its history, something Jordan understood all too well. She'd been adrift ever since her roots had been so mercilessly torn from the earth and stripped of life. She hadn't been able to help her father, but somehow, she had to do something to help Ty. If only she knew what. She'd have to find someone who knew—

An alert tone blasted from her cell and she grabbed it off the desk, staring at the red weather warning. No, that couldn't be right. Frost alert? That couldn't be possible. She bolted from the chair and went outside to stand on the steps of the trailer. The sun was on its way down and the air temp felt at least ten degrees cooler than it had when she'd gone inside just a little while earlier. But frost? This late in the season? No.

She checked the weather reports daily, studied the ten-day forecast every morning over coffee, had multiple weather apps on her phone. None of them had said anything about frost. This had to be a mistake. Spinning around, she went back inside and opened her web browser.

Every weather site said the same thing—after the weather mumbo jumbo was deciphered, the result was the same everywhere. A cold front blowing from the north that had been expected to spin out hundreds of miles away had refused to die, and now it was picking up speed. When the low-pressure front pushing ahead of it hit the warm moist air sitting above them now, the entire northern seaboard was looking at a hard frost. A killing frost for young plantings.

"God." Jordan jumped up, panic grabbing her by the throat. So much to do, and the sun was almost down. She needed to get everything secured by eight at the latest. She needed Ty now, and she couldn't ask her to come back. She was on her own.

She raced to the garden shed, knowing before she got there what she would find. Not enough.

Not enough warning. Not enough equipment. Not enough time.

She stood in the shed doorway as the sun went down behind her,

her heart sinking. Must everything that mattered always end this way—with her alone, helpless and heart bleeding.

Enough self-pity too, damn it. She could do this. She would do this. Somehow.

Her phone buzzed again and she dug it out of her pocket. Unknown caller. She stared, angry at the tiny spurt of hope. Happy endings were not in her forecast. The phone kept buzzing.

Heart pounding, she swiped answer. "Yes?"

"Hey, it's me."

"Kip!" Jordan struggled to catch her breath. "Where are you, are you all right?"

"Yeah, I'm okay. Long afternoon, long story."

"You don't sound all right." She sounded frighteningly beaten and defeated, and not like Kip at all.

"Oh," Kip said, her voice oddly flat and distant. "It's me. This is my other self. The less charming and sexy one."

Jordan laughed, hearing the unsteadiness in her voice. "I call bullshit on that. You're always charming and sexy. Where are you?"

"In a tavern downtown. I was thinking about having a drink. I don't suppose you want to keep me company…"

"Oh, Kip, I can't." Jordan scanned the garden. Kip sounded so vulnerable. What if Kip needed her and she wasn't there? What if…no, that was crazy. Kip was not her father. "I would, I *want* to, but there's a problem here. I'm sorry, I'm so sorry. Is there someone else you can call—"

"What sort of problem?" Kip's voice was suddenly sharper.

"Frost warning."

"Frost? Frost like really cold? Cold enough to kill the plantings?"

"If it gets down to what they're predicting, yes. So I've got a lot to do and I don't have much time."

"I'll be there in fifteen minutes."

Relief washed through her. She didn't even try to pretend she didn't want her to come. "Are you sure? I wouldn't ask you, but—"

"Jordan, I'll be there in fifteen minutes."

"Thank you, I'm sorry, I know it's a terrible imposition."

"It's not. Not if I'm with you."

"Thank you," Jordan said again.

She pushed the phone into her pocket, ignoring the spurt of hope.

She still didn't have enough time or enough equipment, but Kip was coming. She wouldn't be alone and neither would Kip. That was a start, at least.

Kip arrived twelve minutes later, striding through the garden gate as the security lights around the perimeter clicked on. She wore the same khaki work pants, T-shirt, and denim jacket she'd come to work in. She grinned when she saw Jordan. "Did anyone order a couple more hands?"

Jordan rushed over and grasped her shoulders. "Are you really all right? Because I'm taking shameless advantage and I know it."

"Oh, if only you were," Kip replied straight-faced, but her eyes were dancing. "Don't worry about me. Tell me what I should do."

"Never mind that for one minute." Jordan brushed her fingers through Kip's hair. Even in the yellowish glow of the security lights she could make out the shadows under her eyes. She kissed her swiftly. "I was worried half out of my mind."

Kip's arms came around her, and some of the cold that had slowly been making its way through her bones disappeared. Kip's breath was warm against her ear.

"Do that again when we've got all the little seedling babies safe and sound, why don't you," Kip murmured.

Jordan laughed and pressed her face against Kip's throat. Kip's skin was hot. An erratic pulse hammered beneath Jordan's mouth. "It might be a long night."

"That's okay, I don't have anywhere else to be." Kip gently clasped Jordan's shoulders and inched away until their eyes met. "No one else I want to be with. I'll wait."

"There's not much we're going to be able to do." Jordan pushed away completely when all she wanted to do was hold on. "We need to cover everything, and I'm not even sure I have enough fabric on hand to keep everything warm. We'll probably lose the tomatoes."

"No way. Not the tomatoes."

Kip's outrage warmed Jordan and the last of the ice in her chest broke free. Her blood ran hot and steely. She grabbed Kip's hand. "Come on. If I'd known, damn it, I'd have ordered more fabric, but we're supposed to be safely past the last frost date. It'll have to be enough."

"What about those smudge pot things?" Kip followed Jordan to the garden shed and began dragging out the supplies Jordan pointed out.

"Even if we could find a place that still had any, getting them here and getting them set up would take longer than we've got, I'm afraid. They're more designed for trees too, not gardens."

"So what do we need exactly—heat, right?"

"Yes," Jordan said, laughing without the slightest bit of humor. "That's exactly what we need. Since we can't order up some sunshine, we'll just have to wrap everything up as best we can."

"Right. Hold on." Kip set down the roll of garden fabric, pulled out her phone, and punched in a number. After a few second, she said, "Harry, Kip here. I need you to get a flatbed and get me half a dozen portable infrareds ASAP." She shoved her hand in her pocket, started to pace. "How big are they? Yeah, that will probably do. No, I need them before that. Like in an hour." She stopped, laughed. "Fine, double time for everyone, then. Bring the paperwork and I'll sign off."

She pushed her phone back in her pocket and turned around. "Now what?"

"What did you just do?"

"You wanted heat." Kip grinned. "I got us heat. Now we just need to put the blankets on, right?"

Laughing, feeling a little light-headed and just a bit giddy, Jordan threw her arms around Kip again. "I don't know what you're talking about, and I know you're crazy, but thank you for whatever you're trying to do."

Kip kissed her. "Thank me later. Now just put me to work."

An hour later all the beds were double-covered with fabric, and Jordan prayed it would be enough. If the temps stayed below freezing past morning, even the covers weren't going to be enough protection. The sound of a big truck pulling up in the alley outside the fence and a loud horn blast shot her heart into her throat. "Kip?"

"I think those are the boys." Kip jogged over to the fence and swung the gate wide, waving an arm. "Hey, Rafael. Bring that stuff in here. The generators too."

"What can I do?" Jordan asked as four men in hoodies jumped down and congregated around Kip.

"Just tell us where you need the most heat."

"Right." Jordan climbed onto the steps of the trailer and pointed out where they needed to install the ten-foot-tall portable thermal heaters. Six beautiful units with their own generators. Kip and the men had them in position and set up in half an hour. When they fired the generators, the units glowed orange, and heat, blessed heat, flooded down into the garden.

Jordan joined Kip. "How long will they run?"

"All night, easily. What do you think? Will that be enough?"

Jordan laughed. "Are you kidding? The seedlings will be so spoiled we'll probably have to run them every single night."

"That can be arranged." Kip grinned. "What about the chickens? Do they need anything?"

"No, they'll be fine in the coop. Let me get some soil thermometers into the beds so we can keep an eye on the temperatures. Things will get critical around three."

"Go ahead. I'll be right back. I just want to talk to the guys before they leave and sign their overtime slips."

"Whatever the cost," Jordan said, "I'll figure out a way to pay for this."

Kip shook her head. "Consider it a community service."

"Kip, I can't even begin to imagine what this is costing."

"Look, it's not a big deal—"

Oh, but it was. Kip had come when she'd needed her, no questions asked. She'd gone beyond just helping. Jordan's chest ached with the urge to pull her close. She forced herself to finish the job they'd started. "We'll talk about it later. Let me get those thermometers in now."

When the men and the trolleys and the truck had left, Kip closed the gate, leaving them alone in an oasis of warmth and glowing orange light that cast the garden in perpetual sunset.

"How does it look?" Kip said.

"Soil temperature's fine right now. If we can keep things this way as the temperature goes down, we'll be all right."

"How long until we know?"

"We'll need to uncover everything by eight so the plants can breathe and we don't get condensation that might freeze on the leaves."

"I guess I better get us some coffee. Did you have dinner?"

"Dinner?" Jordan laughed. "No dinner, no lunch. What about you?"

"How about pizza?"

Kip's non-answer was answer enough. Jordan caught her hand. "You're sure you're all right?"

"I'm better than I've been in a long time." Kip smiled and the shadows beneath her eyes faded a little. "Can you handle the works?"

"That sounds like heaven."

"I won't be gone long."

Jordan tightened her grip on Kip's hand. "You'll be back?"

Kip cupped her face. "As soon as I can. Don't worry."

"Oh, that's gonna be a neat trick tonight." Jordan gave her a little shove. "Go. Hunt and gather. I'm starving."

"At your service, my lady." Kip grinned. "I'll be back before you know it."

Jordan watched her go, chasing the irrational fears away. Of course she would be back. She couldn't bear to think anything else.

CHAPTER TWENTY

Jordan occupied herself scanning the weather apps while trying not to watch the clock or think about how long Kip had been gone. The apps didn't tell her anything different than they had an hour earlier, and the more she checked the expected lows, the more her nerves jangled. She'd already checked the thermometers twice and blessed the heat pouring down from the portable units. She was never this jumpy, even if she *was* currently facing the potential loss of all their early crops. She hadn't been raised a farmer without having plenty of experience with fickle weather hell-bent on ruining a year's worth of work. When the crops failed, the stock went hungry, the cash stopped flowing, and the tables stood empty. The situation wasn't that dire here yet, and even if it had been, they'd done everything they could for now. She had at least another six hours before the worst would hit.

So she waited.

When she finally heard footsteps, she wasn't sure at first she hadn't imagined them and jumped up to open the trailer door before anyone knocked. Kip grinned up at her.

"You order pizza?"

"I did. Let me help you with that." Jordan reached down for the pizza boxes Kip held out to her. "Two?"

"I figured it would be a long night, and I thought maybe Ty would show up."

Jordan's stomach tightened. "Oh, well, I'm sure we can probably do some damage on these all by ourselves."

Kip climbed into the trailer, shed her jacket, and closed the door. "How are things?"

"As good as we can make them. Thanks to you." Jordan turned on the desk lamp, which was usually plenty of light if she was working on her laptop but barely lit the rest of the ten-by-twenty space. She'd never appreciated how small the place was until she found herself maneuvering around Kip. Every time her shoulder or hip brushed Kip's, her pulse shimmied. They spent hours in the truck together every day, but being alone with the daybed that doubled as a sofa a few feet away made everything seem disturbingly intimate. She balanced the boxes on top of a nearby file cabinet and busied herself hunting up paper towels to substitute as napkins. "I think those heaters might make the difference. I still can't believe you could get them here so quickly."

"The plant isn't all that far away, and loading them up is no big deal."

"Yes, but I can't imagine it's all that simple requisitioning something like that. Or paying for it."

Kip shrugged. "It helps to know the boss."

"Know the boss, or be the boss?" Jordan asked quietly.

"Oh no, not me." Kip looked faintly horrified. "That would be Michael—umpteenth cousin twice removed."

"And he won't mind you using company resources to bail out a friend?" Jordan motioned to the daybed. "Sit down. Go ahead and eat."

"I doubt it." Kip settled into the corner of the sofa with her back against the wall and her legs stretched out in front of her. "And if you give me a receipt for twelve hours of use, we really can write it off as a contribution, gas and all. Win-win, okay?"

"Of course, but I still owe you one." Jordan dragged over a chair and helped herself to a slice. "This is amazingly good, or maybe it's just because I haven't eaten since the scone this morning."

"You're right. And nothing owed. I like helping out."

"You do help."

"Good," Kip said softly.

Jordan was glad for the low light. Kip wouldn't see her blushing. Really? Blushing just because Kip's voice had gotten low and sexy? She cleared her throat. "I've got water in the fridge. Want one?"

"Sure. I thought about getting a couple of beers, and then figured coffee would be a better choice. I'll run out and get some later."

"No need, I've replaced the missing coffeemaker." Jordan handed her a bottle of water. "I'll make some later."

Kip caught her hand. "You doing okay?"

Jordan laced her fingers through Kip's without thinking about it. "More or less. This won't be the first time I've gone to bat against Mother Nature."

"I'll bet."

Jordan slid her hand free and retreated to the safety of her desk chair. "Usually it's the rain that does you in—too much or not enough, and never at the right time."

"At least you're a veteran and not a hobby farmer without a clue." Kip leaned forward to snag a second piece.

"Not many of those volunteering for this—" Jordan's cell rang and she pulled it out to check the number. "Hi, Ty."

"Hey. Are you still at the garden?"

"Yes."

"I saw the alerts. I don't know why we didn't get more warning."

"You know how accurate the weather reports are when it really matters."

Ty snorted. "I'll come back if you need me."

"No, don't," Jordan said a little too quickly, aware that Kip was watching her as she spoke. "There's nothing left for you to do. Everything is covered, and Kip loaned us some awesome heaters. If we don't get a lot of ground condensation, we'll be all right."

"I can at least help monitor temps so you can get some sleep. Otherwise you'll be up all night."

Jordan laughed. "I'm not going to be sleeping, but thanks." She glanced at Kip. "And Kip is still here, so I have company."

Ty was silent a beat. "She's all right?"

"Yes, I think so."

"Good. I'm glad. I'm really sorry about all of thi—"

"Stop. It's fine."

"Call me in the morning?"

"I will. Thanks for checking, Ty. And don't…don't worry, okay?"

"Way past that." Ty sighed. "You don't either. We'll all be fine here."

"Yes," Jordan said fiercely, "you will."

Kip waited until Jordan disconnected. "I was surprised she wasn't here earlier."

"Oh, well…" Jordan sorted through how much she could say without revealing Ty's secrets. "She's got two kids at home, and it's not really her responsibility to show up for emergencies."

Kip studied her. "Why do I think there's something you're not telling me?"

Jordan blew out a breath. "Because there is. And I seem to be crappy at keeping anything from you. But it's not mine to tell."

"But it's something to do with me, isn't it?"

"Why do you say that?" Jordan hedged, but a little curious too.

"She's never been comfortable around me." Kip shrugged. "At first I thought she could tell I was interested in you, and she was jealous."

"Ty?" Jordan laughed at the slight question in Kip's tone, and damn it, she was blushing again. "No, Ty and I are good friends, but there's never been anything more than that."

"So is it just she doesn't trust me because of the arrest thing, or does she think I'm going to hurt you?"

"No, neither. It's not personal, well, it is, but it's not about you and…" Jordan hesitated. You and me? Was there even an *us* in all of this? Did she want there to be? "It's complicated."

Frowning, Kip sat forward, balancing the pizza on the palm of her hand. "If there's something I can do to clear things up, I'll try."

"There might be." Jordan carefully set her pizza aside, her stomach too tied up in knots for her to eat. She needed to be careful. Her focus was too scattered between the weather threat and the constant tug of attraction from just being around Kip. She wanted to protect Ty, but she wanted to see beyond the subtle smoke screen that always surrounded Kip, to understand the woman behind the shield. "You could start by telling me what happened this afternoon when those guys showed up."

"Oh, the men in black?" Kip grimaced. "I'm sorry you got dragged into that."

"Were they from the probation office?"

"No."

"I didn't think so, actually. But you knew them, didn't you."

Kip considered how much she could say without jeopardizing Jordan. Her *friends* had warned her they'd be monitoring the situation, whatever the hell that meant, before they'd thanked her for coming and told her she could go. As if she'd had a choice. Jordan was waiting and she was tired of keeping her at arm's length when she wanted just the opposite. "Let's discuss theoreticals."

"All right," Jordan said slowly. "Why don't we."

"I told you I'm a mechanical engineer."

"Right. Not exactly a car mechanic."

"Not cars, no." Kip grinned. "Not land-based things at all, actually."

"Airplanes?"

Kip went back to eating her pizza.

Jordan made a humming sound. "Okay, things that fly."

Kip pointed a finger. "That will do."

"You are a things-that-fly mechanic," Jordan said. "Right. And?"

"And sometimes I come up with new ideas to make things fly better."

Jordan frowned. "Like designing new and better mechanical parts for the things that fly. Experimental things, basically."

"That's right," Kip said quietly.

"Okay, I think I'm getting the picture. And those men were interested in you...why?"

"Sometimes the people who are interested in new things that make things fly work for the government."

"So they *were* federal agents," Jordan said grimly. "Defense?"

Kip didn't say anything. She'd already said more than she ever had to anyone. Only her father and her team knew what she was working on.

"I suppose that doesn't matter as long as they're not—" Jordan dropped her gaze.

"Not what?" Kip asked quietly. "Jordan?"

"Will they be back?"

"I don't know."

"Are they likely to investigate me?"

"I don't know that either. I'm sorry." Kip rested her hand on Jordan's knee. "I probably should have realized they'd find out about my arrest, but I didn't think they'd show up here."

"Do they think you told me something?"

"No—not you."

"Who? Not Ty." Jordan tensed. "Did they ask about Ty?"

"Ty?" Kip shook her head. "No, why would they?"

"No reason."

Jordan answered too quickly. Something was going on with Ty. Kip considered the options, and there weren't many, especially considering Ty's unusual absence that night and Ty's long-standing uneasiness around her. "I take it Ty would rather not bump into anyone with...official government business."

"That's right."

"Damn," Kip muttered. "Was she very upset?"

"Theoretically," Jordan said, "let's say it's not an association she would like to foster."

"Maybe she'd rather avoid the possibility altogether?"

"I'm afraid so, yes."

Kip stood, paced in the small confines of the trailer. "There's no reason to think they'll be back, and no reason for them to be looking at either one of you. Especially Ty. They were just throwing their weight around."

"Because of you having been arrested."

Kip hesitated. Now they were moving from the professional, where she didn't mind stretching the boundaries a little, to the personal. To Randy, who she never, ever left unprotected. "They wanted details, since I'm not usually prone to getting crossed up with the law."

"Are you in trouble?"

Kip shrugged. "It depends on how you look at it. If they'd wanted, or more accurately, if their bosses wanted to get technical about things, I might get sidelined from the project I'm involved with."

Jordan caught her breath. "Working on those new things that make things fly."

"That's right."

"Permanently? I mean, would it have long-term effects on your ability to do that work?"

"Possibly."

"Oh, Kip. I'm sorry."

"My own fault there." Kip sat back down on the sofa and rested her elbows on her knees. "But you know, I figured something out this afternoon. I really don't care all that much. I like the work, but I don't like the bullshit. And I don't like being pushed around by people who don't know anything about me."

"You're sure you're all right?"

Kip rubbed the back of her neck. "I'm okay. A little tired is all."

"You should go home. There's no reason for you to stay up all night watching the thermometers with me."

"Hey," Kip said, leaning forward to tap a finger on Jordan's knee. "I happen to like hanging out with you in dark, fairly cold trailers."

Jordan laughed. "You could've told me you were cold. I've got an electric heater. Not as big as yours, but big enough."

Kip laughed and she wasn't quite as weary anymore. "I'm sure yours will be perfect."

"Uh-huh." Jordan rose, dragged the heater out from the corner, and plugged it in. "There, this place will be toasty before you know it."

"Almost as warm as outside."

"Those things are amazing. Are they from your work?"

"Yeah, it's not unusual for us to have to work outside on the parts of the bigger things."

"You must be really good."

"I've been waiting for you to say that. Not quite how I imagined it, but—"

"Don't you ever quit?"

"Not when I want something," Kip said softly.

"Your job," Jordan murmured. "You were saying…"

Kip sighed. Timing was everything, and this was not the time. "I like to make things work, and I seem to have a knack for figuring out how to do it efficiently. And efficiency saves money. That makes me desirable."

Jordan smiled. "I can't say that I considered your efficiency quotient in that regard, but I won't argue with the conclusion."

"Careful," Kip murmured. "I'm being on my best behavior, but I can't make any promises if you tease me."

"I wouldn't think of it."

"I didn't say I didn't want you to."

"I can't seem to help it, despite my better judgment. You seem to bring out the worst in me."

"There's nothing bad about what you're doing, except the part where I get all riled up and don't have anywhere to go with it."

"Is that right…riled up."

"Extremely so." Kip edged forward, captured Jordan's knees between her thighs.

Jordan pushed her chair back and escaped. She was breathing quickly. "Well, then we should probably take a circuit around the garden and cool you off."

Laughing, Kip rose and held out her hand. "I don't think it's gonna be that easy."

"No," Jordan murmured, "neither do I."

CHAPTER TWENTY-ONE

"Hey." Jordan sat carefully on the edge of the daybed and gently shook Kip's shoulder. She'd been watching Kip sleep for half an hour, memorizing the lines of her body, the angle of her jaw, the soft fullness of her mouth. She'd never wanted to imprint every atom of a woman in her mind the way she did every time she glimpsed Kip. Even though they spent hours and hours together every day, they were always so busy working they had very few quiet moments together, so tonight even these stolen moments in the midst of a crisis struck her as a gift. Watching Kip uninterrupted was a secret pleasure, and she couldn't even begin to feel guilty about it.

Kip opened her eyes with a slight groan, focused on Jordan, and smiled. Even half-asleep, Kip's gaze spiked Jordan's pulse and woke every other part of her too. She went from weary and worried to wet and wanting in a heartbeat. Leaving her hand on Kip's shoulder an instant longer, she said, "Sorry to get you up. It's almost dawn."

"Hell. I missed my shift, didn't I?" Kip asked.

"Not much to miss. I checked all the generators. Everything's running fine."

"I don't even remember falling asleep."

Kip looked chagrined, which only made her sexier. Jordan bit her lower lip and indulged herself with one brief caress of Kip's jeans-clad leg. Even that slight contact helped ease the aching need to touch her. "We were talking about climate change and you just decided to take a little nap midsentence."

"Oh, that was cool," Kip muttered, rubbing her face. She pushed up and sat with her back against the wall of the trailer, her hip against Jordan's.

The trailer was dark except for the soft light of the desk lamp behind them. The night outside was still black. Jordan would have been happy to stay marooned in this island of quietude for eternity if it meant Kip would keep looking at her like that—like she was desirable and fascinating and the only woman in the world.

"Actually, it was kind of cute," Jordan teased.

"Stop. My ego is delicate."

Jordan laughed. "I know you better than that, remember?"

Kip's expression grew serious and she caught Jordan's hand. "You do. I'm still surprised every time I realize you're okay with me...being me."

"Oh," Jordan said, trying to keep her tone light and failing miserably. God, she had to stop looking at her or she was going to forget about everything except curling up beside her and tasting and touching until she was full, if she ever could be. "I'm much more than okay. I'm quite enamored."

Kip laughed. "You are the worst flatterer ever."

Jordan shrugged. "I bet you're used to much better lines."

"Oh, I am," Kip said darkly. "Which is another reason why I'd rather be here with you than anywhere else. You're real. We're real."

"Are we," Jordan whispered, very much afraid she was falling for her own fantasies. She straightened before she could say or do anything she'd regret. "Speaking of real, I need to check outside."

"How's the temperature?"

"Holding at twenty-four an hour ago."

"Hell." Kip grimaced. "That's not good. We need it to start going up pretty quick, don't we?"

"Ordinarily this low this long would be disastrous." Jordan realized she was still holding Kip's hand and released it with a quick squeeze. "You changed the game with those heaters. Soil temperatures are dropping, sure, and some of the seedlings may shock, but it's not the disaster it might've been."

"Feels pretty terrible to me. Is it always like this, the worry about how the weather and probably a million things I don't even know about will affect the crops?"

"Pretty much every day." Jordan sighed, recalling countless conversations at the kitchen table, over breakfast and supper, her mother and father talking about the heat, the rain or lack of it, and the price forecasts. "I can't ever remember a time it wasn't a main topic of discussion, but I never realized the constant worry that went with it until I was almost grown. I never translated the welfare of the crops into dollars and cents when I was young, and then when I got older and realized what it meant when there was so much rain seeds didn't germinate or too little rain and the corn didn't grow, my father was the one who bore the worry."

Kip caressed Jordan's arm, her hand strong and warm. "You couldn't have taken that from him, you know. The worry."

"I know, but if I'd been there, if I'd only seen—"

Kip sat up and her arms came around Jordan's shoulders. "No, not if he didn't want you to see, and I'm betting he didn't."

Jordan didn't remember moving, but somehow she was in Kip's lap, her arms around Kip's shoulders and Kip's mouth so close, so close and so warm and so perfectly, beautifully strong. Her hand was in Kip's hair, silky strands sifting between her fingers, when she brought her mouth to Kip's.

Kip groaned softly, both hands spanning Jordan's waist. Jordan cleaved to her, wild to climb inside her skin. Kip's heart thudded against Jordan's chest, and hers leapt to match it. When she skimmed Kip's bottom lip and bit down gently, Kip groaned again.

Jordan's stomach flipped. Oh, she liked that tortured sound, liked making Kip unravel. She tilted her head, deepened the kiss, relentlessly demanding. Time, past and present, dropped away and all that remained was the press of Kip's body, the heat of her mouth, the ache of their breasts pressed together. She plundered and teased, her tongue sliding over Kip's, pulling back when Kip would've drawn her in deeper, forcing Kip to chase her, take her, match her need for need. She kissed the edge of Kip's jaw and down her throat, nipping gently at sweet, salty skin.

"Jordan," Kip said, husky and needy. "If you don't stop, I won't let you. Fuck, I'm losing it here."

"Mmm, good. I don't want to stop." Jordan kissed her again, and Kip shuddered. Oh yes. A wave of power spread through her, screaming for her to have and hold and claim. God, she wanted her. She jerked back, gasping. "You like that, don't you?"

Kip's grip tightened, her eyes dark and fierce. "Hell, yes."

Jordan's mind blanked for an instant and all she knew was hunger. "I've never…not like this."

"Yeah, do it," Kip whispered. "Put your hands on me."

"Oh God, I want to." Jordan's breath fled. Her throat closed around a moan. She pressed her forehead to Kip's. "Forgive me, God, I have to stop."

Kip's breath was loud and unsteady in the tiny womb of the trailer. "You know what you're doing to me, right?"

Laughing brokenly, Jordan stroked a finger down Kip's cheek, brushed her thumb over Kip's mouth. "Oh, baby, I think I do. If you're crazy right now, like I am. If you want my hands on you, right now, as much as I want them all over you. If you need me—"

Kip grabbed Jordan's shoulders, jerked her close and kissed her hard, turning them until they were half lying on the bed. Her tongue, skating over Jordan's mouth, hot and hard and urgent, was all the answer Jordan needed. She gripped Kip's shirt in both hands and wrapped her legs around Kip's hips. She opened her mouth and pulled Kip in.

Kip covered Jordan, body to body, and plunged into the hot welcome of Jordan's kiss, her mind ablaze, thoughts incinerated. She heard nothing, knew nothing, only the taste of her and the desperate press of their bodies struggling to join. All she sensed was need. Her breath sobbed out, her stomach pounded, blood pooled in her depths, hot and heavy and making her insane. She raked her teeth down Jordan's neck, tugged open the top button of her shirt, and licked the skin between her breasts. Jordan arched beneath her and cried out, her fingers digging into Kip's shoulders.

Kip slid to her knees on the floor and fumbled open another button. Jordan's flesh was soft and full beneath her mouth. She cupped her breast and pulled her nipple tightly between her lips.

"Oh God." Jordan gasped, fingers locked behind Kip's neck, holding her head down, urging her to take more. Her hips rose in invitation.

Kip pressed her cheek hard to Jordan's stomach and wrapped an arm around Jordan's hips, gathering her close. "One more freaking second and I'm not stopping."

Jordan's hips jerked. "In a second I won't be able to. God, I want you to touch me."

Kip squeezed her eyes shut. Jordan's heart pounded beneath her ear. "I can't believe *I'm* saying this, but we have to wait."

Jordan's laughter was weak and wild. "I know, I do, but I think I might die just the same."

Kip pushed herself up on one arm and leaned over her. "You won't. We're not waiting long. I guarantee it."

"No promises, okay?" Jordan cupped her face, stroked her throat. "You're so beautiful. You make me feel things I've never felt before. Make me want things I never imagined."

"There's more. I swear." Kip took her time kissing her, stroking and caressing every fraction of Jordan's mouth, pouring every ounce of wonder and hunger into the kiss. When she pulled back, Jordan's eyes were glazed, her face soft with desire. "You're all I think about, from the moment I open my eyes in the morning until I close them at night. Everything about you drives me crazy. The way you look holding a plant cradled in your palm, the way you tilt your face up to the sun, the way the wind blows through your hair. I can't stop watching your hands on the wheel. I keep imagining them on me, morning after morning. I want to be that plant in your hands, I want to be that goddamn steering wheel."

Jordan laughed with amazement, running a hand up and down Kip's back. "Baby, you don't have to be anything except you. And if we don't move, you're going to have to lie down next to me and take off your clothes, because I don't care about anything right now except touching you."

"No fair." Kip kissed her again, couldn't bear the thought of moving away from her. Then, with strength she'd no idea she had, she forced herself to stand up. "Come on, the sun will be up soon. Let's check on the children."

"I might need a minute to get my brain working again." Jordan sat up. "I'm not sure I can walk."

"I've got you." Kip held out her hand. It was trembling. Jordan's hand sliding into hers was the answer to a question she'd never known she'd been asking all her life.

❖

Jordan's cell rang a little after six. She checked it and mouthed *Ty*. Kip nodded and knelt by one of the garden beds, sliding a thermometer back into the ground.

"Hi," Jordan said.

"How is everything?" Ty asked anxiously.

"Better than I'd hoped." Jordan smiled over at Kip. The sky had dawned gray and angry, as if affronted by the unexpected weather, but temperatures had started rising a little after six. "We're just getting ready to uncover things now."

"Kip is still there?" Ty's tone was cautious.

"Yes."

After a beat of silence, she said, "I'm glad you had help."

Jordan sighed. "We need to talk."

"I know. I'll call you when I'm back. I'm not home right now."

"Okay. As soon as you can."

"Promise."

"Love to the kids. Don't worry too much, all right?"

Ty laughed harshly. "Talk soon. Bye."

"Bye," Jordan murmured.

Kip stroked her arm. "She okay?"

"I think so. Worried."

Kip winced. "I'm sorry. I'll figure out a way to fix it."

"It's not your fault."

"Her not being here, her being even more scared, that's on me."

Jordan shook her head. "You're not the reason for her fear. You are not always responsible, Kip."

Kip had heard the words, or some variation of them, all her life, but she still knew better. She was part of the chain of events, and what Ty was going through right this moment was her doing. Arguing the point was useless, and right now, when they were both exhausted, was definitely not the time. Kip pressed her hands to the small of her back and stretched. "Do you want something to eat and some coffee as much as I do?"

As if accepting the momentary truce, Jordan nodded. "If you mean bad enough to cry, then I think so."

"Are we out of the woods here now?"

Jordan rolled the tension from her shoulders. "We'll know when we uncover them. If there's condensation and the temperatures are still low, the leaves can get frostbitten."

Kip winced. "I'll make it a quick trip."

"I don't know how I would've gotten through the night without you," Jordan said softly. "Thank you for being here."

Kip shoved her hands in her pockets. Kissing her right now was probably not the best plan. "I meant it when I said I wanted to be here with you. When I'm with you, I feel like I'm where I ought to be."

Jordan's lips parted and her gaze swept down Kip's body. Just that small glance set Kip's skin ablaze.

"You're dangerous when you talk like that," Jordan murmured.

To hell with timing. Now was what mattered. Kip settled a hand on Jordan's waist and kissed her. "I'm not. I'm safer than you think."

"No, you're anything but safe," Jordan murmured against Kip's mouth. "I think we should wait on the coffee."

"What?" Kip's head was light, her brain not firing properly. "God, you taste good."

"Let's finish up here and I'll make you breakfast at my place."

Lightness bubbled through Kip's chest. Happiness, she realized. She'd do anything for Jordan, go anywhere, bring back anything to make Jordan look at her like that forever. Like she was some kind of miracle. "How soon will that be?"

Jordan laughed. "Not too long. I've got plans for you."

Kip let her go, grinning. "So put me to work, boss."

CHAPTER TWENTY-TWO

"You're sure you don't want a room at the Plaza with a big sunken tub and room service?" Kip asked. "You deserve it after last night."

"So do you." Jordan held her apartment door open and let Kip go in first. "And that sounds awesome—I might take you up on it one of these days, but right this moment, I don't feel a lot like waiting for anything, even if it does come with five-star service."

"This looks perfect to me," Kip said, taking in the room. The living room was a good-sized space for New York with tall ceilings that made it seem larger, a set of bay windows facing the street, and a small kitchen visible through a doorway on the far side. Kip guessed the short hallway to the left led to the bedroom and bathroom. The whole place would probably fit into her main living area, but this was far cozier and welcoming than her more luxurious and mostly impersonal accommodations. A well-worn pale blue floral patterned rug covered most of the floor. A pale green sofa that reminded her of the leaves of the young shoots coming up in the garden beds faced the windows. Original art adorned the walls, paintings in an array of periods from earth-toned landscapes to several dramatic abstract canvases filled with slashes of color. An overstuffed chair faced a small brick hearth and open fireplace that took up most of the wall opposite the entrance. A stack of firewood sat beside it along with a set of cast-iron fireplace tools.

"Does that really work?" Kip asked.

Jordan laughed and let the door close behind her. "It does. It's amazing, isn't it?"

"I'll trade you my place for yours. Just so I can have that."

"No deal. I don't know how it managed to survive with all the renovations and the way this place has been cut up for apartments, but there it is." Jordan kicked off her work boots and left them on a boot tray by the door.

"And you really use it." Kip shed her boots with Jordan's.

"All the time. There's something about watching the flames that makes me forget everything that was bothering me during the day." She shrugged. "That's as close as I ever get to meditating."

"I know what you mean. We used to have a lake house when I was small, and my father built a fire pit outside. He dragged these huge logs around it to use for seats. I thought that was the coolest thing." Kip laughed, recalling a time when the lake house meant joy and not sadness. "I could sit there for hours watching the flames. I used to imagine the little bits of cinders that flew into the air were fireflies with wings."

Jordan came up behind Kip and wrapped her arms around her waist, resting her chin on Kip's shoulder. "Same here. We always had a big bonfire after we cleared an area for planting or chased back the undergrowth that was constantly trying to take over the pastures. Huge things that shot flames ten or twenty feet into the air." She shook her head. "Probably illegal now."

Kip turned her head and kissed the corner of Jordan's mouth. "Probably. But I bet there's someplace that you can still build a fire as big as you want."

"Maybe," Jordan said wistfully.

"We'll find a place and sit around watching fireflies dance one of these days." Kip turned, rested her hands on Jordan's waist, and kissed her. "You know, there are three…no, four things I really need right now. That's it. Only four. Give me those, and I'll be a happy woman."

Jordan leaned back, her hips and thighs pressed to Kip's, her hands resting on Kip's shoulders. "Oh? And what might they be?"

Kip grinned at the teasing note in Jordan's voice. She loved the invitation in Jordan's eyes, the confirmation that Jordan wanted what she wanted. Although she doubted Jordan wanted it with the kind of craving that clawed at her insides right this minute. She swallowed, ordered herself to wait. Timing. Timing. Always the damn timing. "A shower, coffee, food…"

Jordan's eyebrow rose as Kip trailed off.

"And you."

"And what would the order be?" Jordan's voice dropped, low and seductive.

"I was thinking..."

Kip paused, and Jordan leaned forward and nipped at her lip.

Kip's stomach tied itself into a knot that only the touch of Jordan's skin on hers was going to untie. "A shower, you. Coffee, you. Food, and..."

Jordan's arms tightened around Kip's neck and they were suddenly body to body, joined everywhere. Jordan's mouth was on her throat, her lips soft and warm as she murmured, "You've got big plans."

Kip stroked her hair, kissed the tender skin below her ear. "Only where you're concerned."

"Then I think we better start with the shower, and get on with it."

"Good idea," Kip growled, fisting her hand in Jordan's hair and tilting Jordan's head back until she could kiss her mouth properly. Timing. Damn timing. She was so damn tired of waiting. "Where?"

Jordan braced her hands on Kip's shoulders and pushed away. Her breath was coming as fast as Kip's. "I'll get you some towels. The bathroom's this way."

"I was thinking maybe you could—"

Jordan grabbed her hand and tugged her along. "I know what you were thinking. But it's not a very big shower and there are quite a lot of things I don't think we can do in there that I'd really like to do."

A buzz saw slashed through Kip's brain and every rational thought splintered into a thousand pieces. "Okay. Sure. Whatever you say."

Laughing, Jordan glanced over her shoulder. Kip looked poleaxed. Oh, how she liked that, throwing the ever-confident, too-sexy-for-words younger woman off her stride. "I'll remind you you said that in a little while."

"I won't be changing my mind."

Kip showered as fast as she possibly could and then realized she had no clean clothes. Well, she wasn't planning on getting dressed again anyhow. She wrapped herself in the largest towel from the stack Jordan had left and stuck her head out the door. "I'm done, but there's no way I'm putting on the clothes I slept in again."

Jordan appeared with a cup of coffee in her hand. "Here, take this. I'll throw your clothes in the wash, but first I have to shower."

"No problem. I wasn't planning on getting dressed right away. If that's okay with you."

"Oh," Jordan said softly, "that's very okay."

Kip sipped the coffee, gauging the heat in Jordan's gaze. She leaned a shoulder against the doorway. The towel opened over her thigh. "Where do you want me to wait?"

Jordan looked down and quickly back up, keeping her eyes above shoulder level. The temptation to pull the towel the rest of the way free and have Kip naked was almost too much to stand. She needed to get cleaned up too, and the instant Kip was naked, she wasn't going to care about anything as mundane as a little bit of topsoil smudging her face. Wordlessly, Jordan pointed down the hall to the bedroom. "Make yourself comfortable."

Grinning, Kip grabbed her clothes and pushed away from the wall. The towel was damp where it stretched across her ass and she could feel Jordan watching her as she walked away. "Don't take too long."

"Don't worry. I won't."

Jordan showered in record time. She wanted about three cups of coffee, but that could wait until…after. Right now only one thing occupied her mind. Wearing nothing but her towel, she padded to the bedroom and paused in the doorway. Kip sat up against the headboard, the sheet drawn to her waist, and, as far as Jordan could see, wearing nothing else. The coffee cup sat beside her on the nightstand. Jordan's heart shot into her throat and her stomach threatened to drop out. She was instantly swollen and wet and practically brainless. She licked her lips. "You do realize I'm in danger of blowing a circuit here. And then where will we be."

Kip flicked down the sheets beside her and patted the bed. "You'd better get over here, then."

Jordan walked to the side of the bed, watching Kip watch her, tracking every movement like a predator in the bushes. Her pulse jumped as if she really were prey and Kip might leap on her at any moment. If that happened she would surrender, exposing her most vulnerable parts, begging for the piercing bite of Kip's claim. She wanted to unleash the storm in Kip's eyes. When she let the towel fall,

Kip surged to her knees at the edge of the bed, her arms snaring Jordan around the waist, her mouth instantly on Jordan's breast.

"Oh," Jordan gasped, gripping Kip's shoulders and pressing her hips forward against Kip's hard stomach to stay upright. Kip's mouth was hot, her teeth gentle as they rasped against her oversensitive nipples. She slipped her hand around the back of Kip's neck and pushed harder against Kip's mouth, wanting to feel her claim, wanting to be taken. "I love the way your mouth feels on me."

Blind to everything but the taste and scent of her, Kip kissed her way from one breast to the other, alternately licking, sucking, and tugging on Jordan's nipples. When Jordan quivered against her, small broken sounds of pleasure escaping her throat, she started all over again. Relentless, driven, insatiable. She stroked the hollow at the base of Jordan's spine and cupped her ass, tugging her hard against her chest. She tilted her head back, found Jordan's unfocused gaze staring down at her. "Ready for bed now?"

"Oh God, yes." Jordan swept her palms over Kip's shoulders, down her back. "Yes, yes, yes."

Kip pulled her down and rose over her, sliding one thigh between Jordan's legs, bracing herself on her elbows on either side of Jordan's shoulders. Jordan was a feast and she planned to explore every inch of her. She caressed and kissed and sucked everywhere, her mouth a constant torment, until Jordan thrashed beneath her, her breath so ragged she sounded as if she was crying.

"I don't think I can stand it." Jordan arched, searching for more contact.

"Not done yet," Kip said, her voice like gravel. She rocked her hips, her thigh sliding over and pressing into Jordan's sex.

The friction, the hard merciless demand, made Jordan ache to come.

"I want you inside me." Jordan dug her fingers into the hard muscles along Kip's spine, wrapping her legs tightly around Kip's, thrusting against her.

"Say it again," Kip said with dark possessiveness.

"I want you to make me come." Jordan bit down on Kip's shoulder. "Damn you. I need you."

Kip straightened her arms and pushed down until her shoulders were between Jordan's legs, holding her thighs apart, open and exposed. Kip's kisses were featherlight where her mouth had been demanding before. Teasing, licking, and sucking until Jordan rode the thin edge of orgasm.

"You're going to make me come," Jordan warned, knowing it was already too late.

Kip raised her head and watched Jordan's neck arch as she entered her. "Yes, I am."

She stroked, deep and slow, feeling Jordan's heartbeat around her fingers, matching her tempo to the rhythm of Jordan's writhing hips until Jordan's breath caught, and she took her hard and fast and over.

Jordan's world exploded in color and flame, the climax leaving her mindless and weak. When she came back to herself and opened her eyes, Kip rested on an elbow next to her, one hand on her stomach, a supremely satisfied smile on her face. Jordan laughed feebly. "I bet that did your ego a lot of good."

"You're amazing." Kip leaned over and nipped at her lip. "You make me feel like a god."

"Oh, I was afraid of that." Jordan curled into her and kissed Kip's throat. "*You* are amazing. I don't think I've ever felt anything like that in my life. No, I know I haven't."

"I'm glad." Kip shuddered and rested her forehead on Jordan's. "I have dreamed about that so many times, but it was never as incredible in my dreams."

"The dream isn't over." Jordan pushed Kip onto her back and straddled Kip's hips, her breasts swaying slightly as she moved. Kip flexed and kissed her breast, but Jordan pushed her back down with a hand in the center of her chest. "I want you to lie there and not move."

Kip's brows rose. Her skin gleamed with a faint sheen of sweat and desire. A barely tamed young animal. "Really."

"Really," Jordan said with quiet command. "I have things I've been wanting to do."

Kip's heart beat a furious tattoo against the inside of her ribs. She'd never been one to be quiet in bed, and for the first time in her life, she wanted to belong to a woman. This one woman. She wanted Jordan to take her. She let her arms fall, palms open by her sides. "All yours."

Jordan pressed Kip's shoulders to the bed and leaned over her,

RADCLY*f*FE

dragging her nipple across Kip's mouth. Kip tensed, but when she would have captured her in her mouth, Jordan sat back up. "Uh-uh. Not yet."

Kip groaned. "You're such a fucking tease. You're killing me."

"You'll live." Jordan laughed, filled with power like she'd never known. Watching Kip's desire made her light-headed, made her swell with urgency, made her want to take and plunder and hear Kip's cries of pleasure. She rocked on Kip's stomach, coating her with the essence of her excitement. Kip grasped her hips as she rode her, arching to meet Jordan's thrusts.

"You feel what you do to me?" Jordan asked, her voice husky and unfamiliar. "I could come all over you right now."

"You're gonna make my head explode," Kip muttered, her hands hot on Jordan's flesh.

"I hope so."

Before she reached the point where she couldn't stop herself from coming on Kip's stomach, Jordan stretched out on top of her, breaking the exquisite contact.

"Why…?"

"My show, remember?" Jordan licked a slow circle around Kip's small tight nipple. Kip's hands played over her back, massaging her ass, guiding her up and down against Kip's thigh.

"I know, I know," Kip groaned, "but I want to see you come again."

"What makes you think I can?"

Kip laughed. "I know you can."

Jordan closed her teeth on Kip's nipple, tugged ever so lightly.

"Damn." Kip hissed and arched. "Jordan. God."

"Like that?" Jordan murmured, holding back a laugh of triumph.

"I dare you to do that on my clit."

Jordan looked up. "You think you could take it?"

Kip's eyes glinted with challenge and need. "Why don't you find out?"

Jordan shook her head. "You can wait a little longer."

Kip cursed and fell back with a groan.

Jordan wanted to make her come more than she'd wanted anything in her life. She would've taken her in the hall outside the bathroom an hour ago, in the trailer the night before, a dozen times before that, and now the want was a ferocious need that terrified her. "I want you to come like you've never come before."

Kip twisted beneath, caught her hand and pushed it down her stomach. "Touch me and I will."

Jordan skimmed her fingers up the inside of Kip's thigh, cupped the heat between her legs, and stroked a finger along her cleft. She found her clit, squeezed her gently between her fingertips.

"Oh yeah," Kip cried, her eyes closed, every muscle rigid. "You know just what to do."

"Don't come until I tell you to."

"I can't wait," Kip gasped. "I'm too close."

Jordan stilled, moved her hand.

"Jordan, Jordan," Kip gasped. "I'm right there."

"I think I promised you something." Jordan shifted again and circled Kip's clit with her mouth. Carefully, she grazed the shaft with her teeth and sucked her against the inner surface of her lower lip.

"You'll make me come," Kip blurted, her voice loud in the silent room.

Jordan grabbed her hips just as Kip exploded against her mouth, bucking with a shout. She smiled against the pulsing heat of Kip's swollen flesh. Victorious, humbled, destroyed.

CHAPTER TWENTY-THREE

W e're going to have to get up soon, aren't we," Kip murmured.
"Mm-hmm." Jordan lay on her back partially covered by
the sheet, the fingers of her left hand entwined with those of Kip's right,
staring at the ceiling and wholly mindless. "Did we sleep or did I just
pass out?"

"I'm not sure." Kip chuckled. "I'm feeling a little destroyed
myself."

Jordan turned her head. Kip's hair was tousled, her face as relaxed
as she'd ever seen it, the starkly handsome lines softened by the
diffuse late-afternoon light and the hours of lovemaking. "You look
phenomenal. Good destroyed or bad destroyed?"

Kip's mouth twitched. "I wouldn't have thought there *was* a good
destroyed until today. But very definitely good." She looked over,
caught Jordan's gaze. "I feel fantastic, other than the fact that every
muscle in my body feels pretty much like a limp noodle."

Jordan hauled herself up onto an elbow, leaned over, and kissed
Kip. "Nothing about you looks limp." She swept her hand down the
center of Kip's torso, over her taut abdomen to her muscled thigh. "You
have a gorgeous body. In fact, I have a thing for it."

Kip's breath kicked up a notch. "I can't believe I'm actually
starting to get turned on again. I would've sworn I was done for a
week."

Laughing, Jordan kissed Kip's breast and brushed her cheek over
her nipple. "Oh no. Definitely not a week. You'll need to be back to full
power in an hour or so."

"Is that a request or an order?"

"Well," Jordan said softly, watching with growing lust as she drew circles on Kip's abdomen and made her muscles twitch, "you're going to have to find a little more stamina than this to keep up with me." She bent down and swirled the tip of her tongue around the edge of Kip's navel, making her gasp. "After all, I'm just approaching my prime. You've still got a long ways to go."

"And she throws down the gauntlet." Kip flexed her incredible abs to propel herself up, grabbed Jordan's shoulders, and whipped her over onto her back. An instant later she was on top of her, pinning both wrists beside her head. She loomed above Jordan, a cocky smile on her face. "And just look who's on the bottom now."

"What you gonna do about it?" Jordan's pulse jumped in her throat, desire an inferno raging deep inside. All it took was one glimpse of the hunger in Kip's eyes, and just that fast, she was ready for her. "I love the way you want me."

"You have no idea," Kip murmured, kissing her throat. "I love to make you come. I can't even describe the feeling, except I could live on it. Never leave this bed. All I need is you."

Jordan's throat tightened. She wasn't sure she wanted to hear those words, knew she wasn't ready to believe them, feared what would happen if she did. She gripped Kip's hair in her fist, pulled until Kip raised her head. "All talk, no action."

Flames leapt in Kip's eyes. "Oh, is that what you think."

"Maybe." Jordan bucked her hips, rolled them in teasing invitation. This she didn't fear. This she could give, this she could take. And keep her heart safe a little longer.

Kip slipped a hand between Jordan's thighs and cupped her. Jordan bit her lip, tightening so quickly she ached.

"Say it," Kip whispered, watching Jordan's eyes glaze. She squeezed ever so carefully until Jordan's back arched. "Say it and I will."

"Fuck me." Jordan stared into Kip's eyes, her voice raspy and low.

"I want to," Kip said, the need a knife slashing through her. "So damn much."

When she entered her, Jordan loosed a sharp cry and Kip whispered, "Feel me."

"Deeper," Jordan murmured, gripping Kip's arm, the muscles

under her fingers tight as steel bands. She wouldn't last more than another stroke, too sweet, too powerful, too perfect.

"That's it, baby," Kip crooned.

"Oh!" Jordan thrashed as the orgasm swept through her.

Kip pressed her forehead to Jordan's breast, quieting inside her, content to stay connected forever. Jordan's fingers played fitfully in her hair while her heart banged against her chest.

"Happy now?" Jordan murmured.

"More than you can imagine."

"Out." Jordan tapped Kip's head. "Out. Done. Done now."

Jordan sighed as Kip gently withdrew and wrapped her arms around Kip's shoulders. Nestled in Kip's arms, she stroked everywhere she could touch. She couldn't stop herself from thinking how right Kip felt in her arms, knowing it was foolish and too satisfied to care. Just for now she would take the pleasure and rejoice.

"Does making me come make you crazy?" Jordan finally whispered, her mouth against Kip's ear.

Kip shuddered in her grasp. "Like you wouldn't believe."

"I might." Jordan kissed her. "How about I see."

Wordlessly, Kip shifted to her side until they were face-to-face. Jordan skimmed lower on Kip's stomach, circled her clit. Kip groaned.

Jordan's heart filled her chest. "Oh, you are ready, aren't you."

Kip laughed, a wild abandoned sound. "I've been ready since the day I laid eyes on you."

"And you have charmed me from the moment I saw you." Jordan kissed her, matching the glide of her mouth over Kip's to the long, silky caresses between her legs.

"Just...charm?" Kip's lids flickered as Jordan stroked her faster.

Jordan couldn't answer, not without telling the truth about all the ways Kip captured her heart and soul, and speaking the truth would make it real. She kissed her harder instead, quickening her strokes even more until Kip rode her fingers in a wild burst of movement, her harsh cries loud in the still room.

"Damn," Kip growled and came in Jordan's hand.

Jordan held her, silent still, her secrets safe.

❖

The ringing of a cell phone woke Jordan, and her eyes flew open. "What?"

"Mine." Kip rolled away from her, fumbled on the floor, and pulled her cell phone from her pants.

"Hey," Kip said, her voice husky with sleep. "What, no. No, no, I'm awake. I'm good. I'm good. Fuck, what time is it?"

Jordan glanced at the bedside clock. Six p.m. Lord, they'd spent the whole day lost in each other. Beside her, Kip sat up abruptly.

"What? Where's Mark?"

Awake now, alert to the strain in Kip's voice, Jordan sat up too. Kip dragged a hand through her hair, her entire body rigid.

"Did you call 9-1-1? Well, I don't know, isn't that what you should do?" She jumped out of bed, snatched her pants off the chair by the bed, and almost fell over trying to put them on while she held her cell phone.

Jordan had never seen Kip rattled by anything, but she was nearly panicked now. Jordan fished pants and an old T-shirt from the top of the clean laundry basket in the corner, pulling them on as she absently registered she'd never actually washed Kip's clothes, and kicked into a pair of boots without bothering with socks. If Kip was in some kind of trouble, she wasn't letting her go off to face it alone again, no matter what Kip said.

"No, don't wait for me. All right, all right, okay. Are you sure? Like how fast?…Okay, I'll be there…ten minutes. Don't do anything until then."

Kip dropped the phone on the bed and spun around, staring at Jordan. "Savannah. Savannah is having a baby."

"Who's Savannah?"

Kip got her pants up and zipped, and yanked her T-shirt on over her head, not noticing it was inside out. "My cousin. I have to go."

"I'm calling an Uber." Jordan fired up the app and put in the request. "Kip, there's time. Focus. Is there someone else you need to call?"

"Later, maybe. She already called her husband. He's way the hell across the country. She's early by two weeks. Is that all right, do you think?"

"Happens all the time." Jordan smiled and pointed at her T-shirt. "You might want to fix that."

Kip glanced down and grimaced. Once she'd fixed her shirt, she took a deep breath and looked moderately less spooked. "Sorry. She's like my sister. If anything happened to her…"

"I'm sure she'll be fine, but you should probably get over there."

"Right." Kip hesitated. "Do you think you could come with me?"

"Of course, if you want me to."

Kip grabbed her hand. "I do. I need you to keep me sane."

"Then I'm coming." Jordan threw an arm around Kip's waist and pointed her toward the door. "Trust me."

The Uber was downstairs by the time they got to the street. Kip gave him the address and told him to hurry. They didn't have far to go, and ten minutes later they were pounding up the stairs to the third floor of a beautiful apartment building overlooking Central Park.

Kip hammered on the apartment door. "Savannah. It's me."

A voice from inside called, "It's open."

Kip pushed inside and Jordan followed. A very pregnant woman lay propped on the sofa, her feet up on several pillows, a watch within reach on the coffee table beside her. She was beautiful, her long blond hair shining, her face slightly flushed, but luminous. She didn't look like a pregnant woman in distress, for which Jordan was immensely grateful. She didn't think Kip could handle anything happening to this woman.

Kip knelt beside the sofa, grabbing Savannah's hand. "How are you feeling? We should go."

"I called my obstetrician and she said there's no rush, that I can head over to the hospital anytime."

"It's time," Kip said quickly.

Savannah picked up the watch, checked it. "Not really. They're fifteen minutes apart still."

"Is this your first?" Jordan asked.

Savannah looked over Kip's shoulder, smiled. "Yes. Hi, I'm Savannah."

"Jordan." Jordan eased a hip onto the arm of an overstuffed chair. "First times can take a while, but not always. You're probably safer to head to the hospital sooner. Wait here or wait there."

"I know." Tears filled Savannah's eyes.

"What," Kip shouted. "What, what hurts?"

"Oh, it's just Mark. He's not here and he's going to miss it."

"I'll video everything," Kip said.

Savannah made a face. "You will not. I'm sure I'm not going to look very attractive at all. I certainly don't want a video of it."

Kip grinned weakly. "I'll just video the baby part, not you, okay?"

"Well, I guess so." Savannah winced and her breathing picked up. "Okay, maybe we should go."

Kip jumped up, her cell phone in hand. "I'm calling...should I call a cab?"

"Call an Uber," Jordan said. "They get here faster than anyone."

She was right. Fifteen minutes later they were checking Savannah in to the emergency room at the hospital. Forty-five minutes later, she was ensconced in a birthing room on the delivery floor.

"Go get coffee or something, Kip. Stop pacing," Savannah said.

"I should let Jordan know what's going on. You're not going to do anything right away, are you?"

Savannah rubbed her abdomen. "According to the nurses, not for a while yet." She gritted her teeth and, after a moment, spoke again. "Hopefully not too long, because honestly? This part is not fun."

"I'll grab something to eat and send Jordan home. Neither one of us has had much sleep in the last twenty-four hours."

"That sounds interesting." Savannah's eyebrows rose. "I could use the distraction. Tell me."

"Um..." Kip could feel herself grinning. "You know I never talk about my conquests."

"You are so full of it. If there's a conquest to be gotten, I'd say it was you."

Kip shoved her hands in her pockets and rocked on her heels. "It shows, huh?"

"I might be delirious now and then, but I'm not so far gone I can't see the way you look at her. She must be special."

"More than special. Amazing."

"Wow, I've never heard you—" She caught her breath.

Kip jumped to her side.

"Okay, that was definitely not fun," Savannah said after another minute.

"I'll stay."

"No. Really. Go get something to eat. I can tell I'm going to be doing this a while longer."

"If you're sure."

"Go find your girl. She's gorgeous, by the way," Savannah said.

"Yeah, I know." Kip could feel her smile spread. "I'll be right outside. I can be back in thirty seconds."

"I know. I can count on you. Everyone can always count on you."

Kip hurried to the waiting room. Jordan was the only one there, settled into the corner of a nondescript dark brown couch reading her phone. She glanced up as Kip strode in, her quick smile a caress to Kip's frazzled nerves.

"How's she doing?"

"It might be at least a couple hours. You should go home and get some sleep."

"If it's all the same to you, I'd like to stay." Jordan leaned over and pulled a cardboard box from a bag and handed it to Kip. "Turkey, apple, and cheddar on wheat. I went for potato salad instead of coleslaw. And a brownie. Eat."

"Oh, man. You're a mind reader. I'm famished." Kip sat down next to Jordan, who opened a box of her own.

"You did burn a lot of calories recently."

Kip smirked. "True. And I hope to do the same again soon."

Jordan pretended to be fascinated by her sandwich. If she looked at Kip right now she was very likely going to make some inappropriate public display. Just the sound of Kip's voice made her blood race. "How are you holding up?"

"Okay. I appreciate you staying." Kip blew out a breath. The fatigue and anxiety of the last day and a half was catching up to her. "I don't like feeling helpless when someone I love is in trouble."

"She's having a baby, Kip," Jordan said gently. "I know it's pretty scary, but it's also just about the most natural thing in the world. And this is a great place. She's going to be all right."

Kip stared at her hands. "I know. I just wish there was something I could do."

"You're here with her, that's what she needs." Jordan leaned close, stroked her shoulder. "You want to tell me what you're really worried about?"

Kip jerked. She hadn't thought she was so transparent, but then Jordan had always seen past her shields. "I was just thinking about something that happened a long time ago."

"I know about the accident," Jordan said. "Well, at least, what the newspapers said. You don't have to talk about it, if you don't want to."

"I've never talked about it," Kip said as a door opened she'd held shut with all her strength her whole life. "Even my father never asked exactly what happened, and I never told him."

"Whatever you say will be safe with me."

"I know." Kip put the take-out box aside and turned to face Jordan. "We were sailing like we did almost every day in the summer. My mother was an expert sailor. Before we were born, before she married my father, she crewed on a competitive racing team."

Jordan waited, said nothing while Kip sorted through the memories.

"I was ten, Randy was seven. He was always a brat." Kip laughed a little unsteadily. "He hated wearing a life vest, and it was a constant battle for him to keep it on most of the time. He was wearing it that day, though. When the storm came, Mom ordered us into the cockpit." She licked her lips. "She told us to stay there, but Randy wanted to see. I should've made him stay, but I didn't want to be down there either. When he opened the hatch, I thought he was just going to look out, but then he climbed out."

Kip shuddered, sweat breaking out on her face.

Jordan wrapped an arm around her shoulders and kissed her hair. "Take your time."

Kip clenched a fist. "I shouldn't have let him do that. He climbed out and I couldn't stop him. And then…" She closed her eyes. "And then I went after him, but he was sliding across the deck into the water and Mom had to go in after him, and the waves were so high, and I couldn't see him. I couldn't see her. I couldn't see either of them. I was holding on and I was about to fall in too. And then Mom was right there and she pushed Randy up onto the deck right at me, screaming for me to hold on to him. To hold on and not let go."

Kip's eyes were wide, filled with old fears. "I didn't. I didn't let go."

"Of course you didn't. You held on just like your mother wanted you to do." Jordan framed her face. "Kip. Kip look at me."

Kip blinked. "Jordan?" Her face flushed. "God, I'm sorry I just dumped all that on you."

"Hey, no." Jordan kissed her. "I'm glad you told me. I'm so sorry."

"It's my fault. I should've kept Randy below deck. She'd still be alive if I had."

Jordan gripped her shoulders, her heart bleeding. "You were a child in a horrible, terrifying situation. There's no way to know what would've happened. You were not responsible."

"I think Randy believes I blame him, but I don't."

"Kip," Jordan said carefully, "sometimes terrible accidents happen, and there's no one to blame."

"Maybe, maybe." Kip sighed. "I'm glad you know. I'm glad *you* don't blame me."

"No, never." Jordan ached to take her pain away. "Are you all right?"

"I'm okay. It helped some, to talk about it."

"I'm very glad you did, and I'm so glad you trusted me."

Kip shrugged. "You're the only one I ever have."

Jordan's throat tightened. She wanted to take her home, keep her safe, protect her from the memories and the hurt. Wished it were all that simple. "Go see about Savannah. You'll feel better if you're with her."

Kip nodded. "Thanks. You ought to go—"

Jordan shook her head. "I'll be right here. I told you I'm not leaving."

Kip rose. "I'm glad."

CHAPTER TWENTY-FOUR

Jordan half unconsciously scanned articles on the internet, most of her attention attuned to the sound of footsteps approaching, signaling Kip's return. Shortly after seven p.m., another family arrived in the waiting area—a nervous-looking young man in a wrinkled white shirt and dress pants paired with mismatched running shoes, a testimony to his probable rush to get to the hospital, accompanied by two older women who Jordan bet were the grandmothers-to-be.

"When are they going to let me go see her," the young man said, his voice high and anxious. "I'm supposed to be coaching. She has to concentrate on her deep breathing."

"They have to get her settled, Danny. Jolie knows what she needs to do. She'll be fine until you get there."

The stout iron-gray-haired woman who spoke wore a dark blue polo with the logo of a major big box store, khaki pants, and sensible shoes. Her no-nonsense look was softened by her tender tone, and she reminded Jordan of her favorite high school teacher—tough but totally devoted to her students. She'd been one of the first to call Jordan after she'd arrived home when her dad had died. Jordan had forgotten that in her zeal to bury the past along with him.

The second woman, tall and thin and equally gray-haired, although her obviously professionally styled coif contrasted with the other woman's practical cut, patted his arm solicitously. His mother, most likely. "Try to relax, honey. Everything is going along just the way it should. They'll be out to get you soon."

"Right, okay," he said, sounding anything but reassured, and continued his circular pacing.

Jordan smiled at the family drama and, nestling farther into the corner of the sofa, closed her eyes. She wouldn't sleep, but her eyes ached from having been awake for too many hours with too little sleep and too much worry. Still, she didn't want to leave. Kip needed the backup, even if all she could offer was company, and she wanted to be the one to provide it. Her rational mind knew the chances of anything going seriously wrong during the delivery were slim, but she worried for Kip, who wasn't exactly rational. Kip's panic had very little to do with her cousin's labor and everything to do with the tragedy she'd suffered, and Jordan wished she could take some of that burden from her. Even knowing that was an impossibility, when Kip hurt, she hurt. If she were anywhere else right now, she'd spend every second worrying about Kip.

She had a feeling very few people in Kip's life had ever protected her. Coming to know her during all the time they'd spent working side by side, she'd seen how quickly Kip stepped in to help when there was trouble, how readily she shouldered any duty. Everything she'd learned of Kip's past suggested she was the one to take responsibility for everything, even when it wasn't hers to accept. Certainly no ten-year-old child could be held responsible for saving the life of another or be accountable for the death of anyone. But Kip had carried that guilt all her life, and as much as Jordan loved her for that strength and sense of honor, knowing Kip was hardwired to take on any burden and blame herself for failures not her own kindled a knot of fear in her belly. She'd watched her father destroyed by that extreme sense of obligation. He had assumed accountability for everything, even the weather, and when the weather and the economy and the false hopes of others had crashed down upon him, he'd broken under the weight of it. She feared Kip was very much like him, and all the things she loved about him were the very things she was still angry at him for.

She rarely let herself acknowledge her anger, torn between grief and betrayal every time she thought of what he'd done. But when she could bring herself to admit it, she accepted she'd been furious from the very moment she'd gotten the phone call from her devastated mother. How could he have done that to them? How could he have not trusted them to help him as a family to get through whatever difficulties lay ahead? But he hadn't trusted them any more than he'd accepted how much they'd loved and needed him. They should have been his greatest responsibility, and he'd abandoned them. She had avoided giving her heart to anyone all these years because he'd broken it. He had taught her that love was not enough.

Jordan rubbed her closed lids. Her head throbbed with more than fatigue and worry. She ached with the old sense of loss and betrayal.

"Hey," Kip said gently, the weight of her body settling beside Jordan on the sofa. "You okay?"

"Yes," Jordan said, opening her eyes and forcing aside the memories. She scanned Kip's face, searching for clues as to how she was doing. Kip was so very good at hiding what troubled her. The anxious lines in her forehead were gone and a bright light leapt in her eyes. Jordan took her hand, her heart easing to Kip's happiness. "Well? Tell me."

A huge grin split Kip's face. "It's a boy. Seven pounds, eight ounces, healthy and hearty. Man, he's got a lot of hair, the same color as Savannah's. Golden and thick."

"Did you get the video?"

Kip made a face. "I did, but boy did he look a mess right at the beginning."

Jordan laughed. "Honey, you're not supposed to take unflattering pictures during the delivery. You're supposed to wait until they get them cleaned up a little bit. I hope you got one of those."

"Yup, all pink and pretty in his delivery blanket and Savannah holding him. They both looked gorgeous."

Jordan kissed her cheek. "I am so happy for everyone. Does his father know?"

"I just texted him a picture. He's in the air right now, so he probably won't get it till he lands. But everything's good."

"How do you feel?"

"Like I just ran a marathon." Kip slid her arm around Jordan's shoulders and pulled her close. "Thanks for being here. It really made a difference during the scary parts."

"I wanted to be here. Kind of like when you were fussing over the seedlings. If it's important to you, then it is to me too."

Kip frowned. "We really ought to head over to the garden. Make sure everything's okay there."

"Maybe you should stay here for a little while. I'll go. You don't need to."

"No way. I'm not backing out now." Kip squeezed her shoulders before moving away. "Let me go talk to the nurses and make sure everything is good with Savannah. They'll have my number and can call me if they need me. Mark should be here around midnight."

"If you're sure."

"I don't plan on letting you out of my sight tonight."

Despite her fatigue and worry, Jordan's spirits soared. She wasn't ready to say good-bye to Kip, either. Even for a few hours.

❖

"What do you think?" Kip said as they walked through the garden beds. They'd turned on the floods and Jordan had a flashlight to get a better look at the young seedlings.

"We've got some frost injury to some of the smaller shoots, but I don't think we're going to lose many, if any at all."

"Ha." Kip shoved her hands in her pockets. "When will we know? Are they gonna be stunted or something?"

"The drop in temperatures might slow down their growth for a while, but it's early, and if we keep the agricultural fabric on them during the day to push the temperatures up, they'll likely catch up. We were pushing things to begin with trying to get an early harvest."

"Yeah, Mr. Liu and his buddies are pretty anxious for that."

Jordan laughed. "Really. They seem to think I can just wave my hand and magically produce vegetables."

Kip stopped, snaked an arm around Jordan's waist, and pulled her close. Kissing her neck, she whispered against her ear, "Well, I think you can do magic with those hands. Although I had something in mind other than making tomatoes grow big."

Laughing, Jordan wrapped her arms around Kip's neck and leaned back to look into her face. "Really? You're not done yet?"

Kip looked confused. "What? That was hours ago. Practically twelve of them."

"Oh, I see. Rapid recovery."

"Hey, you're the one who's in her prime. I'm just trying to keep up."
Jordan leaned in and nipped at Kip's mouth. The playful kiss got away from her in an instant, and she had to have more. She had to taste her, feel her, absorb all that was wonderful and intoxicating about Kip. Which was just about everything. Seconds, minutes passed and she forgot everything except sating the hunger that crashed through her. When she drew back for breath, her heart thundered beneath her breast and her toes curled in her boots. "We need to leave."

Kip's chest heaved. "Yeah, we do."

"You've got some ground to make up."

Kip grinned. "Ready when you are."

"Oh," Jordan said softly, raking her hands through Kip's hair. "I'm ready."

They grabbed a cab on the street and were back at Jordan's in fifteen minutes.

"Are you hungry?" Jordan said as she let them into the apartment. "I've got some pizza I froze just last week."

"Yes, but later for the pizza." Kip dragged her toward the bathroom. "I don't care that the shower's small. I'm all for a little skin on skin right about now."

"In a hurry?"

"Yes." Kip slammed the door behind them. "If Savannah hadn't called, I'd have kept you in bed until tomorrow." She edged Jordan back against the door. "I'm never going to get enough of you."

Jordan's thighs trembled at the heavy look in Kip's eyes. "Why don't you try?"

"Oh yeah, I will." Kip yanked her T-shirt off over her head and shoved her jeans down. Before Jordan could follow suit, Kip was unbuttoning her shirt, kissing her throat and the inner curve of her breasts while her hands roamed lower, tugging Jordan's shirt loose to claim the warm skin of her stomach.

"Pants," Kip muttered against Jordan's breast before pulling Jordan's nipple into her mouth.

Jordan sagged. If the door hadn't stopped her momentum, she'd have slid to the floor. Never. Never had she been wanted this way. "Kip, stop that before I fall."

"Not gonna happen." Kip dropped to her knees and kissed Jordan's stomach. Waiting. Waiting so long. Waiting forever for this woman, this place, this rightness of being. The shell around her shattered and heat flooded the cold dark hallways of her soul. "I need you."

"Take." Jordan unzipped her trousers, and Kip grabbed the waistband and yanked them down. Then Kip was kissing lower, forcing Jordan's legs apart with her shoulders. Kip's mouth closed over her, and Jordan reeled, reaching out blindly for the edge of the vanity. Her head banged back against the door, and she closed her eyes, every ounce of blood pooling in the pit of her stomach, throbbing and aching. She gripped the back of Kip's head with her free hand, guiding her mouth exactly where she needed her.

"I don't think…" Her words were lost as her body took over. She rocked against Kip's mouth, desperate for the heat and the slick torture of her tongue. Lights danced beneath her closed lids. Her breath sobbed out, foreign and wild sounding.

Kip's arms came around her hips, holding her as she plunged and licked and sucked.

"Don't let go," Jordan gasped. Her legs gave way, and she lost touch with everything but the swirling explosion of pleasure. Before the last tremor ebbed, Kip surged to her feet, pinning Jordan against the door with the weight of her body, her gasps ragged and raw. Her back was slick with sweat, her skin hot under Jordan's hands. Jordan stroked her, licked her throat, raked her teeth along the edge of her jaw. When Kip growled approval, a thrill of power shot through her. Jordan laughed unsteadily. "Not bad. Not bad at all."

Kip laughed and kissed her throat. "You are the sexiest woman in the universe."

"Thank you."

"You're welcome."

Jordan draped her arms weakly over Kip's shoulders. "You seem to know exactly what I need."

"You're everything I need," Kip murmured, her breasts pressed to Jordan's, her legs straddling Jordan's.

Jordan rocked into the satin heat between Kip's thighs. "I know one thing you need right now."

Kip shuddered. "You have no idea."

"Oh, I think I do." Jordan clasped Kip's hips and thrust harder. "Shower first? Can you wait?"

"It depends." Kip kissed her. "Are you gonna make it worth my while?"

Jordan laughed. "Oh, you can count on it."

CHAPTER TWENTY-FIVE

Kip woke out of habit at three thirty in the morning. She'd gotten used to being up early to meet Jordan at the garden. Without even knowing it, her life had settled into a pattern that was more natural than anything she'd ever done. Working with Jordan to build the outreach program, toiling in the soil, banging together projects that ran the gamut from the entire greenhouse to a compost bin, were as satisfying as pursuing a hot new idea or chasing an elusive design. Different, but in so many ways the same. Making a vision real was what design was all about. The process was what satisfied her, as much as the product. And the bonus at the end of the day was she'd spent hours with a woman who by turns fascinated, enticed, and surprised her. Jordan was the difference.

Kip turned onto her side and wrapped an arm around Jordan's waist. The change, so gradual she'd only noticed just how titanic when she'd realized she didn't miss a single thing about her previous routine—her previous *life*, was all about Jordan. Jordan was the center of her pleasure, the axis around which Kip's world revolved. She'd never imagined that's what love was like—a solar system of stars and magic, with the sun the smile in a woman's eyes. She nuzzled the warmth at the back of Jordan's neck, inhaled her scent, melded her naked skin to Jordan's. This was what she'd been searching for. This singular touch that reached deeper than flesh, this unique connection to a soul that called to hers as none other. She kissed the triangle between Jordan's neck and shoulder. She recognized these feelings in every corner of her being. This was love.

"Are you trying to wake me up?" Jordan murmured sleepily and pushed her butt into the curve of Kip's hips.

"Only sorta," Kip whispered. "Mostly I was just enjoying you."

Jordan chuckled. "Is that what you're calling it now." She covered Kip's hand where it cupped her breast. "I sort of thought you were trying to seduce me, myself."

"Maybe some of that too." Kip smiled against Jordan's skin and kissed the inner edge of her shoulder blade. She loved every single angle, line, and curve of her body from the satiny soft skin, the work-hardened muscles, and the subtle lift of her breasts to the invitation of her gently surging hips. Her stomach tightened with want and she caressed the faint swell of Jordan's abdomen, feathering her fingers lower.

Jordan clamped down on her hand, stopping her explorations.

Kip grumbled, "Hey."

Jordan half turned and kissed Kip. "Hey, yourself. We have work to do."

"I was getting to that."

Laughing, Jordan tugged Kip's fingers back up her belly and molded them to her breast, holding them there with her hand clasping Kip's. "This is not exactly the *work* I had in mind."

Kip brushed her thumb over Jordan's nipple and Jordan moaned. "You sure about that?"

"All right, I could be convinced, but"—Jordan shifted away— "I'm not going to be. Later for you."

Kip propped her head on her elbow. "Promise?"

The room was still dark, but enough light filtered in from the never-sleeping city for Kip to see the amusement dance in Jordan's eyes. Something else danced there too, a kindred fire to her own. Her belly warmed, knowing she was desired. Patience had never been her long suit, and she'd never wanted a woman the way she wanted Jordan. Waiting, she was discovering, was a pleasant torture all its own when the woman she was waiting for was Jordan.

"I don't have to promise." Jordan leaned closer and kissed her, slow and deep. "You already know, don't you? That I want you? And I'll be looking forward to it? Because if you don't, I'm doing something wrong."

"Believe me," Kip whispered, "you're doing everything right."

"You're sure?" Jordan stroked Kip's cheek.

"Positive." Kip didn't doubt Jordan's desire. She read it in her eyes, in every touch of her hands, in the subtle glimpses she could feel on her skin throughout the day. Being wanted was a heady pleasure and one she believed was about her and not her name or her position. But being wanted wasn't enough. For the first time, she wanted far more than that, and when she'd worked off her community debt and settled her obligations to the feds, she would make her intentions known. For now, she was just going to be happy she'd gotten so damn lucky.

Sighing, Kip said, "Well, we should probably get going, if we're going to get our chores done."

"Our chores. I haven't heard that in a good many years." Jordan laughed and caressed Kip's back. "You probably would've been a good farmer. Could've kept the tractor running."

Kip pulled her close and took what she needed to make it through the day, tasting her, absorbing her heat, memorizing the lines of her body. When Jordan trembled in her arms, she gently drew back. "I can keep a lot more than the tractor running."

Jordan nuzzled Kip's breast. "So I see."

"Okay. Now we really need to get up." Kip sat up on the side of the bed and surveyed the pile of clothes on the floor. "And I am not wearing those for the third day in a row."

"Why don't you run home before you come by the garden. We can wait an hour to get started."

Kip ran a hand through her hair. "You sure?"

Jordan sat up beside her, tossing the sheet aside. "Yes, of course. Go. Get a shower, check your mail, grab clean clothes. We'll plan on heading out at five thirty."

Kip pulled on her rumpled clothes and kissed Jordan good-bye. "I'll make it sooner if I can. I miss you already."

Jordan thrust her hands into Kip's hair and pulled her head down for a long, hard kiss. "Remember that while you're gone."

"Oh yeah," Kip muttered, head reeling. "I will."

❖

Kip's apartment seemed sterile and soulless when she walked in, shedding her clothes on the way to the bedroom. She liked the place, on the surface. She'd chosen the colors and the furniture and the decor, but the place felt like what it was—a place to sleep and eat and stop over when she wasn't working. Nothing about it spelled home, not the way Jordan's place had from the second she'd walked in. Because Jordan lived in that place, just as she lived in the garden, just as her spirit touched everything around her. And now she lived in Kip's heart, rooted deep and bright.

She showered quickly, and grabbed jeans and T-shirt from her dresser. As she sat down on the side of the bed to pull on socks and boots, her cell rang. She smiled to herself. Jordan must be missing her too. She grabbed the cell and frowned when she saw the number.

"Dad?"

"Catherine." Her father sounded awake and businesslike.

"What's wrong?" She checked the time. A minute after five a.m. Her father kept early hours, but he never called her at this time of day, even for business. His admin made those calls.

"I'm afraid there's a problem with your brother."

Kip's chest tightened. "What do you mean?"

Randy hadn't been very communicative, even after his period of imposed no outside contact had been over. He'd emailed a couple times, taken one of her calls, and hadn't had much to say. His replies to her questions about the rehab program had been brief and vague, and she'd chalked the underlying discomfort and evasiveness in his conversation to embarrassment over the incident that had landed him in there and earned her a stint of community service. Not that she'd minded how that had played out. She'd met Jordan, after all. Still, maybe she should have paid a little more attention to what he'd been saying or, rather, not saying. Most of the time when she tried to reach him, he'd been in session or unavailable. The intermittent progress reports from her father had said he was doing fine, and she'd taken that at face value, too caught up with Jordan and her own exciting revelations. "Has he had some kind of setback?"

"Your brother signed himself out of the center just before midnight last night."

Kip's stomach dropped. "Where is he?"

"That's something quite a few people would like to know. I don't suppose you've heard from him?"

"No. What about the latest girlfriend—Lindsay?" She did some quick mental calculations. Randy was over halfway through his three-month program—longer than he'd made it the first two times. Knowing him, he'd just gotten bored and decided he'd done penance enough for his latest folly. "He's either going to contact her or one of his other exes."

"I have our security people checking with her now and any of the others we know of." His voice telegraphed his distaste for Randy's frequent liaisons, another source of recurrent strife between the two. "But if he contacts anyone, I would assume it would be you. If he continues true to form, and I see no reason that he wouldn't."

"What are you talking about?"

"You've always been his protector. If he's in trouble, he'll expect you to continue to take care of his problems."

Kip bit back the automatic retort that maybe if her father had been a little more protective, she wouldn't have had to be, but that wasn't altogether fair. She had always been Randy's shield, even before the accident, and that had only become more pronounced after they were left on their own, or so they'd felt. In grade school she'd intervened on his behalf when he'd gotten involved in schoolyard skirmishes, and later, in high school, she'd smoothed over the hurt feelings of the girls he'd played and unceremoniously dumped. By the time they'd become adults, helping him out with his run-ins with the law had just seemed natural. She couldn't argue that her father was wrong now. "I haven't heard from him. His attendance was voluntary, right? So he hasn't actually broken any rules by leaving."

"Technically, yes, although he and I did have an agreement, not that that would matter to him. There's another problem, however."

"Don't tell me he stole a car."

"Fortunately, no," her father said, "but there may be a possibility that he is party to the theft of a number of drugs from the facility pharmacy."

Kip jerked. "What? How could he possibly have done that?"

"We're not entirely sure he's involved, but the evidence is suggestive."

"What evidence?" Kip closed her eyes. *Oh, Randy. No. Don't let this be true. You can't be that stupid, you just can't.*

"One of the night med techs did not show up for their shift. And coincidentally, although the authorities obviously do not think it's a coincidence, a number of narcotics and other drugs are missing."

"Why do they suspect Randy? Like you said, it could be a coincidence."

"The med tech is an attractive twenty-five-year-old woman who worked in the wing where he resided, and at least several residents said they were close." He made the word *close* sound faintly obscene.

Kip refused to keep grasping at straws. Randy had screwed up and was headed for very big trouble. The time for finger pointing and recriminations would come later, and she'd own up to her part in enabling him all these years, but right now they had to find him before he compounded the problems. "What do you want me to do?"

"Call him. Let him know that you're worried about him, and help us find him."

"Don't you think your security guys can do that a lot better than me? I'm no detective."

"They are searching, as are, unfortunately, the authorities. But there's every possibility he will contact you first."

"All right. I'll try to reach him."

"If you're here when he contacts you, we can put our people on damage control and we might be able to…circumvent…official channels."

"Like keeping him out of jail? Again." Kip sighed. "I'll come over there."

"I think that would be best." He hesitated. "Thank you."

Kip disconnected and sat on the side of the bed, the phone cradled between her palms, staring at the blank screen. If the authorities were looking for Randy, they were going to interview her sooner or later too. She couldn't go to the garden now. The last thing Jordan or Ty needed was more official attention on them. She pushed Jordan's number.

"Hey," Jordan said, "running late?"

"I'm not going to be able to make it this morning."

"All right," Jordan said, a cautious note in her voice. "Are you all right?"

"I…" Kip rubbed her eyes. *No, no, I'm not all right at all. I don't know what I should do anymore. I don't even know what I want to do. But I know one thing—I don't want you or anyone you care about in danger.* "I'm okay, but there's a problem with my brother. I need to get it straightened out and I don't know how long it's going to take."

"Is there anything I can do?" Jordan asked.

"No, I'm really sorry about this. But I think it's better if I don't come around until this is resolved."

Jordan was silent for a long moment. "Are you trying to tell me that I'm not going to see you for a while?"

"I hope it's not for very long. I just need to find out what's going on and get this mess straightened out."

"And that's something I can't help you with?"

"I'm not going to drag my problems to your door. If anyone comes around asking questions, it's best you don't know anything at all. Including where I am."

"Are you in danger?"

"I don't think so." Kip hesitated. "I'm not sure how this will affect my community service obligation."

"Kip," Jordan said slowly, "I thought we were more to each other than this."

"We are," Kip said. "I just…I need you to trust me on this."

"I'll try," Jordan said, "but I can't be someone who stands by and watches you be hurt or hurt yourself. You have to know that."

"I'm really sorry. More than you know."

"Yes," Jordan said quietly. "So am I."

"I'll call you," Kip said softly.

The silence when Jordan hung up was the loneliest sound she'd ever heard.

CHAPTER TWENTY-SIX

Jordan sat in the corner of her sofa, arms wrapped around her drawn-up knees, watching steam waft from the teacup on the coffee table in front of her, replaying the conversation with Kip over and over again. She could make sense of all the words, but she was still struggling with the message beneath them. Kip had a family problem, and she understood family problems as well as—she gave a mental grimace—*better* than almost anyone. Kip was needed at home, and she understood that too. She'd never try to stand in the way of anyone taking care of family. All of that was obvious from what Kip had told her. But what wasn't obvious, and what she was forced to put together from murky clues and reluctant half explanations, was exactly why Kip had to keep all of these things a secret, and why whatever obligations calling her home meant she had to deal with all those things alone.

Of course, everyone had private battles. She got that too. But when people loved each other, they supported each other in their struggles, even if all they could do was offer comfort and warmth in the dark. Kip hadn't even let her close enough to do that. She'd shut her out, the same way her father had shut her and her mother out, while he fought his demons alone and lost. Kip was not her father, she knew that too, but that didn't stop the hurt or the anger or the fear. If they'd been friends, *just* friends, she might've understood Kip's silence, but they were more than that. At least she'd thought so, had begun to let herself believe so. The words hadn't been spoken, but their actions had, more than mere words ever could, at least for her. Maybe she'd misinterpreted Kip's feelings, and it surely wouldn't be the first time she'd missed clues. Maybe her own desires had blinded her to how Kip really felt about what they'd shared. Maybe she'd only heard in her head what she'd wanted to hear in her heart.

She didn't know anything, and her questions had no answers. She finally took the cooling tea into the kitchen and dumped it down the sink, collected her keys and her wallet, and headed out as she did every morning to her comforting routine. This morning, the routine was anything but a comfort. Kip was not there waiting for her, exclaiming over the morning's selection of pastries; would not be a few feet away in the truck cab, outlining plans for a new irrigation system or a solar panel for the greenhouse; would not be anywhere in her day, catching her off guard with a smile or a long, appraising glance that set her heart racing. Kip might never return at all.

Driving through the morning stops alone, with the silence in the cab growing ever more dark, left her feeling empty and abandoned. Beneath the sadness, anger simmered. She did not deserve to be left out in the cold like this, and she really had no one to blame but herself. She'd risked her heart and now she was paying for it.

After the tenth time she'd checked her phone, she zipped it into the inside pocket of her coat where she couldn't reach for it without thinking. She was behaving like a jilted teenager, pining over a girl who didn't return her feelings in the same way. Those irrational feelings had no part in her life today, and she ought to have known better than to even open the door to the possibility. She wasn't being fair to Kip, and beneath all the tangled emotions, she knew it. Kip wasn't behaving any way other than the way she'd always behaved—she kept her problems private and didn't share her pain with anyone. They might have gotten closer, close enough to share a bed, and that was what she needed to remember. Sex was safe, and in this case, where her relationship with Kip began and ended. She'd let herself forget that and had broken her own rule. She'd promised herself after her father died and her mother followed soon after, a broken woman with a broken heart and broken dreams, she'd never let herself be in a position where someone else could push her aside, leave her out of the most important decisions in their life, and abandon her. Better that she relearned that lesson now before it was too late.

When her phone rang inside the pocket of her jacket, she dashed to the fence post where she'd hung it, fumbled to find the zipper, yanked it down, and jerked out the cell. "Kip?"

"Jordan?" Ty asked, surprise and concern in her voice. "You okay?"

Heart sinking, Jordan leaned back against the post, her energy draining into the ground like rainwater down a gully. "Yeah, sorry. How are you?"

"Bored to death. I really miss you."

"I miss you too." Jordan dragged a hand through her hair. "Are the kids okay?"

"They're fine. They're going to school just like always, and they like staying…here."

"I'm glad."

"How is everything there?"

Jordan glanced over the quiet garden, weak sunlight coaxing the seedlings to reach for the sky. "Everything pretty much survived intact. We'll have to replant a few of the tomatoes, but overall, we got lucky. Thank goodness we hadn't rushed the peppers in too." The hulking heaters stood silent sentry, their faces blank eyed and cold. She supposed someone from Kip's company would come and pick them up. No one had contacted her about them.

"Is Kip still there helping?"

Jordan blew out a breath. "No. Something came up."

"You're there all by yourself? With all that has to be done—that's crazy."

Jordan smiled grimly. "It's okay. I don't have anything else to do."

"You never do, but that still doesn't mean you can manage everything. I'm going to come back to work."

"No," Jordan said quickly. "Not for a little while."

Ty paused. "Why? What's going on?"

"Nothing. Well, something, but I'm not sure what. Kip has some kind of family situation and isn't going to be here for a while."

"What's a while?"

Jordan closed her eyes. "I don't know that either. I don't know what the situation is or what she needs to do or why she's not coming here." She shook her head. "No, that's not entirely accurate. She's not coming here because she thinks that might bring unwanted attention to you and me."

"She might be right," Ty said gently. "You know there's something she's not telling you about why she was here in the first place. That woman is no criminal."

"I know." Worry warred with frustration and anger. "If I knew more of what was happening, I'd be able to judge better. But I don't know a damn thing."

"I'm really sorry."

"Yes. So am I."

"It sounds like she's trying to protect you," Ty said tentatively.

"I don't need to be protected," Jordan snapped.

"I know that, and I bet Kip does too, but some people are just made that way. It takes a lot of practice to undo the instinct to protect someone you care about."

"Oh, I know, but damn it, Ty, if she cared about me she'd let me help!"

"I'd say it's pretty obvious she cares about you."

"If she cared about *me*, the person I am, she wouldn't just walk away like this. Obviously, she doesn't know me at all."

"Maybe you're being a little hard on both of you," Ty said. "Why don't you wait to see what she says about it all."

"It's not like I have much choice about waiting." Jordan's stomach clenched. "Kip has already made the choice for both of us."

"Let me know when I can come back," Ty said.

"I'll contact you as soon as things settle down. I don't want you getting caught up in the middle of something when we have no idea what's going on."

"All right. But you call me if you need me."

"I will." Jordan drew a breath, forced the cloud of fear and anger from her mind. "Just take care of yourself and your family."

"Okay. Talk soon," Ty said.

When Jordan disconnected, she vowed to set her loneliness and anxiety aside until she knew what she was dealing with. Ty was right about needing to wait until Kip explained. No matter what else happened, she knew Kip would not just disappear without a good-bye. She worked through lunch and was making good progress on transplanting some of the greens into larger beds when two men came through the gate. She straightened and frowned. The men in black were back. Wonderful.

"Help you?" she called.

The smaller one, the one who had climbed into the back of the SUV with Kip when they'd taken her away, was in the lead. He smiled as if happy to see her again. Yeah, right.

"Ms. Rice," he said collegially. "We're looking for Ms. Kensington."

"Why is that?"

He smiled, his lips pressed together in a thin line that looked anything but friendly. "Just some follow-up questions we need to ask."

"I'm sorry, but she's not here. I don't expect her back anytime soon."

"Have you had any contact from anyone else in the Kensington family?"

Jordan couldn't help but look surprised. Kip had been right about keeping the details from her. She really had no idea what the hell was going on. "No, why would I?"

He raised a shoulder as if the answer should be obvious. "Anyone looking for her is likely to stop by here."

"Well, no one has. Sorry. I can't help you out there."

He smiled again, his eyes growing hard and threatening. "You'll be sure to call us if you do have any visitors looking for her."

"It might help if you were a little more specific."

He didn't even bother trying to smile this time. "We're specifically interested in her brother, Randolph."

"Why? What has he done?"

"Oh, nothing that we're aware of." He watched her as if expecting her to help him out. "We're just interested in talking with him."

"Yes, you seem to do a lot of that."

He laughed, an edge of darkness cutting the sound short. "We find it more productive to start out that way."

She didn't really want to think about what steps came after discussion. "You can leave your number. If anyone comes here looking for Kip, I'll pass it along to them. I'm not a message center."

"No, but you are close to Ms. Kensington, aren't you?"

Heat flared in Jordan's throat and she lifted her chin. "We're friends."

"Well then, I'm sure you want your friend to avoid any appearances of compromise. Ask her to call us."

"I'd think you'd be able to find her."

"Oh, we know where she is."

They turned without saying good-bye and left the garden gate ajar behind them. Jordan followed, closing and latching it. What did they think Kip had done to warrant such attention? But she didn't know, because Kip hadn't told her.

❖

Kip paced the expansive gardens behind her father's estate, walking down toward the sound, the wind buffeting her through her light windbreaker and jeans. The wet air left her skin cold and clammy in its wake. The last fifteen hours had been endless. Private security in black SUVs pulled in and out of the drive around the clock, grim-faced men and women rushing into her father's study. No calls from Randy. Her father didn't need her advice or her company. She was powerless and useless on top of that, and all she could think about was Jordan. She missed her like a part of her was absent. The hole inside her wept and bled. She stood with her back to the house, her hands in her pockets, staring out at whitecapped slashing seas. A storm was coming. *Just don't let it be snow.* The gardens couldn't tolerate a late snow, not after what they'd gone through already. Her fingers itched to grab her phone and call Jordan just to hear her voice. She would've been happy to hear her breathe.

God, she missed her. Jordan had sounded hurt and angry, and that scared her. She didn't want to put Jordan in the middle of this manhunt, especially when the feds were likely to get involved. They had a way of digging into everyone's lives for whatever leverage they could find, and Jordan didn't need that. Ty for sure didn't. No. She had to stay away from Jordan until she got Randy home, but the thought of losing Jordan gutted her.

She hunched her shoulders against the wind and ignored the tears leaking from the corners of her eyes. Just the wind. When her phone rang, she glanced at the readout, her heart sinking when she saw it was a private caller, not Jordan.

"Kensington."

"Hey, sis. What you doing?"

For an instant, rage warred with relief, leaving her mute. She took in a ragged breath. "Where are you?"

"Well, that's kind of a problem. I'm not exactly sure. I slept most of the way to wherever I am. I smoked a little weed that hit me a lot harder than I expected. Lost my tolerance, I guess."

Kip gritted her teeth. "What else have you done?"

"Not much. Southern Comfort and some coke. Forgot how much I liked that stuff."

"You need to come home."

"I don't really think that's a good idea right now."

"Randy, the police are looking for you. Are you with the girl from the center? The pharmacy tech?"

"Lucy? Yeah, Lucy. Not anymore. She kinda took off early this morning. So I don't have any wheels or any money, and I'm running out of essentials."

Meaning drugs and alcohol. "I'll come and get you. Where are you?"

Randy laughed. "I think I'm somewhere in the Catskills."

Kip squeezed her eyes closed. "Check the map app on your phone. It'll tell you where you are and text me the screen shot. It'll take me a couple hours to get there."

"How's the old man?"

"Like he always is."

"How much trouble am I in?"

"I don't know, Randy. What the hell have you done?" She looked over her shoulder just to be sure she was still alone. Her phone wasn't tapped, as near she could tell, but she didn't want to have this conversation where anyone could use what Randy was about to say against him. That's why they had lawyers, and he at least deserved the degree of protection the law said he was entitled to.

"I don't really know."

"Well, you need to figure it out, because one way or the other, you're going to have to talk to the police when we get back."

"I was kinda hoping you could take care of that."

"I'm not a fucking magician," Kip said wearily. "This time you'll have to do the explaining yourself."

"You'll be there, right?" His voice suddenly seemed smaller and younger.

Kip flashed back to all the times he'd come running to her for comfort and help, the lost little boy who'd never grown up. She'd always been his hero. "Your text just came through. Don't go anywhere. I've got the address. I'll be there as soon as I can."

"Thanks, sis." His laughter echoed hollowly. "I always knew I could count on you."

"Right." Randy rang off and Kip was left with the phone in her hand, staring at the angry sea, filled with frustration and regret.

CHAPTER TWENTY-SEVEN

Randy's hidey-hole turned out to be a roadside motel off the interstate an hour out of New York City and twenty minutes from the rehab center. Randy and the girl hadn't run very far before they'd stopped to celebrate. Kip pulled into a long, narrow, potholed lot ringed with scraggy pines a little after midnight and sat with the engine idling, scanning the generic twenty-unit, single-story building that looked like any of the thousands of others she'd passed in her life. A battered pickup truck, a mud-splattered Volvo station wagon with a bumper sticker featuring a school soccer team, and a low-end sedan were the only vehicles parked in front of the faceless doors. Most units were dark. Light spilled out of a grimy plate-glass window in the far end unit where a flickering red neon sign spelled out the word *Office*. She didn't see anything that suggested the place was being watched and finally parked in the corner of the lot beneath a wooden utility pole with a burned-out bulb that cast a small circle of shadow. She texted Randy. *What unit are you in?*

When he didn't answer her text after two minutes, she called his number. Her call went to voice mail. Hell. He'd either let his phone battery run down or he was sleeping. Or stoned. She wasn't going to draw attention to them by asking at the office if a young woman or couple had recently checked in. She kept calling and he finally answered, his voice hoarse and his words slurred.

"Yeah?"

"Randy, it's me. What unit are you in?"

"Uh. I don't know. I haven't been outside."

Right. They'd have to do this the hard way. "Is there a light on in your room?"

"The TV. No lights."

"Okay, go turn on the closest light and I'll tell you if I can see it." She watched the small windows beside the doors for any flicker of illumination.

"Yeah, okay," Randy muttered. "I just did it."

"Okay, I've got you. Number twelve. I'll be there in a second. Be ready to go."

"Yeah. Thanks."

"Don't thank me yet," she muttered, but he'd already gone.

He answered the door wearing jeans a size too large and a rumpled T-shirt with the logo of some band she didn't recognize. The ill-fitting clothes looked like they'd been slept in more than one night, which they undoubtedly had. His hair was tousled, his face creased, and in the faint yellow light from the bedside table lamp, his hazy eyes barely focused.

"Do you have your stuff?" Kip didn't try to hide her impatience or her disappointment. He'd squandered whatever benefit he'd gained from rehab—worse than wasted his time and everyone else's since he'd managed to get tangled up with a staff member in who knew what kind of trouble. Her anger was fueled by heartsick disillusionment and bone-deep fear of what lay ahead for him. This time she could not, would not, rescue him. She had come to get him to be sure he was delivered safely to the authorities. She didn't trust him to go on his own and wasn't sure he'd go with anyone else. The last thing she wanted was for him to run and make matters worse, or get himself hurt in the process.

"I didn't exactly have luggage with me," Randy scoffed. "And I dumped the prison uniform as soon as I was out of there." He looked down at himself. "Lucy brought me the clothes."

Kip examined his bare feet. "Did she bring you shoes?"

He grinned, and for an instant an image of the bright, winning little boy he'd once been shone through. "I had them. They're around here someplace." He ran his hand through his hair like she'd seen him do countless mornings when she'd go in to wake him up for school. He turned in a slow circle and grunted. "There they are."

"Grab them and…is that your backpack?"

Looking confused, he followed her gaze to the army green bag hidden half under the lopsided bureau and shrugged. "Yeah."

"Grab it and let's go, then."

"Okay. Yeah. I guess we have to go home, huh?" His voice held a hopeful note.

"Randy, where else would we go? You have to get this mess straightened out, and you have to get yourself straightened out. It's on you this time."

"I just wanted out of there," he said.

"And you couldn't have waited another, what, five weeks to complete the program? You had to escape in the middle of the night like a jailbreak?"

"Hey, I did everything they wanted me to do. I was a good boy. But I'd had enough talking." He kicked into the unlaced sneakers. "You have no idea how boring that place was."

"That's the problem, Randy. You're not a boy anymore." Shaking her head, she watched her brother slowly gather his scant belongings. He wasn't a boy anymore, and they both had to accept that. She couldn't keep standing between him and trouble. She loved him, but she wasn't helping him.

She texted her father while she leaned against the closed door. *I have Randy. We're going to the nearest police station.*

She'd just reached the car when her phone vibrated.

Bring him home. Attorneys will handle it from here.

"So what now?" Randy asked as he dropped into the front seat.

"We're going home." Kip slid behind the wheel and tucked her phone away. She backed up and turned toward the highway. "Then you're going to talk to—"

A police cruiser, lights flashing, pulled into the parking lot, blocking the exit. Ten seconds later a second and then a third patrol car pulled up.

"Fuck," Kip whispered. A cold hand clamped around her heart and squeezed so tightly she almost couldn't breathe. She slammed on the brakes and sat blinking into the bright lights shining through the windshield. She slipped her phone out and quickly replied to her father's last text. *Staties just stopped us.*

Randy jolted upright beside her. "What the fuck?"

"Police. Just stay where you are, don't say anything."

"Damn Lucy," Randy snarled.

Kip cut him a look. "What are you talking about?"

"If she hadn't left me here with no wheels, I'd be safe in the city by now."

Kip didn't bother pointing out if Randy hadn't left the rehab center with Lucy, he wouldn't be in this situation at all. And if these officers were here for Randy, she would bet Lucy had done more than walk out on him and leave him stranded. She'd probably been picked up herself and used him as a bargaining chip. "Just keep quiet and do as they say."

Two officers got out of the closest vehicle, their black forms silhouetted against the blinding lights in a gut-churning déjà vu of her first arrest. Kip broke out into a clammy sweat. She rolled down her window before the officer reached her, her wallet already in her hand.

"License and registration, please." The male state trooper's face was obscured in shadow, a blank void of power and intimidation.

Kip handed the items out the window and returned both hands to the steering wheel, staring straight ahead. Another officer walked around to Randy's side of the car, stopping a few feet back from his door. She tapped on Randy's window, calling for him to step out of the vehicle.

"Would you step out of the vehicle, please," the officer said after a moment.

"Yes." Kip swallowed. "My brother and I were on our way to the police station. We're happy to cooperate."

"Please just step out of the car," the officer repeated.

"Yes, sir. Randy, get out of the car."

"What? Why? They can't just—"

"Just do it."

Kip stood next to the open driver's side door while Randy fumbled with his door and finally exited. He slouched against the side of the vehicle as the second officer ordered, "Put your hands on top of the car."

Kip watched, her pulse pounding in her throat. Randy didn't move.

"Randy," Kip said sharply, "do what the officer says right now."

He looked over the top of the vehicle at her, his eyes fear filled, but he put his hands where he was told. Kip gritted her teeth while the officer beside her shone his Maglite around inside the vehicle. "What's in the backpack?"

Kip pictured the bag Randy had tossed at his feet when they'd gotten in the car. "Clothes."

He continued to stare. "That doesn't look like clothes to me."

Before she could reply, he grasped her wrist and snapped a cuff onto it. Across the top of the car she saw the other officer doing the same with Randy. The eerie tableau of the last time she and Randy had been together replayed as she stumbled numbly toward the nearest cruiser, a foreign hand pushing between her shoulder blades, a palm on the back of her neck directing her into the backseat. She sank down in the dark and closed her eyes, the red glow from the light bars the perfect backdrop to the familiar nightmare.

The county jail was unwelcomingly similar to the one in Manhattan, although cleaner and less populated in the middle of the night. The officers were no less formal and no more polite, but so far they'd skipped the booking procedure and left Kip in a holding cell. She'd been allowed to call her father, but she hadn't seen Randy and no one would tell her where he was.

"Don't say anything," her father said. "They have no grounds to hold you."

"All right." She knew better than to ask him for information while she was in custody and might still be questioned. The less she knew right now, the better, but being helpless was a suffocating cloud choking her every breath. She had to trust he would send an attorney to sort things out. All she could do was wait.

Kip sat up on the side of the narrow cot, with its familiar coarse cotton sheet and thin wool blanket, and stared at the bars. She had fervently prayed never to be locked into another small, dank, soulless room again, and here she was. Alone, and though she knew it wasn't true, abandoned. She couldn't even tell if she was under arrest. Occasionally a low murmur of voices filtered down the hall, presumably from other cells, but mostly it was quiet. Sweat trickled down the back of her neck even though the cell was cool.

How long this time? Another night, half a day? Time lost all meaning when all she could hear was the beating of her own heart and the echoes of despair. She'd told the first officer she had been taking her brother to the authorities, but she had no idea if he'd cared or mentioned it to anyone. How had the police even known they were there? And why was she in a cell? Because she'd been with Randy, who she wasn't even sure had committed a crime? Signing himself out of the rehab center was stupid, but not criminal. She remembered the green knapsack she hadn't even thought to check, and her stomach plummeted. If Randy had been carrying the missing drugs, they were both in trouble.

Two hours later, a female officer in a tan trooper's uniform with a large ring of jangling keys opened her cell door.

"Come with me," the officer said. "You can collect your things."

Kip stared. "I can leave?"

"You're being released."

"What about Randy? Randolph Kensington, my brother?"

The trooper shook her head. "I don't know anything about him." She gave Kip a long look. "Just be glad you're getting out."

Kip didn't argue. All she wanted was out of that cell, out of that corridor, out of the building with its nightmares lurking in every corner. She didn't see anyone when she signed the forms and collected her belongings. They kept her keys because her vehicle had been impounded. If their father's attorney was around somewhere, he was probably with Randy. That was fine with her. She'd had enough of everyone related to the legal profession. She probably ought to call her father, but no matter what was happening right now, she couldn't change it. She'd done the best she could for her brother. She'd tried, all her life.

Fifteen minutes later she was standing outside an hour before dawn with nowhere to go and no way to get there.

CHAPTER TWENTY-EIGHT

Jordan was already awake when the phone rang. She hadn't slept much, her dreams fragmented and anxious. Every time she twisted awake, she thought about Kip, thought about calling her, and knew instinctively she shouldn't. Kip was trying to protect her, trying to do the right thing, and as much as she disagreed with how Kip was going about it, she couldn't stay angry.

On the second ring, she rolled over and grabbed the phone. Relief, like a long-awaited kiss, rolled through her. Finally, she saw the readout she needed to see. "Kip? Are you all right?"

"Not really," Kip said, sounding more exhausted than Jordan had ever heard her.

"Where are you? Are you hurt?"

"No, but I'm stranded outside a police station in Westchester." Kip read off the address to her. "I know it's crazy of me to ask you, but could you come and get me?"

Jordan was already out of bed, scrambling for her pants. "Of course. Yes. You're at the police station? Are you sure you're all right?"

"I will be as soon as I get out of here."

"I'm on my way." Jordan grabbed keys and her bag.

"There's a Denny's I can see maybe a half a mile down the road from here. I'll go there and wait for you."

"Be careful, all right? I'll be there. Just…be careful."

"I'm sorry."

"Kip," Jordan said softly, "shut up."

Kip's laughter was a little weak, but she sounded more like herself. "Okay, I'll do that."

❖

At six in the morning, the Denny's parking lot hosted a smattering of pickup trucks, several eighteen-wheelers idling off to the side, and a few cars. She pulled the truck into an empty slot close to the front doors and hurried inside. Kip slouched in a booth at the far end of the diner, looking worse than Jordan had ever seen her, even after a night with little sleep tending the generators and coaxing the seedlings through the late frost. She wore only a light windbreaker, a rumpled button-down-collar shirt, and jeans. The shadows under her eyes were almost as dark as her carelessly ruffled hair. She gripped the coffee mug between two hands and stared straight ahead, as if watching some movie playing inside her head. Her gaze flickered up as Jordan approached and recognition slowly sparked a light in her eyes. Jordan slid into the booth opposite her and reached for her hand.

"First, tell me you're not hurt."

Kip nodded, swallowing, her words feeling like sandpaper in a dry throat. "I'm in one piece. Thank you for coming."

"I could almost be angry at you for saying that, but you get a pass this time because you look like you had a rough night."

Kip laughed bitterly. "You could say that."

Jordan stroked the top of Kip's hand, wishing she could gather her up right that instant and take away the pain that rode so hard in her eyes. "Can you tell me what happened?"

Kip closed her eyes and nodded. "My brother went missing from a rehab center near here and I came to pick him up when he called me. The police were looking for him too, and we both ended up at the station. He's still there."

"They let you go?"

"Yeah. Either he or my father's lawyers convinced them I had nothing to do with this latest escapade."

"I'm sorry," Jordan said. "That sounds horrible."

"Not something I wanted to do again, that's for certain." Kip shuddered.

"Do you need anything? Some food? More coffee?"

"All I really need right now is you."

Despite her resolve to keep some kind of sane distance, Jordan couldn't turn away from the raw need in Kip's voice. "I came as quickly as I could. Now you're coming home with me."

"I don't have any right to ask for that," Kip said quietly.

"You have more right than you know, but now is not the time to talk about it. Come on, I'm taking you home."

Kip got wearily to her feet. "You have no idea how good that sounds."

Jordan drove through the increasingly heavy morning traffic as Kip rode silently beside her, her head back and her eyes closed. Jordan would've thought she was sleeping if she hadn't been holding her hand. Tension radiated through Kip's grip. Her fingers were icy despite the heater going full blast. Jordan recognized the numb cold that followed shock and pain. Time would help, but so would someone to remind Kip she wasn't alone. Jordan was that someone, and trying to tell herself anything different would just be a lie.

"Kip," Jordan said quietly. "We're here."

Kip slowly turned her head, searched Jordan's face. "I don't have to stay."

"Yes, you do. And you're not going to get too many more passes if you keep saying ridiculous things to me."

"I'm not used to good luck, and I'm sure not used to miracles. You feel a lot like one to me."

Jordan leaned over and kissed her. "Trust me, I'm no miracle, but I'm real. And I'm taking you inside to bed."

Kip's smile almost reached her eyes. "I must be bad off, because I ought to have a line ready to answer that, but all I can say is yes, please."

Jordan jumped out, locked her door, and came around to Kip's side. She held out a hand when Kip opened her door. "You can save your sexy lines for after you've had some sleep. Come on upstairs."

"I ought to shower," Kip muttered, keeping pace on wooden legs.

"Can you stay awake long enough?" Jordan asked as she opened the door to her apartment.

"Just barely." Kip hesitated. She needed to sleep, but she couldn't forget she'd left Randy alone, and she was afraid if she closed her eyes, Jordan would disappear. "Are you going to work?"

"No." Jordan locked and chained the door. "I'm going back to bed with you. I'll be waiting."

Jordan had pulled the blinds and the room was dim, almost as dark as night. When Kip crawled into bed naked, Jordan curled around her. The sensation was unfamiliar, to be held, to be protected that way. Kip couldn't ever remember anyone doing that, or wanting anyone else to take care of her the way Jordan had. She grasped Jordan's hand and cradled it between her breasts, slipping her fingers between Jordan's.

"I fucked up a lot of things," Kip whispered. "I'm afraid I'll fuck things up with you too."

"Not if I don't let you." Jordan pulled her closer and kissed the back of her neck. "We'll talk when you wake up."

"I love you," Kip said. "I've wanted to tell you that for a long time. I need you to know that."

Jordan pressed her forehead between Kip's shoulder blades, her heart pounding so fast she couldn't hear her own thoughts. She wanted her, oh, how she wanted her, and all the love she offered. She wanted to wrap herself around her, inside her, and live every moment flooded with the passion and wonder of her. But if she let herself fall, there would be no ending to her wanting, to her need, to the longing and desire and hunger for her. She would never be able to go back to the safe shelter she had made of her life. "I know. Now sleep."

Kip closed her eyes surrounded by Jordan's scent and, for once in her life, was unafraid to dream. For now, that was enough.

❖

Kip woke stiff and with a pounding headache. The bed was empty. She shot upright and fumbled on the bedside table where she'd left her phone. The battery was dead, and she had no idea what time it was. She felt like she'd slept a year. A clean T-shirt and a pair of sweats rested on the foot of the bed. After tugging them on, she walked barefoot out to the living room. A fire burned in the fireplace, and Jordan sat curled up on the end of the sofa, a steaming cup of coffee in her hands. She smiled up at Kip, and the knot in Kip's chest relaxed. "Hi. What time is it?"

"About five. There's more coffee in the kitchen."

"Thanks." Kip poured a cup and carried it into the living room. She sat on the coffee table facing Jordan and took a deep breath. There was nothing to say but the truth. "So, this is the second time my brother and I have run afoul of the law. The first time I was driving the vehicle my brother and his girlfriend *borrowed* from her neighbor, and that's how I ended up with community service. I was lucky, but I'm embarrassed, ashamed, that you know that about me."

"I never thought you stole it," Jordan said. "Why didn't you explain the circumstances when you were arrested? You didn't know it was stolen, did you?"

"No, but I was at least guilty of being stupid enough not to ask them whose car I was driving." Kip winced. "And I wanted to protect Randy. He's been in trouble before, and I was afraid he'd end up in jail. He promised he'd stick it out in rehab this time. He didn't."

"And last night?"

Kip told her what she knew of Randy's latest escapade. "If he had anything to do with taking those drugs, he probably will get jail this time. My father's lawyer is with him now. Part of me feels like I should be there right now, but I know that won't help him. Maybe if I hadn't covered for him the last time, this wouldn't have happened."

"Kip," Jordan said gently, "you love your brother and you wanted to protect him. That's who you are. But he could have spoken up too. He could have protected you."

"It's hard to let him face this on his own, but I know I have to." Kip sighed. "I'll contact my father soon and find out what's happening, but not until I take care of what matters most of all."

"What do you want to do?"

"I want to make love with you for about a million years, and then I want to go to the garden and deliver Mr. Liu's vegetables and finish the shelves in the greenhouse." Kip ached to touch her, feeling as if her future balanced on the edge of a knife blade. If Jordan turned her away she would never stop the bleeding.

"I can get behind quite a lot of that," Jordan said, "but I'm not sure I'm ready to."

Kip's stomach somersaulted and dropped into free fall. "I don't blame you."

"Not for the reasons you probably think," Jordan said, running her finger around the rim of her cup. "I'd like nothing better than to walk out that door with you, back into a life I've come to enjoy a lot more because you're part of it." She raised a shoulder. "Actually, that's not quite right. First, I'd like to go to bed and stay there for the rest of the day—minimum. I've missed you, and I want to feel your body on mine, your skin under my hands, your mouth on me."

"God, Jordan." Kip raked a hand through her hair. "You have no idea how much I want that too."

"Oh, I think I do." Jordan's breath was coming faster and she needed to keep her brain in gear and her body in check for a little while longer. Kip's gaze was searing, the look that made Jordan feel—no, made her *know*—she was the only woman in Kip's world. Another second and she was going to give in and beg for Kip to turn that look into action. She couldn't afford to surrender to the need pounding deep inside her, not yet, not when everything mattered so much. "I want that just about every second that I'm breathing, but I want something else even more."

"What more do you want?" Kip emphasized each word as if the world hung on Jordan's answer.

"I want the next time I'm in bed with you to be the beginning. I want to know there'll be a next time, and a next time, and a next time. I want us to have a life together."

"You don't know what you'd be getting with me." Kip swallowed. "My life is messy."

"Everyone's life is messy." Jordan set her cup aside and leaned forward, both hands on Kip's thighs. "Do you want me in your life?"

"With every beat of my heart."

"Then I want your promise that no matter what happens in the future, we are in it together. That if there's trouble, you don't go off on your own to take care of it. That I matter, that *we* matter, more than anything."

"I might need some help."

"We'll both need to help each other. I'm no expert at this either." Jordan shook her head. "It is insane. You're way too young. And—"

Kip gripped her shoulders, pulled her forward, kissed her. "Calling bullshit."

Jordan laughed against her mouth. "I know. I know. As if that were the only issue."

"That's the only thing that isn't an issue." Kip framed Jordan's face and kissed her again. "I want you, I want to build a life with you. I need to make some changes before I can do that."

"All right. That's a good start." Jordan's voice was calm and steady. "What does that mean?"

"I have to fulfill this contract for the—" Kip winced. "The details aren't important and it's better if they stay that way."

"The men in black. Yes, I get it. Will that get rid of them?"

"Probably. I'm just a small part of a big project that my father's company is involved in, and once my input is completed, what I know about it won't have all that much value to anyone. Which means I won't be that important."

"What about the next projects?"

Kip shook her head. "There aren't going to be any. I'm quitting."

"You're quitting? Because of me?"

Kip caught her hands. "No. Because of me. And because of us. I don't want that life. I want something else."

"What?" Jordan was having a hard time breathing. She'd always told herself dreams did not come true, but right at that moment, she was beginning to believe she'd been wrong. Maybe the dreams you made, the dreams you shared, could be real. Maybe sometimes, when love was real, life was as simple as two people sheltering each other in the night.

"When the garden project is at a point where you can leave," Kip said slowly, "I think we should start a bigger garden project. You and me. On a farm."

Jordan laughed, the happiness making her light-headed. "You want to be a farmer?"

"Well, I was thinking more you would be the farmer and I would be tech support."

"Tech support." Jordan stroked her cheek, leaned to kiss her, had to taste her just a little. "I hope that includes manager, mechanic, and business consultant."

"Jordan," Kip said thickly, "I'll wear whatever hat you want. Just please let me touch you soon."

"That life will be nothing like what you've been used to, you know," Jordan murmured, reveling in the want in Kip's eyes.

"What, you mean getting up at four in the morning and spending all day hustling for accounts and watching the weather reports and working outside with you? Because if it's even like that half the time, I'll be plenty happy." Kip shifted over to the sofa and pulled Jordan into her arms. She kissed her until the memory of ashes and loss was replaced by the bright, clear sunshine of hope. "And if I can have you in my arms every night, I'll be complete."

"You haven't asked me if I love you," Jordan whispered, her hands under Kip's T-shirt, stroking possessively.

"I was hoping if you didn't, I could convince you."

"You could convince me of anything," Jordan whispered, "but it so happens I love you madly, insanely."

"Then will you come away with me and be my only love?"

"Yes. Always."

CHAPTER TWENTY-NINE

Kip grabbed her briefcase and suit jacket, thanked the Uber driver, and headed down the alley. The closer she got to the garden gate, the stronger the feeling of coming home, of rightness, of familiarity laced with excitement. Two weeks cooped up in an office sixteen hours a day had felt like two years. She was pale from lack of sunshine, and on top of the work stress, short-tempered from too little sleep and constant worry over Randy's sentencing. Only the few stolen hours on the nights she'd been able to spend with Jordan had kept her going. But she was done with it now, done with the life that had been a prison all its own, built of guilt and misplaced responsibility and lost dreams.

She lifted the latch she'd repaired the first day she'd met Jordan and, smiling at the memory, pushed open the garden gate and stepped inside to sunshine and green and the scent of hope and promise. Ty leaned over a long row of young seedlings, talking to an older woman Kip didn't recognize in a big floppy straw hat and faded denim overalls. A dapper man in carefully pressed trousers, white shirt, and suspenders pushed a wheelbarrow filled with compost toward another bed that looked ready to be planted. Ty glanced over, nodded, and pointed toward the trailer. Kip gestured for Ty to join her, and after a moment, Ty came over. They hadn't spoken in the time she'd been away, but Jordan had told her Ty had come back to work. The wariness was gone from Ty's eyes, only a curious question there now.

"Looks like you got some new help," Kip said.

Ty smiled. "Yes, and more have signed up after we held an open house last weekend."

"That's great."

"It's coming together." Ty paused, hands tucked into the pockets of her canvas work pants. "How are you?"

"Coming together." She pulled a card from her pocket, handed it to Ty. "You can trust this guy, when and if you decide it's time. I think having the kids will help, and he'll know the best way to work things."

Ty glanced at the card, tucked it into the breast pocket of her work shirt. "Thank you."

"You're welcome. If you need anything, anytime, let me know."

"You're coming back to work, aren't you?"

Kip grinned. "Just as soon as I can."

"Good." Ty turned away, hesitated, and looked back. "We can use a good mechanic around here."

Laughing, Kip headed for the trailer, her pulse kicking the way it always did when she was about to see Jordan. When she climbed to the top step, Jordan's voice reached her.

"I'll be out to help just as soon as I finish this bleeping budget. God, I hate spreadsheets."

"I kinda love them myself," Kip said.

Jordan swung around and jumped up. "Kip!"

Kip stepped all the way into the dim trailer and closed the door behind her. "Hi, baby."

Jordan kissed her, one hand running through her hair. "I didn't expect you. Is it over?"

Kip tossed her briefcase and jacket onto the daybed and pulled Jordan into her arms. She rested her cheek against Jordan's hair and breathed in the cool, clean mystery of her. "It's over."

"What happened?" Jordan asked quietly, running her hands up and down Kip's back.

"For once my father didn't pull strings for him." As hard as it had been to admit, she agreed with her father's decision. "Randy got a year with the chance of parole in three months."

Jordan's breath caught. "I'm sorry."

"It could be a lot worse. And he'll be in a minimum security place where he'll get treatment as part of his incarceration."

"And the rest of it?" Jordan leaned back, her arms looped around Kip's neck. "What about you?"

"I signed off on the designs last night. I've still got a few more hours of community service to pay off, so I'm yours for the rest of the summer. Or as long as you need me here."

"Oh," Jordan said softly, "I'm sure I can find something for you to do."

"Good. I'm back to khakis and work shirts from now on."

"I'm very glad," Jordan said, skimming her hands down Kip's shirtfront. "Although I do like you in a suit."

Kip laughed. "I'll wear one for you whenever you want."

"I like you out of it a lot better." Jordan opened the top button of Kip's shirt, spread the soft linen folds apart, and kissed her chest.

Kip closed her eyes, buried her hand in Jordan's hair. "No fair. We have work to do, don't we?"

"Always."

"Then you'd best stop."

"For now." Laughing, Jordan rubbed her cheek against the curve of Kip's breast. "You're coming home with me after work."

It wasn't a question.

"I rather thought I might do that every night," Kip murmured, "if you don't mind."

"Oh, not a bit." Jordan looked up. "As long as it's every night for always."

"I think we can count on that," Kip said, and kissed her.

About the Author

Radclyffe has written over fifty romance and romantic intrigue novels, dozens of short stories, and, writing as L.L. Raand, has authored a paranormal romance series, The Midnight Hunters.

She is an eight-time Lambda Literary Award finalist in romance, mystery, and erotica—winning in both romance (*Distant Shores, Silent Thunder*) and erotica (*Erotic Interludes 2: Stolen Moments* edited with Stacia Seaman and *In Deep Waters 2: Cruising the Strip* written with Karin Kallmaker). A member of the Saints and Sinners Literary Hall of Fame, she is also an RWA/FF&P Prism Award winner for *Secrets in the Stone*, an RWA FTHRW Lories and RWA HODRW winner for *Firestorm*, an RWA Bean Pot winner for *Crossroads*, an RWA Laurel Wreath winner for *Blood Hunt*, and the 2016 Book Buyers Best award winner for *Price of Honor*. In 2014 she was awarded the Dr. James Duggins Outstanding Mid-Career Novelist Award by the Lambda Literary Foundation. She is a featured author in the 2015 documentary film *Love Between the Covers*, from Blueberry Hill Productions.

She is also the president of Bold Strokes Books, one of the world's largest independent LGBTQ publishing companies.

Find her at facebook.com/Radclyffe.BSB, follow her on Twitter @RadclyffeBSB, and visit her website at Radfic.com.

Books Available From Bold Strokes Books

The Sniper's Kiss by Justine Saracen. The power of a kiss: it can swell your heart with splendor, declare abject submission, and sometimes blow your brains out. (978-1-62639-839-9)

Divided Nation, United Hearts by Yolanda Wallace. In a nation torn in two by a most uncivil war, can love conquer the divide? (978-1-62639-847-4)

Fury's Bridge by Brey Willows. What if your life depended on someone who didn't believe in your existence? (978-1-62639-841-2)

Lightning Strikes by Cass Sellars. When Parker Duncan and Sydney Hyatt's one-night stand turns to more, both women must fight demons past and present to cling to the relationship neither of them thought she wanted. (978-1-62639-956-3)

Love in Disaster by Charlotte Greene. A professor and a celebrity chef are drawn together by chance, but can their attraction survive a natural disaster? (978-1-62639-885-6)

Secret Hearts by Radclyffe. Can two women from different worlds find common ground while fighting their secret desires? (978-1-62639-932-7)

Sins of Our Fathers by A. Rose Mathieu. Solving gruesome murder cases is only one of Elizabeth Campbell's challenges; another is her growing attraction to the female detective who is hell-bent on keeping her client in prison. (978-1-62639-873-3)

Troop 18 by Jessica L. Webb. Charged with uncovering the destructive secret that a troop of RCMP cadets has been hiding, Andy must put aside her worries about Kate and uncover the conspiracy before it's too late. (978-1-62639-934-1)

Worthy of Trust and Confidence by Kara A. McLeod. FBI Special Agent Ryan O'Connor is about to discover the hard way that when you can only handle one type of answer to a question, it really is better not to ask. (978-1-62639-889-4)

Amounting to Nothing by Karis Walsh. When mounted police officer Billie Mitchell steps in to save beautiful murder witness Merissa Karr, worlds collide on the rough city streets of Tacoma, Washington. (978-1-62639-728-6)

Becoming You by Michelle Grubb. Airlie Porter has a secret. A deep, dark, destructive secret that threatens to engulf her if she can't find the courage to face who she really is and who she really wants to be with. (978-1-62639-811-5)

Birthright by Missouri Vaun. When spies bring news that a swordswoman imprisoned in a neighboring kingdom bears the Royal mark, Princess Kathryn sets out to rescue Aiden, true heir to the Belstaff throne. (978-1-62639-485-8)

Crescent City Confidential by Aurora Rey. When romance and danger are in the air, writer Sam Torres learns the Big Easy is anything but. (978-1-62639-764-4)

Love Down Under by MJ Williamz. Wylie loves Amarina, but if Amarina isn't out, can their relationship last? (978-1-62639-726-2)

Privacy Glass by Missouri Vaun. Things heat up when Nash Wiley commandeers a limo and her best friend for a late drive out to the beach: Champagne on ice, seat belts optional, and privacy glass a must. (978-1-62639-705-7)

The Impasse by Franci McMahon. A horse-packing excursion into the Montana Wilderness becomes an adventure of terrifying proportions for Miles and ten women on an outfitter-led trip. (978-1-62639-781-1)

The Right Kind of Wrong by PJ Trebelhorn. Bartender Quinn Burke is happy with her life as a playgirl until she realizes she can't fight her feelings any longer for her best friend, bookstore owner Grace Everett. (978-1-62639-771-2)

Wishing on a Dream by Julie Cannon. Can two women change everything for the chance at love? (978-1-62639-762-0)

A Quiet Death by Cari Hunter. When the body of a young Pakistani girl is found out on the moors, the investigation leaves Detective Sanne Jensen facing an ordeal she may not survive. (978-1-62639-815-3)

Buried Heart by Laydin Michaels. When Drew Chambliss meets Cicely Jones, her buried past finds its way to the surface. Will they survive its discovery or will their chance at love turn to dust? (978-1-62639-801-6)

Escape: Exodus Book Three by Gun Brooke. Aboard the Exodus ship *Pathfinder*, President Thea Tylio still holds Caya Lindemay, a clairvoyant changer, in protective custody, which has devastating consequences endangering their relationship and the entire Exodus mission. (978-1-62639-635-7)

Genuine Gold by Ann Aptaker. New York, 1952. Outlaw Cantor Gold is thrown back into her honky-tonk Coney Island past, where crime and passion simmer in a neon glare. (978-1-62639-730-9)

Into Thin Air by Jeannie Levig. When her girlfriend disappears, Hannah Lewis discovers her world isn't as orderly as she thought it was. (978-1-62639-722-4)

Night Voice by CF Frizzell. When talk show host Sable finally acknowledges her risqué radio relationship with a mysterious caller, she welcomes a *real* relationship with local tradeswoman Riley Burke. (978-1-62639-813-9)

Raging at the Stars by Lesley Davis. When the unbelievable theories start revealing themselves as truths, can you trust in the ones who have conspired against you from the start? (978-1-62639-720-0)

She Wolf by Sheri Lewis Wohl. When the hunter becomes the hunted, more than love might be lost. (978-1-62639-741-5)

Smothered and Covered by Missouri Vaun. The last person Nash Wiley expects to bump into over a two a.m. breakfast at Waffle House is her college crush, decked out in a curve-hugging law enforcement uniform. (978-1-62639-704-0)

The Butterfly Whisperer by Lisa Moreau. Reunited after ten years, can Jordan and Sophie heal the past and rediscover love or will differing desires keep them apart? (978-1-62639-791-0)

The Devil's Due by Ali Vali. Cain and Emma Casey are awaiting the birth of their third child, but as always in Cain's world, there are new and old enemies to face in Katrina-ravaged New Orleans. (978-1-62639-591-6)

Widows of the Sun-Moon by Barbara Ann Wright. With immortality now out of their grasp, the gods of Calamity fight amongst themselves, egged on by the mad goddess they thought they'd left behind. (978-1-62639-777-4)

Arrested Hearts by Holly Stratimore. A reckless cop who hates her life and a health nut who is afraid to die might be a perfect combination for love. (978-1-62639-809-2)

Capturing Jessica by Jane Hardee. Hyperrealist sculptor Michael tries desperately to conceal the love she holds for best friend, Jess, unaware Jess's feelings for her are changing. (978-1-62639-836-8)

Counting to Zero by AJ Quinn. NSA agent Emma Thorpe and computer hacker Paxton James must learn to trust each other as they work to stop a threat clock that's rapidly counting down to zero. (978-1-62639-783-5)

Courageous Love by KC Richardson. Two women fight a devastating disease, and their own demons, while trying to fall in love. (978-1-62639-797-2)

One More Reason to Leave Orlando by Missouri Vaun. Nash Wiley thought a threesome sounded exotic and exciting, but as it turns out the reality of sleeping with two women at the same time is just really complicated. (978-1-62639-703-3)

Pathogen by Jessica L. Webb. Can Dr. Kate Morrison navigate a deadly virus and the threat of bioterrorism, as well as her new relationship with Sergeant Andy Wyles and her own troubled past? (978-1-62639-833-7)

Rainbow Gap by Lee Lynch. Jaudon Vickers and Berry Garland, polar opposites, dream and love in this tale of lesbian lives set in Central Florida against the tapestry of societal change and the Vietnam War. (978-1-62639-799-6)

Steel and Promise by Alexa Black. Lady Nivrai's cruel desires and modified body make most of the galaxy fear her, but courtesan Cailyn Derys soon discovers the real monsters are the ones without the claws. (978-1-62639-805-4)

Swelter by D. Jackson Leigh. Teal Giovanni's mistake shines an unwanted spotlight on a small Texas ranch where August Reese is secluded until she can testify against a powerful drug kingpin. (978-1-62639-795-8)

Without Justice by Carsen Taite. Cade Kelly and Emily Sinclair must battle each other in the pursuit of justice, but can they fight their undeniable attraction outside the walls of the courtroom? (978-1-62639-560-2)

21 Questions by Mason Dixon. To find love, start by asking the right questions. (978-1-62639-724-8)

A Palette for Love by Charlotte Greene. When newly minted Ph.D. Chloé Devereaux returns to New Orleans, she doesn't expect her new job and her powerful employer—Amelia Winters—to be so appealing. (978-1-62639-758-3)

By the Dark of Her Eyes by Cameron MacElvee. When Brenna Taylor inherits a decrepit property haunted by tormented ghosts, Alejandra Santana must not only restore Brenna's house and property but also save her soul. (978-1-62639-834-4)

Never Enough by Robyn Nyx. Can two women put aside their pasts to find love before it's too late? (978-1-62639-629-6)